THE SPLENDID OUTLAW

JACKSON GREGORY

SAGEBRUSH
Large Print Westerns

First published in Great Britain by Hurst & Blackett, Ltd.
First published in the United States by Andrew Melrose

First Isis Edition
published 2020
by arrangement with
Golden West Literary Agency

A catalogue record for this book is available
from the British Library.

ISBN 978–1–78541–863–1

Published by
Ulverscroft Limited
Anstey, Leicestershire

Set by Words & Graphics Ltd.
Anstey, Leicestershire
Printed and bound in Great Britain by
TJ Books Limited, Padstow, Cornwall

This book is printed on acid-free paper

THE SPLENDID OUTLAW

Hal, a Bear Track Ranch top hand, is a good-looking, decent young fellow when sober, but ᵢn wheels when drunk. In Queen City they call "Outlaw" and hate to see him coming. He ᵢs to escort a party of boss Oscar Estabrook's ᵢes and friends to the ranch, where Old ᵢey Estabrook has put Oscar in charge, hoping ᵢallenge will cure his son's gambling habit and ᵢ man of him. While Hal waits for the train, in ᵢr drunken rage he tangles with Big John ᵢ a powerful itinerant preacher who takes a ᵢo him — and will soon be an asset when they ᵢhat Oscar is deep in debt to dapper, heartless ᵢe" Victor Dufresne, a clever gambler and ᵢrer. Can Hal and John spoil Victor's game ᵢe Oscar and the Bear Track from sure ruin?

JT12344/

TO
MY MOTHER

TO
MY MOTHER

Contents

1.— A Storm Brews...1
2.— Threatened Danger 12
3.— Hal Shoots – To Kill..21
4.— The Mountain Road 36
5.— A Double Hold Up...56
6.— The Bear Track...71
7.— A Man and a Horse 83
8.— Moon Madness and Music 91
9.— Distrust and Suspicion 105
10.— Schooldays Again..118
11.— Tragedy and Premonition.................................129
12.— A Chance Spark in the Darkness 138
13.— A Shattered Idol 153
14.— The End of a Dream..171
15.— The Work of God, Nicodemus,
      and John Brent 182
16.— Black Days 191
17.— The Gates to Paradise 202
18.— Shadows in a Man's Soul 217
19.— What Hal Found in the Ravine 234
20.— Certain Light Upon the
      Bear Creek Robbery..247
21.— What the Mountains Have
      Hidden They May Disclose 257
22.— The Prince Calls for a Show Down 270
23.— A Wager With the Sheriff 283

24.— Estabrook Takes His One
    Desperate Chance...292
25.— And at Last is a Man 300
26.— The Blue Sky for a Limit.........................308
27.— The Valley of the Waterfalls.......................321

CHAPTER
ONE

A Storm Brews

He called himself a man, a real bad man at that. But when he forgot himself with a friend and laughed, or when he was looking on at life rather than being looked at, his eyes gave him away for the boy he was. When men looked on he made his eyes stern and forbidding; take him unaware and they were clear and untroubled. He was at that age which is at once the ending of boyhood with its ideals and the beginning of man's estate with its responsibilities. He was but going through the debatable land, passing through the mists where all things are formative and wherein one finds himself. Youth is prone to take itself seriously and he was no exception after all.

The great outdoors had cradled him, nursed him, blessed him with the things which are hers to give. He was a lithe, slim waisted, splendid young man-animal, as light of foot as the big cat of the mountains, as quick of eye, as graceful. With straight black hair, keen black eyes, a skin burned to a coppery, burnished brown, with the free, undulating grace flowing from the supple strength of the range-born, he looked almost the Indian.

1

He hooked his gloved fingers into his belt and stood in the wide door of the Eagle Stables looking meditatively down the one and only street of Queen City. There was for a moment a certain indecision in his manner, in the very way he held himself balanced upon the ball of his foot, which hinted at a mental cross-roads. There was in his whole being, the way he carried his shoulders as well as in the expression of his face, a something which indicated that he was not the sort to debate long with himself. With his kind decision comes in one flash, action in the next. He pulled his hat down over his eyes, adjusted his neck-handkerchief with a careless jerk, and strode off towards the little railroad station, whistling softly. Resting his arm upon the shelf under the ticket window, he peeped in at the telegraph operator.

"Say, Marshall, when's the Overlan' due, d'you reckon?"

The man manipulating the electric keys swung about quickly.

"Why, hello, Hal," he said. "You in town again?"

"Yes, I'm in town." The reply was gently spoken, the voice seeming to come from deep down in his throat, at once calm, quiet, softly musical, and vaguely truculent. "Got any objections?"

The telegraph operator came to the window.

"Objections? No." He laughed easily and put out his hand. "Glad to see you, Hal. In town for a little recreation?"

"I'm on business for the Ol' Man." He did not appear to notice the hand which Marshall had offered and now allowed to drop with tapping fingers to the little shelf running along below the window. "An' I don't know why you're glad to see me. I rec'lect askin' quite a while ago when the Overlan's due."

"The Overland? Which way?"

"From the East."

"It's late again as usual. Twelve hours late. They generally make up time, though, the last three hours. It should be in about four o'clock in the morning."

The cowboy swung upon a high heel, and without a word to Marshall walked slowly down the street towards the double row of rough board shacks.

"When a man ain't glad to see you, why in hell does he say he is?" he muttered to himself in a tone of deep disgust.

Marshall, the telegraph operator, had stepped quickly to the window, peered after the departing form a moment, and then hurried back to his keys. It took him but an instant to get Jefferson Junction, a score of miles away. His message was brief:

"Victor Dufresne: Hal is in town. Marshall."

Upon the porch of Uncle Parker's grocery store four or five men were lounging in idleness and ease, taking advantage of the little shade cast by the afternoon sun in the flat, treeless environs of Queen City. A little flicker of interest ran over their placid faces and brightened their somnolent eyes as the dark man swung past.

"Hello, Hal," spoke one, and, "It's Hal, from the Bear Track," added two others. He lifted his head slightly, very slightly, let his black eyes run carelessly, almost unseeingly over them, dropped his head in what may have been a nod, and passed on.

The street was all but deserted. The young man's heels echoed lonesomely upon the crazy board sidewalk. He met a woman, a little, bird-like matronly woman, who looked up at him swiftly, smothered a half-choked gasp, and, gathering her skirts as though from contamination, hurried on. He had glanced at her as he had at the men upon the porch, and lifted his hat with no flicker of a smile, no indication of the head, no sign of recognition beyond the careless sweep of his hat. A man coming out of the post office with a handful of papers greeted him casually, turning as he passed to look at him. As he came abreast of the Round Up saloon, the half-doors swung open under the attack of a heavy shoulder, and a man in drooping, tawny moustaches and shaggy chaps came out with dragging spurs, wiping a pursed mouth with a dingy shirt sleeve. He stopped dead in his tracks in mild surprise.

"Well, I'm damned!" he burst out in a voice which could be heard at the store. "Ol' timer, how goes it?"

His outstretched hand was grasped warmly in, the vice of the gauntleted one.

"Hello, Ches!" A quick smile went with the greeting, the fine white teeth fairly flashing in sudden contrast to the darkness of skin and eyes, the tone and manner one of boyish pleasure. "Where'd you drop in from?"

4

"Workin' at the yards down to the Junction. Heard about the las' visit you made here, you ol' son of a gun." Ches chuckled gleefully, thrusting a big cracked thumbnail into the other's side. "If you're plannin' on another like it, I guess I'll be gittin' out."

The young fellow laughed, a low-throated, mellow laugh of candid amusement.

"There ain't no danger, Ches," he said, drawing off his gauntlets, which he caught up under his arm, and reaching for his tobacco and papers with a hand which, while sinewy, was remarkably slender and small, as shapely and white as a girl's. "I'm in town on business for the Ol' Man this trip. An' I guess I got to be good. Anyway I ain't hardly got time to moren' limber up. Let's have somethin'."

Ches followed him into the saloon. The weary, Methodist preacher-looking bar-tender looked up, and a light of interest drove the weariness out of his pale yellow eyes.

"You here?" he grinned. "Well, I'm taking my day off."

"Git out!" cried Hal, his smile growing broad and spilling over from his eyes and mouth into the little network of lines. "I'm on a peaceable erran'. I jes' hooked up with Ches here an' he looked like he was dyin' of thirs', so I trotted him in to git revived. Trot out your company medicine, Eddie."

The ecclesiastical-looking bar-tender reached a long arm out to the shelf behind him and singled out from its neighbours a round-bellied, red-labelled bottle, setting it on the bar with a couple of glasses.

"How'd that strike you?" he asked, his elbows again on the bar. Hal took up it carefully and gazed long at it with something of affection in his regard.

"It shore looks all right," he admitted slowly. "But jedgin' whisky by the looks of the label is damn poor politics, Eddie. It's something like sayin' a man's hones' 'cause he's got a long bunch of fly-away whiskers. Try it on, Ches."

Ches emptied his glass at a gulp, throwing his head back with the scientific gesture betokening much practice, and made the usual wry face on top of the proceedings, vowing, when he had gotten through choking, that it was good stuff. Hal drank more slowly, more thoughtfully; one would have said, with more appreciation. He made no face thereafter, but putting his glass gently on the bar, smiled reminiscently, nodded, and poured himself another glass.

"That ain't water you're drinking, young feller," admonished the mild-eyed bar-tender.

"A man oughtn't to mention water in the same breath with this," said Hal, with something of gentle reproach in his tone, his eyes admiringly upon the red label.

After the second drink he and Ches moved to one of the three little circular tables at the rear of the long, bare room and dropped into desultory conversation over their cigarettes They had not seen each other, it appeared, for six months or so, and in consequence they had no end of trivial experiences to swap. Ches brought the news he had gleaned along the railroad, giving it in exchange for months-old happenings of the

6

back-lying cattle country seventy and a hundred-and-fifty miles removed from the smoke of locomotives.

Gradually as they talked and the late afternoon wore on, other men began to drop into the saloon. Several greeted Hal casually, receiving from him the briefest of nods, generally with a spoken word of greeting. Many merely looked at him and turned to mutter something, unheard by him, to the men at the long bar. Only one or two did he accost with any warmth. It was on the surface that Hal was a man of few friends, and certainly not a favourite in Queen City.

It grew out of Ches' bantering remarks and suggestive questions that Hal's latest visit to Queen City had been a couple of months ago, and that it had been memorable. He had had some money, and had spent it in the only way he knew, and freely. He had lost heavily in a poker game to a man named Victor Dufresne, a professional gambler widely known as Prince Victor, and had had trouble with the man who, he claimed, had robbed him. After the game he had enough money remaining to keep on buying whisky, and before morning had launched himself upon one of his famous tempestuous drunks, going *fey* with the blood-burning liquor, running amuck of established law and order, whirled into a mad, brutal, murderous frenzy of intoxication. He had been gathered in by Dan Nesbit, sheriff, only when his guns were emptied and he himself was falling to the floor in the senseless stupor of alcohol. He had sobered up in the ten-foot square jail, and had been allowed to go on his way the next morning, and asked to remember that his presence in Queen City was neither requested nor desired in the future.

"I guess I was some het up," he admitted to Ches, with a grim smile. "It was some drunk, they tell me."

Ches grunted by way of assenting comment.

"What are you in for to-day?" he queried.

Hal frowned.

"Business for the Ol' Man," he retorted. "An' rotten business too. There's a herd of folks comin' in on the Overlan', and I got to meet 'em and pilot 'em out to the Bear Track. Eastern jaspers."

"Them Eastern jaspers is sure a rare bunch," mused Ches.

The two men moved along the bar, Ches returned many greetings of the men they elbowed, Hal seeming to see no one, and called again for the bottle with the red label. And again, with slow thoughtfulness, Hal drank two brimming glasses. Ches saw what his companion did not appear to notice: every man in the saloon paused in his talk or in his own drinking for a brief moment as his eyes turned towards Hal. And Ches understood the meaning of the silence with which the men turned from Hal and looked at one another.

"Come on, Hal," he suggested, with quiet tact, "I want to show you a hoss I bought off'n a man for thirty bones."

Men stood aside for them as they passed out with no word, followed them with stern eyes as the doors snapped open to their shoulders, and turned silently to one another when they had gone. One of them spoke sharply to the bar-tender.

8

"How many jolts has he took, Eddie?"

"Only four yet," answered Eddie, pausing for a moment in his languid mopping of the bar. "But he's takin' 'em slow like you saw, an' he's takin' 'em up to the brim. That's the way he begun las' time."

The man who had spoken, a heavy-set, short man, with a grave face and a quiet air of determination, was Burt Walsh, a big cattle owner and the father of one of the few families in Queen City. He was the man who had been elected by his peers during the last invasion of Hal to tell the young fellow that he was not a desirable citizen in the little village. He made no answer to Eddie's reply, but put down his glass and left the room.

Meanwhile Ches had led his friend towards the stables, his brows drawn thoughtfully, speaking no word. They were half-way to the stables when he finally cleared his throat and said carelessly:

"Them Easterners frien's of the Ol' Man?"

"Sure. Mother, a couple a sisters, an' some other long-horns. Why?"

Again Ches cleared his throat, shot a quick, sidelong glance up at the man beside him, and answered, coming to a sudden halt:

"I want to talk with you, ol' timer!"

Hal paused as Ches had done, lifting his eyes with a swift flicker of surprise at the other's serious tone.

"Go ahead," he replied lightly. "What is it?"

"How long you got to be in town, Hal?"

"Until the train gits in. Four o'clock in the mo'nin."

A third time Ches cleared his throat, shifting his feet a bit uneasily.

"It ain't none of my funeral," he blurted out at last. "An' I reckon you're ol' enough to look out for yourself. But I'm passin' it straight to you jes' the same. This here town got a bellyful of you las' trip, Hal, an' if I was you I'd go powerful slow with the red eye. I seen Burt Walsh sizin' you up all the time we was in there, an' —"

Hal cut him short with a low laugh.

"I'm obliged, Ches," he said smoothly. "But as you says, it ain't your funeral in the firs' place, an' I'm ol' enough to han'le myself in the secon'. Let's look at that cayuse of yourn."

"The hoss can wait. I'm shootin' my wad anyways an' you can do as you like. I've heard a lot of talk, Hal, an' I know what you're up against if you cut loose again. A lot of family men lives in Queen City nowadays, an' a man with a wife an' little kids ain't strong for raisin' hell like you turn loose when your'e het up."

A black frown distorted the young fellow's face, his eyes glowing dully.

"Dam' the sof'-footed married men," he snapped. "It's sure gittin' to be the hell of a country when a man can't go out an' git drunk if he wants to. Whose business is it?"

Ches shook his head.

"They're makin' it theirs," he answered, something of disappointment in his voice. "An' I don't know as I blame 'em none neither."

Hal jerked his head up, flushed a trifle under his thick tan.

10

"What do you mean, Ches?"

"I mean what I say," maintained Ches stoutly, his eyes frankly upon Hal's. "These folks lives here, an' it's up to them to make what laws they like for this town. An' if they say what outsiders can't do — well, she goes as she lays, that's all."

"Outsiders, hell! Ain't I lived here long before Burt Walsh ever saw the place? An' I'll be here a long time after he gits himself planted for stickin' his nose in strangers' business. An' I'm goin' back now for a drink. Comin', Ches?"

"No," answered Ches with quiet emphasis. "I ain't goin' to have no more drinks with you to-day."

The quick anger which always lurked so near the surface sprang up red in Hal's eyes. About to speak, he changed his mind, and with a short laugh swung on his heel and walked back towards the Round Up saloon.

"Which is diggin' his own grave," muttered Ches disgustedly. "Well, it ain't no grub off'n my plate."

CHAPTER TWO

Threatened Danger

Like many another well-meaning person before him, Ches had interfered to do good and had but spoiled the thing to which he had put his hand. No one knew better than Hal with what peaceful intentions the Bear Track man had entered Queen City, the memory of his recent trip being strongly with him. The short-worded hint he had had two months before had remained in his brain and had had its effect. Even now it was against his will that he came back to the town he had wrecked in his last orgy. There was the possibility that he might have spent the hours of waiting for the Overland as quietly as even Queen City could wish. But now he felt that the peace-loving denizens of the community had not contented themselves with a hint, but were telling him like a naughty child what he could do; and what like a dare to a hare-brained boy? With his head up, his eyes all but hidden under his drooping lids, he made his way, with a non-chalance that was vaguely insolent, through the group of men at the Round Up and called upon Eddie for a drink.

One swift glance assured him that Burt Walsh was not there. The men fell back silently from the end of the bar where he stood, keeping their eyes steadfastly away from him. There was something ominous in the wordless way in which they took their drinks which he did not seem to notice. Nor did he seem to observe that as they put down their glasses, they all of them turned and left the saloon. As the doors snapped back after the last of them Eddie leaned forward across the bar and said in a voice which had dropped almost to a whisper:

"Take a tip from me, Hal, an' don't take on too much booze this trip. It ain't healthy."

"Take a tip from me," snapped Hal, his teeth showing under a lifted lip, "an' keep your mouth shut. If there's any jasper in this town —"

Again the saloon doors swung open to the heavy-set frame of Burt Walsh. And as he whirled on his heel with some sudden premonition of danger, Hal saw that the man who had been unarmed ten minutes ago now had a heavy gun at each hip.

"Hal," said Walsh, speaking evenly and quietly and slowly, "we been hopin' you wouldn't make no more mistakes. The boys has asked me to let you know how we ain't ready to stan' for any high hand from outsiders. You better go easy this time Hal."

"Ain't I goin' easy?" retorted Hal bellicosely. "Have I stepped on anybody's toes yet?"

"No," answered Burt Walsh with the same stern quietness, "you ain't. An' we're hopin' you ain't figgerin' on cuttin' loose. You're welcome to do as you please as long as you don't make no breaks like las' time."

13

"Well, wait 'till I make a noise in your Sunday school, will you? There's time to howl when you're hit. Gimme a drink, Eddie."

Eddie, with a suggestion of hesitation, glanced at Walsh, and seeing him shrug his shoulders and turn to leave the saloon, put the bottle down upon the bar. Hal poured another glass, full to the brim, and drank it with slow thoughtfulness.

"That's prime liquor, Eddie," he said with reminiscent satisfaction.

He had seen the interrogatory glance directed towards Walsh, and understood that if an order came from the men of Queen City for Eddie not to sell him any more whisky, Eddie would obey orders. With a shadow of a smile he spun a dollar on the bar.

"Gimme two flasks of that, Eddie," he said casually.

"Can't I feed it to you fas' enough?" demurred the bar-tender.

"You might run out'n it," laughed Hal. "Anyway, I ain't taking no chances of dyin' of thirs'. A flask for each hind pocket, Eddie."

Six o'clock, supper-time for Queen City, came, and Eddie, relieved by a boy from the grocery store, slipped on his coat and went up to the hotel. Hal shook his head at Eddie's invitation to come with him.

"I ain't got no time to eat," he grunted.

Only two times did he leave the saloon for the street, shouldering his way along in a sullen silence, his hat low over his restless eyes, turning out for neither man nor woman, speaking no word to any one. He had gone the first time to the stables to look after the horses, the second time to the station to ask for the latest report on the Overland. The slow hours of the afternoon, save for these two exceptions, he spent in a brooding silence in the Round Up, drinking a great deal of raw whisky or sitting alone at the little poker-table in the rear of the room. During the whole afternoon he had been as much by himself as if he had been out in the heart of Bear Track range.

At seven o'clock he was still drinking heavily, sullen and silent; his eyes alert and suspicious and beginning to show little red veins. Still there had come no further word from Burt Walsh, whom he saw now and again in the saloon. Walsh was not drinking, and was as silent and quick-eyed as the man over whom all Queen City was watching. The Bear Track man saw that more than one man who had been without weapons in the early afternoon was carrying a belt with dragging revolvers now. That for a brief moment amused him. Then his amusement died in a surly muttering, and a growing anger replaced it.

At eight o'clock he was moving always with his back to the wall, swaying slightly as he walked, his hands nervous, near his hips. He saw Burt Walsh beckon to two men, calling them outside; noticed that they were two who had armed themselves during the last hour, and withdrew quietly to the far corner of the saloon, behind a poker-table, his back to the wall. His eyes, lost in the shadow of the brim of his hat, were cat-like in their quickness as they flashed back and forth from the front doors to the narrow door at the back.

When the front doors were pushed open his hand, toying with a deck of cards on the table, grew still and very tense ready to leap to the grip of his gun if it were Burt Walsh and the others looking for trouble.

The man who entered had not been in Queen City for upwards of ten minutes. He had stepped down from the local train from Jefferson Junction and hurried to the one-storey hotel where he had dropped his grip, signed the register, "Victor Dufresne," in a slight, girlish hand, and then had walked briskly down to the Round Up, as though upon urgent business. Only at the door had he dropped into a saunter, entering the saloon with a quiet lounging step.

He was a man as dark as Hal and almost as handsome in a heavier, bulkier way. A man of middle age, with a sprinkling of white in the black of his temples and the short-cropped moustache, his jaws clean-shaven and firm, his cheek-bones prominent, his nose as perfect as a Greek god's, his manner quiet, his carriage superb. His appearance, natural and sartorial, the immaculate frock-coat, the carefully creased grey trousers, the silk hat and gold-headed cane, the sparkling diamond upon his stubby little finger — these things had given him his name in cattle land where such things were rare. After the way of names bestowed as his had been, the name stuck. And Victor Dufresne took a mild pride in his title, Prince Victor.

He knew every one, and every one was willing to shake by the hand and drink with the man with whom he was too well acquainted to play cards. Now, when he stepped to the bar, his hat in his hand, his cane under

16

his arm, his face smiling, he was accompanied by three men whom he had called in from the door. His eye, roving over the room, as bright and black and round as a bird's, found out the slouching form of Hal in the far corner.

"Hello, it's Hal!" he cried warmly. "Have a drink, Hal."

Since he had left Ches no man had offered to buy him a drink, no man had spoken cordially to him, all men had shunned him openly. The men with Prince Victor looked swiftly to see what answer Hal would make. And Hal, seeing the look, feeling the tide of rebellion surge higher and higher within him, chose to forget his last meeting with Dufresne, and came forward. He reeled once and caught at the bar, and his eyes were quick to see that his lurching gait was noticed by all. Steadying himself, making no move to take the hand Dufresne put out, he answered slowly, steadily:

"Hello, Prince."

"What are you having, Hal?"

Hal lifted his arm, his forefinger pointing out the nearly emptied bottle with the red label.

"Same thing," he muttered gutturally.

The three men with Prince Victor drank hurriedly, and with a brief word left his side and moved across the room, leaving the Prince and Hal alone. Hal noticed and laughed loudly, drinking his glass slowly, thoughtfully, after they had gone.

"They ain't in love none with drinkin' with me," he said musingly. "I reckon they're afraid some one'll see 'em. You ain't scared, are you, Prince?"

Victor Dufresne did not answer Hal's question or the sneer which went with it, as he spun a gold piece on the bar.

"If any man," he said, his eyes upon the shimmering disc spinning before him, his voice lifted so that it could be heard anywhere in the quiet bar-room, "is too proud to drink with a man I invite to have something with me, he can go to hell."

His words fell crisp, clear, resonant with a note of challenge in them. The three men who had moved back looked at one another, spoke in low tones, and shrugging their shoulders, went out. Hal turned bright, suspicious eyes upon Dufresne.

"I guess there's trouble in the air," he said quietly. "But I ain't askin' no help from you."

The gambler laughed softly.

"It's just as well you are not counting on it, my dear fellow," he said frankly. "Because you wouldn't get it."

Hal muttered his answer, his words unintelligible. Dufresne had swept up his change and was turning away when the other flung a dollar on the bar, saying sharply:

"Here's a come back. Have one on me."

Again they drank. Hal's glass, for the first time that night, spilling a few drops of the fiery liquor; Dufresne sipping slowly the light red wine he had ordered.

Again the swing-doors opened and Hal turned quickly, with his back to the bar, his thumbs hooked with seeming carelessness and actual eagerness into his cartridge belt. It was Burt Walsh this time and the two men whom he had called outside. With never a glance at Hal, a slight nod to the Prince, Burt Walsh stalked down the room to the end of the bar, called Eddie to him. His words, low spoken, were not guarded, and reached the man whom they most concerned with quiet distinctness.

"You won't sell him no more liquor, Eddie. Jim Bradshaw an' Spike Wallace'll jes' sit back of the bar with you. I'll be around if there's anything doin'."

Quietly Bradshaw and Wallace moved back of the bar, leaning their elbows on it and seeming to look anywhere save at the man whom in reality their eyes never left. Walsh dropped back and stood near the door, his hands upon his hips, his eyes sternly upon Hal's. And Hal, in the heights of a supreme impudence, laughing, whipped a flask from his pocket, tilted it high, and drank slowly, thirstily.

Dufresne had watched and listened with a quiet smile, saying nothing. As Hal lifted the bottle to his lips the Prince stepped, equally without haste and without delay, out of the line of possible danger, still smiling slightly, still sipping his glass of wine. The silence was complete, and save for the slight altering in the position of Dufresne, no man moved so much as a finger. Both Wallace and Bradshaw turned quick questioning eyes upon Walsh. Walsh merely shook his head, and his lips seemed to frame the word "Wait." Hal had put the flask, half-emptied, back into his hip pocket, and moved unsteadily along the bar, his eyes never resting as they swept from one of the three points of threatened danger to the other two and back. From the end of the bar he stepped backward, without turning his eyes, until he had reached the poker-table in the corner. There he had dropped into the chair behind the table, the corner at his back, his face hidden, his eyes lost in the black shadow of his low-drawn hat.

CHAPTER
THREE

Hal Shoots – To Kill

Prince Victor finished his glass and gently set it back upon the bar, yawning. As he did so a man standing near the door pushed forward and called to him. It was Marshall, the telegraph operator.

"Mr. Dufresne," he called laughingly, not seeming to have felt the tension in the atmosphere, "Papa Clark is in town and he is looking for you."

Dufresne turned mild, uninterested eyes upon Marshall.

"And," went on his informer rapidly, "he says he has seven hundred dollars in his pocket."

Dufresne laughed.

"Tell him that his money is safe this time," he replied, his voice as lacking in interest as his eyes had been. "I am taking the Overland to Reno."

"But the Overland is late," continued Marshall. "It won't be in before four o'clock."

Dufresne looked at his watch with the first flicker of interest.

"Where is he?" he demanded abruptly.

"I saw him up at the hotel. He just got in and is eating. He'll be down here in a minute."

"If you see him," replied Dufresne, putting his watch back into his vest pocket, "you might tell him that if we get started by nine o'clock there will be plenty of time to finish by four. Seven hours — that is only a hundred dollars an hour!"

"Eddie," cried Hal, who had been listening as had the other men in the saloon, "how much of my money have you got lef'?"

Two months before, when Hal had so disturbed the peace of Queen City that he had been told to move on, he had had nine hundred dollars, proceeds from the sale of a piece of land in California left him by his father. He did not know even now how much of it he had thrown away in that one wild night of recklessness and dissipation, the major part of it drifting across the table to the two men who were to play tonight. In lieu of a bank he had deposited the remainder in the hands of the bar-tender for safe keeping.

Dufresne laughed quietly at Hal's question.

"Not this time, Hal," he replied decisively. "You take a friend's advice, and let Eddie keep it for you."

Advice again! Advice to a man who was now in a state where a natural violence abetted by the urge of alcoholic fumes made any suggestion the one thing to be opposed with the blind stubbornness of a drunken man! Advice from the man who seemed so confident of winning that seven hundred dollars that he did not want to share a cent with a third man! Advice from the man who had robbed him once and now would deny him the gambler's right to satisfaction! If they had invited him to play, the stupid cunning of intoxication

22

would have brought a jeering, insulting refusal to be robbed again. Every man there, excepting Hal, understood as well as did Prince Victor himself.

"Damn your friend's advice!" cried Hal, swaying to his feet, his flushed face thrust forward angrily. "Ain't I got revenge comin'?"

"Yes," responded the Prince with a quiet smile that but stung Hal's growing temper. "Whenever you are ready," he added significantly.

"Then it's now. Give me my money, Eddie. I'm ready now."

Dufresne shrugged his shoulders.

"I don't think so," he said, moving towards the door.

"Why not?" screamed Hal, his eyes flaming redly. "You damn hold-up gambler, why not?"

"Because," the answer came crisply, "you're too drunk to see the cards in your hand. I wouldn't play you to lose, and I don't want to win off a man in your condition."

Men who did not know Victor Dufresne well looked at him with wonder and something of admiration. Men who knew him well looked rather at the young fellow in the corner, their stern faces showing something that was almost pity. When the door opened and Papa Clark came in, a stalwart old man with a square beard and glinting, cold blue eyes, as hard a gambler as Dufresne, all men, there, excepting the man most concerned, saw the "frame up," and knew that Hal, with all his bluster, was as a harmless, buzzing fly in a mesh of two merciless spiders. And when the spiders combine against the fly the battle is likely to be short.

Papa Clark, after a curt greeting to Dufresne and a sharp glance at Hal, joined his voice to Dufresne's with short emphasis.

"Young man," he snapped, "you better git to bed, where you can sober up 'stead of measurin' your horns with grown-ups. Come ahead, Victor."

Hal's obstinacy when sober was proverbial. When drunk it became an aggressive Rock of Gibraltar. His tongue loosened in a tirade of imprecation, he gave reins to the rage within him which had so long fumed for an outlet, and for the first time that day broke into open insult and threat.

"Drunk," he stormed, lurching forward from his corner, all memory of Walsh and Bradshaw and Wallace gone before the sting of the new opposition. "Drunk, am I?" He laughed loudly, his lips drawn back from his white teeth. "You damn rabbits never saw a *man* drink before! I'll drink any sober two of you drunk now, an' be sober at the end of it! Drunk, huh! I'll show you if I'm too drunk to see straight!"

His right hand had jumped to his hip. As he moved, two guns leaped out from behind the bar in the steady hands of Wallace and Bradshaw, and Burt Walsh dropped his hand to his belt. Their eyes were steely and watchful upon Hal's.

At the far end of the bar was a picture, a ballet girl in pink tights. On the heels of his last word came two quick reports. The boy jammed the gun back into his holster before the smoke had cleared away, calling loudly:

"Can I see straight? Damn you, am I too drunk to see straight?"

A little gasp, not unmingled with admiration from the younger men, went up as the smoke cleared. The picture was thirty feet away and the eyes of the pink ballet girl were no bigger than dimes. Yet the two speeding bullets had found them.

"Let him in," snapped Papa Clark, moving towards the poker-table at the back of the room. "If the fool wants to give us his money, let him do it."

Hal laughed with blatant satisfaction, and swept into his two hands the gold and silver Eddie poured out upon the bar, not stopping to count. The three men with no further word, Prince Victor merely smiling and shrugging his shoulders, sat down together.

Clark toyed much with his white beard and sat long with pursed lips over each bet. Prince Victor, his hat and cane laid carefully upon the chair at his side, sat with inscrutable face and restless eyes, smiling slightly at each hand which was dealt him, good or bad. And Hal, his wide hat very low over his eyes, sat slouching forward, never lifting his head, turning merely the corners of his cards which he let lie, face down, upon the table.

The bystanders moved slowly back towards the table, exercising their prerogative in Queen City of watching the game which custom said should be played in the open. Bradshaw and Wallace stepped quietly to the end of the bar, the crowd falling aside unbidden so that the two men could see, and so as to be out of the line of fire if trouble should shoot, hissing, into their midst.

Cutting for the high card, Clark had won the first deal. Each man tossed a five-dollar gold piece into the pot without looking at his hand. Dufresne offered a bet of ten dollars after calling for cards. Hal saw it. Clark, with pursed lips, his fingers meditatively lost in his beard, added another ten dollars. The man on his left threw down his cards. Hal came in. Clark exposed his hand, three queens, and without a word Hal tossed his five cards into the discard.

Dufresne dealt. Hal, without looking at his cards, shoved twenty dollars to the middle of the table. Clark, with pursed lips, tugged long at his beard and finally, with a sigh, threw down his hand. Dufresne, smiling as ever, with the swiftest of glances at his hand, gently shoved twenty dollars into the pot, following them with another twenty. Hal turned the corners of his cards, stooping farther forward to look at them, and called. And again he lost, this time to aces and tens.

It was Hal's deal. He had already, in two minutes of fast play, lost seventy dollars. He shuffled the cards slowly, cutting them and reshuffling before he passed them to Dufresne for the final cut. The three antes of five dollars each were made simultaneously, before any man had looked at his cards. Clark made an opening bet of ten dollars after due reflection.

Dufresne came in for a like amount and raised the pot another ten. Hal slipped in the twenty they had called for and bet another fifty. Clark called the fifty and raised it fifty. Dufresne dropped out, still smiling. Hal called for a show down, and lost, one hundred and twenty-five dollars loser on the hand, one hundred and ninety-five dollars on the game.

In the fourth hand, moved to caution, he threw down his cards, not even coming in with the ante. Clark won a small amount. In the fifth hand Hal again refused to bet, Clark again winning on a small hand. Then Hal dealt again, and fingered his coins slowly while waiting for "action."

The game had been conducted in absolute silence save for the chink of gold and silver pieces and the ruffling of the cards, the two guns at the bar looking ridiculously unnecessary and even out of place. A sudden thundering voice from the doorway, snapping into the almost unnatural stillness, made every man in the saloon start and wheel towards the figure that had just entered.

"This gambling hell, this den of iniquity and vice, is held up for twenty dollars and five per cent, of the winnings of any and all games now in progress!"

The man standing on the threshold, his empty hand out-flung in wide gesture, was a giant even in the land where men grow big. Six feet four and broad in proportion, endowed with a bull's voice, a cavern for a mouth, big knotted hands, an arm swelling in his shirt sleeves like a blacksmith's, a face like a prize-fighter's, deep, steel-grey eyes under tangled, hanging brows, a weight of solid bone and sinew which made the floor creak, as shaggy as a shepherd dog from a bed in the thicket, ungainly, ill-dressed, belligerent. A great shock of upstanding hair seemed at once to assert its own rebelliousness and its master's.

"Even as Samson, come to the vineyards of Timnath," thundered the great voice from the cavern of a mouth, "took from the carcass of the dead lion honey that he might give of it to his father and his mother, so do I take from the mouth of the lion, which is this corner of hell, money for my children that I may please God, Who is my Father and my Mother!"

The men who had started at the first booming, clarion note of his voice, laughed. The big man came forward, his strides heavy, his boot heels making the floor groan beneath him. Hal, looking up, demanded angrily:

"Who is he?"

"Who am I?" thundered the big man, his voice like the rumble of distant thunder. "What man of this God-cursed Gomorrah does not know me? Me, who am the trumpet of the Lord God Almighty, the shepherd of straying herds, the disciple of Jesus! Me, who ask but my dues when I wrest from the very claws of Beelzebub bread and raiment for my suffering poor. I am John Brent, Brother."

He had paused, his hand unlifted, his eyes bright with a righteous wrath. Now again he strode forward in the noise of his big, tan laced boots, which he had brought with him from the last mining camp into which he had carried the Word, and which were far fitter objects for the pile of cans and bottles and discarded raiment behind the saloon than for the feet of man.

Hal's swift, grunted comment lost itself between his own jaws. Big John Brent had turned away from him and gone straight to the bar-tender. Eddie, with no

28

shadow of hesitation, had snapped open his till and slapped a twenty-dollar piece on the bar.

"I thank you, Brother, I thank you," bellowed John Brent, thrusting the gold coin deep down in his pocket. "In the name of our Father on high, I thank you. May God be with you this night."

"Ten dollars," remarked Papa Clark quietly, as he shoved his five dollars and another ten out on the table.

"*And* ten," smiled Dufresne, putting out two tens and a five.

"An' fifty more," snapped Hal, thrusting seventy-five dollars of his diminishing pile from him.

"I pass," smiled Dufresne.

"I — call," said Clark after long meditation and much pursing of lips. "What have you got, Hal?"

Hal had dealt himself two kings and had drawn a third, with two fours making a full hand. He threw down his cards, face up, and looked swiftly at Clark. The old man stopped for a grave whistle at Hal's luck, then showed his hand. He had four nines. Hal merely dropped his head, seeming to take no further interest in the pot which the horny hand of Clark drew slowly to the opposite side of the table.

"Five per cent., Brother," thundered Big John Brent, standing over Clark. "Five per cent, for my poor. One hundred seventy-five dollars. Five dollars for the Church, Brother."

With no murmur of dissent, merely the habitual pursing of lips, Papa Clark slipped five dollars across the table to the preacher.

"I thank you, Brother. In the name of our Heavenly Father, I thank you."

There was a man in the crowd about the table named Simon Tolliver, a newcomer in Queen City who had not heard of John Brent, disciple of Jesus, and who was gifted with a longer tongue than brain and with no shred of respect for the cloth. He laughed contemptuously as he saw Brent pick up the silver. Opening his coarse mouth to the man at his elbow, he said loudly:

"Damn beggin' thieves of preachers, why don't they work for a livin' like other men?"

Big John Brent turned slowly, looking across the heads of the men about him.

"Brother," he said mildly, "guard thy lips against criticism of those appointed by the most high God to be His shepherds here on earth."

The man laughed again, turning a sneering face upon the giant minister.

"Your high God is the God of Graft," he retorted. "An' I ain't takin' no sermons from no big, lazy —"

"Brother," interrupted the preacher sternly though not unkindly, "it is not well to deride a seeker after Christ. You should learn courtesy to the meek and lowly, Brother."

The men, always ready as boys to laugh lightly at what diversion the world presented them, guffawed loudly, chiding. Simon Tolliver with ready jests. Tolliver, having more tongue than brains, tried to cover his discomfiture in hurling the oath which came readiest to him at the man who declared himself meek and lowly. The epithet he used was the one epithet that men at any of the four corners of earth do not swallow if they be men.

There was a great bellow of wrath as John Brent ploughed through the knot of men who fell away from him like flies before a plunging horse. His great right hand, clubbed like a sledge in the grasp of a veritable Samson, rose and fell once only, striking the man who had an unguarded tongue fairly in the sneering mouth, felling him to the floor where he lay still, the life in him all but crushed out of his prone body.

"I am a preacher," Brent roared, and the rafters trembled with the vibration of his powerful voice. "And I am a man of God, and try to serve my Heavenly Father as best I can, and lead His sheep unto His fold — but I am not going to crawl to Him on my belly like a snake!"

They carried Tolliver to the front of the room where he gradually regained consciousness, and whence he slipped muttering, to the street. Meanwhile the game went on serenely. The preacher had seen the man slink away, and had returned quietly to the poker-table.

Hal continued to lose almost steadily. The two men against whom he had pitted himself were men who had been known throughout a wide part of the West as professional gamblers years before he had ridden his first horse. They did not play for amusement. The money they put into a game was as the money a Wall Street man puts into his bigger but similar game. With them poker was no longer a game of chance but one of almost pure skill and science. They were men whom long practice had made almost uncannily clairvoyant, seeming to see through the backs of the pasteboards, judging their opponents' hands almost as swiftly as they read the values in their own hands. They were men who never drank heavily, never tasted whisky, never allowed alcohol to dim the keen instinct without which a gambler is no gambler, but an ox in the shambles. Now they were so seriously in earnest that they did not even go to the trouble of losing small sums that their prey might be encouraged and led on. They had won hand after hand, or refused to play when the fickle goddess seemed to have drawn away from their winning elbows. And Hal, still losing, his face hidden from them, his breath coming sharp from between his set teeth, played recklessly, stung by each loss into madder sallies that he might recoup. But still the tide of that thing which is called luck never swung about to drop its golden silt at his hand.

Bradshaw and Wallace had come from behind the bar, their guns in their holsters, and stood near the table, watching. Prince Victor was dealing, smiling his eternal inscrutable, dark smile. Hal straightened a bit in his chair and cast a scowling look at the men about him. His bleared eyes encountered Burt Walsh's, and he sneered openly. Openly he whisked the flask from his pocket, drank the little whisky remaining, and flung the bottle to the floor where it shivered into clinking bits.

For the first time, as Hal put his head back to drink, Big John Brent saw the dark, flushed face.

"Who is he?" he demanded of the man at his elbow.

"It's him," was the response. "The man from the Bear Track, — Hal."

A great surprise dawned in John Brent's deep grey eyes.

"That the man!" he cried in amazement. "That the man all Queen City whispers about! That the 'Outlaw!' Why, man alive, he's only a boy!"

Only a boy! And Hal, twenty-four years of age, had prided himself for many a day that he was not only a man but a bad man, a man from whose approach timid mothers drew in their children like fussing hens clucking their broods under their wings when the fell pirate of the air sent his piercing hunting cry earthward. Such wild nights as to-night, when he felt that every man about him was watching him with something of fear and a ready gun, were common with him.

"Why, man, he is only a boy!" There was more of pity than of censure in the big man's voice which had dropped into an incredibly low tone, vastly more.

Not fear, not the horror which a wild life might have been expected to awaken in a man of the Church, not even surprise and a shock of repugnance; merely a vast, yearning pity. The blood surged hot in his scowling face as Hal dropped his head again. They had called him the "Outlaw," he had won his title by his lawless life, and he was proud of it, perhaps because — he was only a boy after all!

His last forty dollars were shoved out into the centre of the table. He had not looked at his hand, he had no intention of looking at it. If he was only a boy at least he would lose with his studied, insolent carelessness and indifference. He drew the second flask from his pocket and forced a mouthful of the fiery stuff down his rebelling throat. His eyes were more than bleared, they were blood-shot, and seemed to peer redly out from the veil of a film of drunkenness. Both Clark and Dufresne put in their forty dollars and looked to him to show his hand.

He flipped over his cards, half rising from his chair, reeling forward across the table, laughing unsteadily. For the first time that night he had won a pot worthwhile. The faithless gods of chance had veered to him at the last moment. He had not looked for it, he had in no way expected it. Perhaps that is why the change came.

"Five per cent. for the Church's poor!" thundered Big John Brent, reaching out a long arm, his fingers touching the money.

Hal whirled upon him, caught in the grip of a blind unreasonable drunken rage.

All night long the flood of rebellion within him had been surging higher, threatening to break the bounds set against it, whipped into a white froth with restriction and advice and surveillance. And now at last, when he hardly knew what he did, when his soul was drugged and deadened, when alcohol, rampant, held undisputed sway over his body, now came a man against whom his flaring rage could direct itself.

"Take that, you damn preacher!" he screamed.

Before a man could reach him to knock the gun from his hand, before Walsh or Bradshaw or Wallace could grasp his swift purpose, he had fired. Big John Brent, not four feet away, threw his arms wide out, and, with a look of dismay upon his face, fell heavily to the floor.

And Hal, before a man could draw his gun, crumpled up, and fell unconscious across the table.

CHAPTER
FOUR

The Mountain Road

Sibyl Estabrook was the sort of woman a man's eyes find swiftly, almost intuitively, the sort of woman who first holds his eyes and then his interest, and if he be impressionable, may drag the very heart and soul from his body. She was tall, superbly, magnificently tall, and deep breasted, with splendid throat, lithe, supple waist, perfect swelling hips, and a certain grace of movement almost like his own who looked upon her. To Hal she seemed purely feminine, richly womanly, a high specimen of the human female. She was serene, would be serene under all circumstances, he thought subconsciously. Her colour was ivory and dull gold. The masses of her loose-gathered hair were a deep tawny yellow. Her large eyes were of the same colour, cool and calm and tawny. Such satin-soft, smooth, white skin he had never seen. Nor such even, milky teeth when she smiled. Nor had he ever dreamed that a woman could have to such a superlative extent the essence of that intangible thing which so clearly bespeaks the female of the species.

He turned from her to his horses. He did not even see the men and women crowding politely after her. He grew dizzy with something which was not the fumes of last night's debauch. And he had never thought before of woman save as an institution, a requisite to the world that man-children might continue to be born, an inferior, negligible animal, the mere mother and nurse of the man-child, a necessary mammal, a keeper of the kitchen, a maker of bread, a lay figure somewhere upon the plane upon which Mohammed had placed her. As a proper mate for a man — the idea had not occurred to him. As man's superior — there were heights and depths upon the wide-reaching, misty borderland of which his strictured mind had not wandered.

He was in haste to be gone. The memory of last night was not a pleasant thing to him. He knew that he was alive to-day only because the men who had picked him up from the table where he had sprawled were not the men to lift their hands against an unconscious man; that before he had regained dizzy understanding Big John Brent had floundered up from the floor with a bullet hole in his shoulder from which the blood was still running; that the preacher had taken into his own lap the head of the man who had shot him, and with snarling lips had defied a man of them to lay hand upon him.

"He hurt no one but me," the big man had bellowed, forgetful in his rage at them of his own bleeding wound, and brandishing the gun which had dropped from Hal's fingers. "He belongs to me. He shall not be harmed this night. Would you have him reel this way drunken and blasphemous into the presence of his

Maker! For shame! And you call yourselves men! Mother of God! Can't you see he is only a boy?"

Yes, he remembered something of it. He knew how the preacher had worked with him. The hot, stinging shame still crept red into his cheeks. He had laughed and mocked and jeered; he had called the preacher a fool and a soft-hearted baby: he had got dizzily to his feet, the oaths dripping from his lips. But all of his bluster, all of his threats, all of his curses and swagger to show them the real badness of him, had not sufficed to wipe from his memory the sting of the preacher's words, the sting of the knowledge that the unarmed man whom in that blind moment he had hated and tried to kill, was the man who had saved his life for him and who had spoken softly of him, almost motherly, saying to the wolf-eyed men about him, in hushed tones of pity:

"Why, he is only a boy!"

It was five o'clock now and at last the Overland had come. Two heavy spring wagons, each with four restless horses were waiting at the stables. Hal called to the nine people, who got down together from the train to follow him, and stalked off towards the stables, carrying the two suit-cases he had snatched from somebody's hands.

"The Easterners" trooped after him, their sleepy eyes brightening in the dawn-sweet air, a lively curiosity in their glances and ejaculations alike. Hal had cast one comprehending glance at the group, singling out no individuals after he had stared for a dull moment at the glorious creature whom he promptly guessed to be

Sibyl Estabrook, the "Old Man's" elder sister, totalling his Easterners as he would have surveyed a herd of range cattle. His curiosity seemed to have surged up suddenly, and to have died down as swiftly.

But for these men and women who had stepped from their luxurious surroundings in the heart of New York a few days before, and who found themselves like excited, wandering children in a new land of romantic possibilities, every detail, great or small, that went towards making up the sum total of the romantic West they had come so far to see, came in for much examination, sharp scrutiny, and endless criticism. Therefore it was but natural that the man who stalked on ahead of them, a lithe, slim-wasted, handsome young fellow, himself unconsciously the most brilliant bit of "local colour" in the landscape, with his high-heeled boots, the revolver peeping out of his hip pocket, his bright red knotted neck-handkerchief, the free swinging grace of his stride, the dark, dare-devil dash of him, came in for no little of the interest so ready to be lavished upon anything of the West.

"He is splendid!" It was the magnificent young woman, Miss Estabrook, speaking to the sandy-haired, fair-eyed young man at her side. "Did you see his eyes? Do you notice the *je ne sais quoi* of his carriage, bespeaking him the wild, untamed, untameable, very spirit of the West! Isn't he splendid?"

"My dear Sibyl," expostulated her companion in mild mock-terror. "You aren't going to fall in love with the chap and throw me over, are you?"

She laughed gaily at him, but without taking her eyes from the slim figure head.

"I don't know, Louis," she told him merrily. "Would you be entirely broken-hearted if I did?"

"I'd just die, you know," replied Mr. Louis lightly.

"You tragic lover," she laughed at him, deigning for a fleeting second to transfer her regard from the cowboy to the fair, placid face at her side. And then, still lightly, but with a substratum of seriousness under her bantering tone, "I don't believe that *he* would do a thing like that. It would be more his part to remove his rival than quietly to die himself!"

"I shall never go unarmed, by mine honour!" quoth Mr. Louis Debner.

The two four-horse teams were fighting their bits, furrowing the ground with their sharp, impatient hoofs, enveloped in the dust of their own making, in haste to be gone. Dick Sperry, blue-eyed, horny-handed, bronzed, and sinewy — another puncher from the Bear Track — sat already upon the seat of his wagon, his eyes and hands alike busied with the nervous horses, the four reins jerking in his grip. He had no eyes for the "Easterners," but waited silently for Hal to assign half of them places in his wagon so that he might give his horses their heads. A stable boy, standing at the heads of the horses harnessed in the wagon Hal himself had driven, cried sharply that he couldn't "hold 'em all day." Hal tossed the two suitcases into the bed of the wagon, climbed to his own seat, unwrapping the reins from the brake, and called sharply:

"All right, ladies and gents. Half of you can climb aboard this wagon, the rest on Dick's wagon. We better be startin'."

"You'll perhaps ride in this one?" suggested Mr. Dabner to Miss Sibyl. And, Miss Sibyl, with no answer to him, allowed Mr. Dabner to help her to a place beside Hal. When safely ensconced upon the seat which was already swaying, she turned demure eyes upon him and said smilingly:

"You can take the rear seat, Mr. Dabner, I have no doubt. Perhaps Yvonne will ride with you. Mr. Cushing, will you take care of mamma and Fern?"

A very round, very short, very florid little gentleman of middle age and affable manner put his puffy little hand upon the unresisting elbow of a thin, sharp-faced woman who had tagged along in seeming weariness and ennui and despondency at the end of the little procession, helped her to a seat in the second wagon, stepped to the side of a pretty, blue-eyed, black-haired girl, and then took his own seat.

Mr. Dabner performed a like ceremony for a girl whom Hal had hardly seen, a slender, girlish girl of perhaps twenty, brown haired, with big soft grey eyes, and a manner quietly unobstrusive. Hal merely glanced at her now, noticed her slight limp as she came slowly forward, and promptly forgot her in the presence of the woman at his side. Two other men, servile and patently servants of the boot-licking order, together with a little French-looking girl, as patently a maid, half hid under her armful of wraps, put other suit-cases and grips into the two wagons and took places themselves with murmured apologies by the sides of their masters.

"All right?" cried Hal, after a swift survey of the two teams. It was the girl at his side who answered for them all, saying, "All right."

He threw his leaders around and out into the road, the stable boy jumped back, the wagon lurched suddenly, and his four horses plunged forward in their slack traces. The dust swirled up, cloud-like, from under the racing hoofs, the slack traces jerked suddenly tight, the whole wagon rocked and quivered under the strain put upon it. And Hal, sitting straight, his hat far back upon his head, his hands tight in their gauntlets upon the tugging reins, his eyes upon his galloping leaders, forgot that Queen City was being hurled back into the distance behind him, forgot even Big John Brent and the ignominy of last night, remembered only that his elbow touched the wonderful creature at his side.

The four horses on the dead run, the wagon shot rocking and creaking down the one street of Queen City and towards the open valley to the eastward. The steady hand upon the jerking reins swung the leaders sharply to the right at the first corner and out into the country road, the wagon making the turn upon two wheels, the four occupants beside the driver gripping the seats to save themselves from being hurled out. Hal half turned his head, saw the girl at his side, her lips parted, a little smile upon her face. Merely glimpsing her in his sweeping regard, he turned and looked back. The little scream of the French maid he passed over unnoticed. Dick Sperry behind them, giving his own half-tamed horses the rein that they too might indulge in their first pent-up eagerness before they be gradually pulled down to a trot, allowed no gap to widen between himself and the first wagon. So they swept into the open road, and Hal, finding the wild burst of speed exhilarating and even soothing at the same time to his frayed, irritated nerves, kept his eyes upon his horses and upon the road, and drew the breath of the morning into his lungs.

He threw his shoulders back, unconscious that he did so, knowing only that it was good to have the town behind him, far behind. Now and then his voice, low toned, musically sweet, called to his horses, soothing them, drawing from them the terror which young horses feel when new to the harness, setting them into a steady, hammering trot. He did not again turn to the girl beside him. She was an Easterner, she was of a world set apart from his world, she, like the rest of them, would look down upon him from the cool serenity of her social heights, as an entomologist looks upon an insignificant but rather interesting bug.

The sun wheeled up through a mass of gold and crimson clouds, the morning breeze sprang up rollicking and died away whispering, the dust rose higher and higher about the swiftly rolling wheels, the horses ceased to snort and fight their bits. Queen Creek sprawled and flashed and babbled across the road, and its yellow line of frail willows grew indistinct behind them. The little valley had closed in about them in a seemingly impassable wall of rocks and steep sides, and then with a suddenness almost magical a narrow pass opened up before them and the wagon went rocking and jerking through it. The four horses took the grade and the steep climb at the same swinging pace, eager to thrust their stubborn necks deep into their collars. Fifteen minutes later they had shot out of the far end of the pass and were pushing down hill through another valley, narrower, with steeper boundary-defining hills than the first.

Hal now thrust the reins under him, holding them with his hip, whipped off his gauntlets, and began to roll a cigarette. His eyes, even now, were alert upon his horses. There were still red flecks in his eyes, which smarted no little. It was only by a masterful exertion of his will that he kept his fingers steady upon his wheat straw. His throat was dry, beginning to ache from the thirst engendered by the alcohol he had poured down it so few hours before. He regretted now that he had not thought to secure another flask against the day's ride, a ride upon a road where houses were many miles apart. Even water would taste good now, he thought with a shrug. But it was ten miles to the next water.

Meantime few words had been spoken. Mr. Louis Dabner and Yvonne evidently had little enough in common. The girl sat looking somewhat wistfully out over the long stretches of country which unrolled before them, offering no remark herself, rarely replying to Dabner's sallies by more than a smile and a nod or by a monosyllable. Dabner once or twice leaned forward with a light word to Sibyl, and although her spirits were light and a-wing, she herself did hardly

44

more than answer. Three times, not to be reduced to silence, he had tapped Hal upon the shoulder and asked some question regarding the country through which they were passing or of the Bear Track range. The first two times the cowboy had snapped out monosyllabic answers. The third time he had swung about and, with eyes flashing angrily, had snarled:

"I ain't no guide, mister. An' besides, I'm busy."

Whereupon Miss Sibyl had smiled at the rocky range of hills, and Mr. Dabner, sinking back with a sigh, had lighted a cigar and accepted at last the burden of silence.

There was a curious light in Sibyl's eyes as she covertly watched Hal roll and light his cigarette before drawing on his gauntlets again. She saw the small whiteness of his shapely hands, saw in them what she believed was a keynote to the character of a man who was at once an uncouth puncher and who had the hands and the eyes and the bearing of this one. And again, her own eyes again running out over the valley and the rim of hills blue in the east, she smiled with something of contented amusement.

The man who was the cause of the smile did not see it. He had not once glanced at her during the last five miles. Upon the heels of the compelling admiration he had at first felt for her there now surged up in him as swift an anger. An "Easterner"! Was that not enough? Did he not know the breed? Did it not mean that he or she who came from the rim of the ocean which sees the sun rise from its own dirty waters was of a different world? Was not she like the rest, a sort of human snail

45

with a shell which the Westerner could never pierce, a shell into which she would retreat at any second, leaving outside the fool who dared think of her looking upon a cold, adamantine exterior? Again he thought bitterly of the bug under the finger of the cold-blooded scientist. She would have just so much interest as served to probe into a new species; but to think of the man whose elbow her own elbow rubbed, as a man — he flung his whip out over his horses' backs, jerking angrily away from the physical contact with her.

During the first three hours of the morning Sibyl Estabrook remained enwrapped in a musing silence. She had not once addressed her taciturn, black-browed seat fellow, having perhaps read his nature better than Dabner, or having forgotten him altogether, or having at least profited by Dabner's lack of success in drawing the cork of conversation from his stubborn silence with the old corkscrew of question. Save for the crunching of wheels, the noisy rattle of hoofs upon stones set rolling, or an occasional shriek from Mimi the Parisienne, the drive was a silent one.

The rock-ribbed hills gave roothold to scant vegetation — here and there a patch of scrubby, dry, grey brush, an occasional scrub oak or dwarf cedar. But as the road writhed and twisted like a mammoth serpent, even higher upon the foothills drawing into the fastnesses of the mountains, a peculiar floral growth of no little dignified grace began to make its appearance in the rockiest, seemingly most barren spots. A green stalk perhaps three inches thick at the base, springing out of a nest of iron-dagger-like leaves, stood straight up, some five or six feet, the top of it hung with great white bell-like flowers. It would have been a beautiful flower in a king's garden. Here upon the bleak aridity of a desert mountain its loveliness was something transcendent. The golden eyes of Miss Sibyl Estabrook lingered upon each far-away flower, softly speculative as she saw that as the road wound ever higher and higher so did the strange cactus march continually nearer.

"What is the name of those flowers?"

Her question, put in as few words as possible, the first remark directed to Hal, was coldly impersonal, and a something in her assured tones left no chance for evasion, no opening to say as he had said to Dabner, "I'm no florist — an' besides, I'm busy." So Hal answered, not turning towards the face which had not turned towards him, crisply and shortly:

"Spanish bayonet."

She did not seem to notice the short, almost surly note of the reply, nor to greet indifference otherwise than with indifference. She did not thank him, merely repeating softly to herself, her eyes still upon the superb cactus which had drawn her question, "Spanish bayonet." After a silent twenty minutes she spoke again. At a turn in the road they had come to the largest, most perfect specimen she had yet seen, standing like a sentinel upon the brow of the hill not fifty feet away.

"Stop a minute. I want that one."

The same impersonal note, the same tone of command and of assurance. Hal, almost automatically, slammed on his brake and jerked his horses to a sudden standstill.

"Get it for me," she said quietly, putting out her hands for the reins.

Hal turned upon her, something of surprise in his eyes.

"I'm drivin'," he answered as quietly as she had spoken and with as much determination in his voice.

"I can drive," she told him steadily, the black lines of her brows arched over her grave golden eyes." "The horses are quiet now."

Her hand was still outstretched for the reins, her eyes still steadily upon his.

"I ain't lettin' no woman drive these hosses. If you want to git that flower there you can. An' I ain't got long to wait."

Slowly her hand dropped to her. lap. She drew her eyes from him, a slight flush in her cheeks, her lower lip caught up between her teeth. Mimi the maid shuddered and gasped, "*Oh, mon Dieu!*"

"Louis," she said quietly, "will *you* get it for me? Or has a three hours' sojourn in the cattle country stolen away all of *your* gentlemanliness, too?"

Dabner, his eyes twinkling, his averted face showing much inner satisfaction, scrambled down and obeyed his lady's behest. Not knowing the plant and its own peculiar methods of defence and self-preservation, he was repelled from the first joyous assault with prickling hands and ankles. It was only after a second and more cautious attack and a great deal of hacking with a diminutive penknife that he came away victorious, the long bell-crowned stalk over his shoulder. He had hardly more than thrust it into the wagon and put his

48

foot upon the step to climb in himself, when Hal snapped back the brake and sent the horses forward.

The thanks bestowed upon him were short, neither himself nor the flower coming in for any flattering attention of the imperious young woman. For it was perhaps the first time in her life since wilful babyhood that Sibyl Estabrook had called upon a man for a favour which had not been granted with alacrity. Still Mr. Louis Dabner, wiping his soft-skinned hands upon a dainty handkerchief, seemed in no wise disgruntled. Instead, he continued to smile complacently upon the broad back of the driver, and it would seem that he was not without a certain sort of humour. Nor yet without discretion. Miss Sibyl looking straight ahead into the distance did not see the smile.

It was an hour after noon when they swept down into a green little valley and Hal slammed on his brake. He had swung his horses out of the road and under a wide-branching oak tree. Fifty yards away was a creek he had been longing for, no less on account of his own burning throat than for his horses. All about them the blue tops of mountains shot skyward, the ineffable stillness of the mountains brooded.

"An hour off to rest the hosses," he announced to no one in particular. "Pile out."

Yvonne looked about her with a little cry of delight as her eyes grew bright and wide with the glory of the mountains shutting in this little "Happy Valley." Mimi lifted her ample bosom in a great sigh of fatigue. Mr. Louis Dabner glanced from the expressionless face of this type of "hired man," new to him, who so ordered his employer's guests about, to the face of Miss Sibyl. And Miss Sibyl banished her slight frown with a quick, light laugh, as she prepared to obey orders.

Lunch baskets were dragged out, Hal waiting with unconcealed impatience until the little party turned away to make camp under the tree, and then drove off towards the creek. He had unhitched and led his horses to the water when the second wagon drove up and allowed Mrs. Estabrook, Fern Winston, Mr. Cushing, and the two men-servants to get down.

Mrs. Estabrook, a great weariness in her face and bearing alike, allowed Mr. Cushing of the puffy hands to escort her to a seat upon a pile of wraps against the tree trunk. And with a great quivering sigh the fatigued lady sank down to rest and bemoan her fate.

"I am half dead," she moaned almost tearfully.

"Yvonne, you will never, never understand all that I have sacrificed for you in making this horrible trip west."

"For me, mamma?" Yvonne looked to her mother in mild surprise.

"Yes, for you, you ungrateful child," whimpered Mrs. Estabrook dolefully. "And I'm sure I don't know if I'll ever come out of it alive. Not that you will care." She dabbed a delicate lace handkerchief at her eyes and shook her head moaning.

Mr. Cushing mopped his florid brow with a pale lavender handkerchief and dropped limply and moistly to a seat between Fern and Yvonne. Firefly and two men-servants, Cushing's man Bates, and Dabner's retainer, Crofton, were bringing a varied lot of tinned

50

meats and fruits from the depths of two wicker baskets, and spreading the lunch upon the fragrant grass.

"What do you think of Hal, the 'Outlaw'?" queried Mr. Cushing, finally dragging his eyes away from the spread and turning them upon Sibyl. She paused a moment in her superintending to ask what he meant. Who in the world was Hal, the "Outlaw"?

"Don't you know?" He lifted the thin, straw-coloured lines which served him for eyebrows. "He's the man you rode out with, your driver."

Sibyl wheeled about suddenly, a light of interest springing up into her eyes, to demand quickly:

"What? And why, pray, the *Outlaw*?"

"Evidently he isn't an egoistical chap," responded Cushing. "Now, I rode alongside of our driver and he told me a whole lot about himself — his name's Dick Sperry — and about his brother wild man. Your driver is certainly an interesting figure, more interesting than desirable, perhaps. Eh, Mrs. Estabrook?"

Mrs. Estabrook took down her hands to shudder.

"Theophile," she admonished weakly; "I wish you wouldn't mention such things."

"Tell me," insisted Sibyl. "What about him?"

"You see," sighed Dabner, removing his cigar for a moment in order to be sufficiently mock-serious. "I wanted Sibyl to marry me before we left New York. Already she is getting interested in this romantic-looking wild man. Mrs. Estabrook, do you think that she is going to throw me over for him?"

51

Shocks and shudders seemed to be that lady's chief stock-in-trade; she both shuddered now and looked shocked, very, very shocked.

"Louis!" she cried. "How can you!"

Sibyl stamped her foot.

"You foolish people," she cried impatiently. "Mr. Cushing, tell me about him."

"After lunch —" began the stout gentleman, only to be interrupted by Sibyl's emphatic

"Not a bite do you get to eat, Mr. Cushing, until you gratify a very natural curiosity. I want to know about this man, and why he is called the Outlaw."

Mr. Theophile Cushing lifted his fat shoulders and smiled his fat smile.

"Dear Sibyl," he drawled, "you are *so* energetic and *so* insistent. As to the young savage who has acted as your driver this morning: I should say that he is called the Outlaw for the simple reason that these peculiar people of the West have the bad habit of calling a man just what he really is. It seems that about two months ago he ran a-foul of the charming populace of that equally charming Queen City, and that he came pretty close to killing somebody or other. That the good citizens drove him out and told him that if he showed up again they would put some six feet of alkali soil on top of his dashing self. That he was foolhardy enough last night to get into another mix-up. He shot a man a very few hours before we got into that delightful town. And —"

"And —" cried Sibyl impatiently.

"And now I think I have earned my luncheon."

"Go on first. What more?"

"Really nothing much. He seems to have a reputation which he has made well known over a thousand square miles of cattle country, a reputation as a bad man, a reckless gambler, an out-and-out drunkard."

"Didn't I tell you?" cried the impetuous young lady, swinging triumphantly upon Dabner. "Didn't I say that he was the very embodiment of the spirit of the West, untamed and untameable?"

"He doesn't look to be vicious," smiled Yvonne, bringing her eyes back from the blue shreds of sky.

"Yvonne!" cried Mrs. Estabrook. "How can you say such things! You want to kill me with them. I know you do."

Yvonne's eyes grew grave as they went back to the strips of sky. She made no reply.

The hour sped by; the two Bear Track men smoked their cigarettes and Hal dozed in the shade. When Dick Sperry awoke him with a gentle poke in the ribs the two men watered their horses and hitched up. The guests scrambled to their feet, Bates and Crofton and Mimi attending to the baskets and wraps, and the two wagons swung out into the road again, the horses picking up their feet in lively eagerness for the afternoon's work.

Little by little the road grew rougher, steeper, more and more ill-defined. Hardly ten teams had travelled it in as many months. Here and there, where the last winter's rains had torn out the side of the mountain, the road was almost lost. The maid cried out more frequently now, and in the second wagon Mrs.

Estabrook whimpered continually to Mr. Cushing, whom she had begged to sit in the rear seat with her. She was very positive that she was never to come out of it alive, and she was equally convinced that Yvonne would never, never thank her for it.

At times there was hardly more than a cattle trail along the steep slope; at times the wagons left the road which winter had made impossible and picked a jolting, hazardous way over rocks and bushes and stumps. Progress grew slower constantly, the ten-mile clip of the morning being cut down to about three miles an hour now. Three times did Hal throw on his brake, and with no explanation, command his passengers to "Git down an' hoof it a bit." As they had followed him over the battle-scarred iron breast of the mountain, had seen the great cuts gouged into what he was pleased to term a road, and looked shudderingly down half a thousand feet into a rocky chasm into which the wagon seemed always on the verge of slipping, no explanation was needed.

And still over such places Hal drove with what speed was possible, his cigarette sending aloft its serene signal, his face and mien undisturbed, confident. Following close behind him, once they had seen the hind wheel of the wagon slip over the edge of an embankment, had felt their hearts in their throats stifling them, had seen him throw out his whip and call quietly to his leaders, jerking the wheel back upon the "road," as calm about it as though the fall were five inches instead of as many hundred feet.

"The way that man drives," muttered Dabner to Sibyl at his side, "is commentary sufficient upon his character. He's as reckless as the very devil."

"You'll observe," smiled the young lady, "that with all his recklessness, which is so obvious, he goes over dangerous places and comes across them alive. There is a certain competency not so apparent but none the less active under that recklessness. We have a type of the man animal here, my dear Louis, that is a new type to you and me and our kind of people. And I am going to study it!"

CHAPTER
FIVE

A Double Hold Up

At one moment the red ball of the sun was resting upon the mountain tops, soft and molten, broadening and flattening under its own weight as it slipped downward upon the rocky ridge. A second later its liquid fire had burst into a stream, cascading through a tangle of fir-tops, the burning torrent plunging down into the shadows upon the far side of the mountains, a glint of ruddy gold winked back for a moment, and, as though it had been, a signal for the invasion of the legions of the night, the darkness swept into the narrow passes of the mountains, leaped and charged up the steep slopes, conquered the far-reaching fastnesses and flung far out the black banners of night. The stars shot out, new signal fires of the new conqueror, and the whole aspect of the landscape was changed.

The light was gone, swept up into dim twilight, leaving deeper, softer tones upon the vague horizon. The hard, bleak faces of the giant cliffs grew suddenly softer, less sternly unyielding, touched as though with a gentle hand into a beauty no less majestic, only made tender with something almost like human sympathy. From far off in the heart of the darkness came the

56

whisper of a breeze, fragrant with the balmy incense of the pine-tops, picking up their night song upon its sighing lips, telling of a flashing waterfall, of the stirring of branches, of the last sleepy chirrup of a drowsy bird, a wonderful song, fragrant, musical. The weird calls of night-waking beasts and birds, prowling hunting calls, the long-drawn, sobbing scream of a panther, mingled indescribably with the perfume of the wooded heights. Hal's quick cries to his horses went billowing through the night, caught up and tossed back and forth by the two sides of the canyon, as though the rocky pinnacle here and the one yonder were playing ball with his voice. And even Hal's tones had taken on an intangible difference, a soft weirdness, a something which made them strangely at harmony with the other night calls.

The stars were thick strewn across the dusky velvet of the moonless sky, the ground underfoot lost in black nothingness, the mountains merely sheer walls of ebony, when the Bear Track man swung his team about a well-remembered bend in the road. The moon lifted an arc over the mountains in the east, and now the Easterners, looking down, saw the moon and the stars looking back up at them from the floor of the valley. Yvonne cried out aloud, a little ecstatic cry of delight, like a child's. Mimi choked, "*Oh, mon Dieu, mon Dieu!*" and crossed herself. Surely the earth itself here was a plaything of the devil.

Cutting into the silence so sharply, so abruptly that the enrapt guests were startled by it and the French maid threw her arms around Mr. Dabner's neck, shocked into a shriek of terror, Hal's piercing yell went

57

flying out over the valley. The echoes went mad with it, the two sides of the canyon which they had just left breaking the sound into a thousand fragments, the rocky cliffs playing at their eerie game of ball more frantically than ever. As he called they saw one of the stars far below begin to move along the side of the strange mirror which had caught the reflection of the sky, and knew that they were directly above Swayne's Lake and Swayne's Road-house. The runaway star had resolved itself into a lantern, swung in a circle about a man's head, and an answering voice told them that Swayne was waiting for them.

Still it was half an hour before the four horses could bring them to the lakeside. For the road was bad and seemed needlessly long in its cautious windings down the mountain side. His passengers were fearfully thankful that Hal was thirsty. Once upon a stretch of level valley road, he turned his team towards the rambling old house which stood outlined against the lake, shook his reins out loosely, and gave his horses their heads.

The Estabrook party lost no time in admiration of the flashing jewel placed here, high in the emerald setting of the mountain valley, but hastened stiffly into the house. The short greetings of their new host were lost in the furious barkings of a dozen dogs, and went unanswered. Sibyl Estabrook slightly in advance as usual, they entered the long, low-ceiled front room of the squat, log building, found rough, home-made chairs and benches by the light of a dim, evil-smelling kerosene oil lamp, and dropped thankfully upon them.

Outside the heavy voice of Swayne, Hal's short laugh in reply, and presently the rolling wheels and pounding hoofs of the second team. Inside a heavy, restful silence. A very long room with a deep, rough stone fireplace upon one side, crudely constructed benches upon the other. A lamp hanging from a staple in the rough-hewn ceiling, the chimney allowing the dimmest of rays to straggle through long-accumulated dust. An uneven floor, a long table made of planks ripped out of oaken logs with an axe. Upon the table a dozen plates, no two of them alike, a varied assortment of thick ware cracked and chipped into amazing designs. Tin cups, pewter cups, several glasses, and the proper number of black-handled knives and three-pronged forks. Mrs. Estabrook, entering dolefully, gave one sweeping glance at the preparations which had been made for their entertainment and shuddered herself to a bench, upon which she continued to shudder at intervals moaning dismally about the ingratitude of one's children.

Swayne, standing in the open doorway, his big hands upon his hips, the curl of his pending moustaches concealing the curl of his lips, surveyed his guests for the night with cool critical scrutiny. If he were greatly pleased with them, if he felt the honour which he surely should have felt, he at least gave no sign. In fact, his only vocal utterance was suspiciously like a sniff of disapproval. Turning his back upon them for a moment he commanded a half-dozen dogs at his heels to "dry up an' git out," and then stalked into the room, leaving the door open.

"Well, ladies an' gents," he drawled, "you're here, are you? You're welcome. Make yourse'fs to home. Supper'll be ready in about ten minutes. You kin find a place to wash up out there. An' the bar's right in yonder. The drinks is on me."

Poor Mrs. Estabrook! She at last could find no word in her vocabulary adequate even to hint at her emotions. She sighed, and her sigh being lost in the noise of Swayne's boots as he strode through the room, sighed again and louder. Mr. Cushing got to his feet with an alacrity astonishing in one of his slothful nature, and trotted along after the broad-shouldered form of the host. Mr. Dabner, with a murmured apology which Cushing had forgotten, followed the fat gentleman. And Bates and Crofton, seeing their masters accepting Swayne's invitation, took the swift advantage of conditions which the servile in service are prone to take, understood that here man was as good as master, and hurried after the others.

Swayne struck the door with his shoulder, leading the way into a second room as long as the first and wider. Along one side of the room was a painted redwood bar, behind the bar several shelves of bottles, glistening dully under the rays of a second oil lamp. Swayne stepped behind the bar, gave it a professional swipe with a dingy towel, and said brusquely:

"What you takin', gents?"

Since there was only a choice between beer and whisky, it did not take long for them to name "their poison." Having replied to Swayne's hearty, "Here's how," they drank with him. Bates and Crofton standing

60

elbow to elbow with their masters. And then having accepted the other invitation to "wash up "outside where the barrel of water and the basin and towels were, they returned considerably refreshened to the dining-room — by way of the bar-room, at Cushing's suggestion.

A Chinaman, slant eyed and with shuffling feet, brought the dinner in, and disappeared to the kitchen, leaving those at the table to wait upon themselves. Swayne called to them to "Set in," dragged his own chair up to the head of the table, leaving his guests to perform like services for themselves, and began to carve the steaks piled high upon the platter in front of him. Supper went on smoothly, until Mrs. Estabrook received the final and crowning shock of the day. Mr. Cushing, his epicurean tongue made unusually sensitive by the long fast of the afternoon and the two raw whiskies, had passed his plate back for a second steak, asking what kind of meat it was.

"This here?" queried Swayne, holding a large piece suspended and dripping with his own fork. "This here, stranger, is bear meat. Eatin' this'll put hair on your ches' and make you scrap tigers."

Naturally Mrs. Estabrook shuddered. I don't know that one should blame the dear soul. Mr. Cushing, being anxious to cover up the declaration of the road-house keeper, continued swiftly:

"Bear meat? It's fine. You kill him?"

"Yep." Swayne nodded. "An' time I did, too."

Mr. Cushing looked mildly interested.

"Yes? How's that?"

"He was a bad one. A man killer. I had two Chinks workin' for me las' week. I only got one now. This same ol' bear had et all one side — leg an' arm an' —"

As daintily, as ladylike about it as a lady could be imagined to be under such circumstances, Mrs. Estabrook delicately removed the particle of meat from her mouth with a lace handkerchief. Even Mr. Cushing grew suddenly pale and left his second steak marooned upon the edge of his plate, pushing it gingerly away from contact with his potatoes.

"Hem," remarked Mr. Cushing with a weak, sick smile. "Remarkable."

Hal and Dick Sperry, entering together, tossed their hats to the floor in the corner and sat down, their lips twitching. They had had time to wash and plaster their hair down upon their foreheads in the approved and unbecoming style of their fellows, and now came in through the bar-room, wiping their lips upon their shirt sleeves. Dropping into their seats, they passed their plates up to Swayne and partook generously of the "man killer" steaks. Their heads down, intent upon the business of eating, they plied knife and fork swiftly, and in silence.

"An' now, ladies an' gents," said Swayne, having finished his own meal and being engaged now in picking his big strong teeth with one of the three-pronged forks which he did not lay aside to address his guests, "if you'll jus' stick aroun' a little you kin make yourselves to home. Purty pronto my Chink'll have your rooms ready for you. I got to go out an' shut up my stock."

He pushed back his chair noisily, floundered to his feet, and went lumbering out of the room. His guests finished their dinner one by one shortly after he had left, and withdrew from the table to sit upon one of the benches or deformed chairs. Hal, his appetite little, his thirst a thing of fire, pushed his chair back, leaving untasted much of his portion, and sweeping up his hat as he went, strode into the bar-room. He selected a bottle from the bar, poured out his two customary drinks which he took with slow appreciation, giving no sign that he knew Sibyl's eyes were fixed upon him through the open doorway. Having put the bottle again in its place he tossed a coin into the little drawer under the bar, and strolled away to the stables, making a cigarette as he went. Dick Sperry, having no thirst but a working-man's appetite, made a hearty meal, eating swiftly with no regard to the science of mastication and thirty-two bites per mouthful when his strong jaws and teeth could do the business in two, and followed Hal to the stables.

Mrs. Estabrook, who had watched him gulp down his meal, fascinated by the horror of this style of eating which suggested cannibalism to her delicate nerves, the more so since the biography of the *pièce de résistance* had been read, wore an expression of face very much resembling that which might be supposed to visit the countenance of a fastidious diner who had mistaken the vinegar for the light sherry. Mr. Cushing tilted his chair against the wall, his little fat legs a-dangle, his drop open. No doubt he was on the very verge of a snore. Mr. Dabner, the thin blue spiral of smoke climbing aloft from his cigar to the rough, smoke-blackened beams across the ceiling, carried his musing eyes with it as he too leaned back in after-dinner peace. Fern Winston, the pretty girl with the black hair and blue eyes, was watching Mrs. Estabrook and seemed to find amusement in the look that lady wore.

Yvonne, half sitting, half reclining upon one of the long benches, looked dreamily out through the door and to the little lake sprinkled with stars. She was hardly more than half conscious of the presence of her companions, or of her complaining mother's querulous voice, something deep down in the depths of her city-bred soul expanding, awaking, rising upward to the surface, swimming upon the vague rim of her consciousness, answering to the call of the world outside and to the night and the stars.

"Why did your father send us 'way out here?" Mrs. Estabrook was half sobbing, her tearful eyes upon Yvonne. "And why did Oscar send two such savages for us? Oh, don't tell *me*: I know a few things, I hope. They are cut-throats, I know; butchers, wild men. If they eat the bears that eat their Chinks, whatever kind of servants Chinks are, who knows but that they eat each other? And they have brought us to this unheard-of low place where they could rob us and kill us and —"

"Hands up, gents! Look alive! Jes' set still, ladies. The first one as makes a move gits his brains spattered all over!"

The voice was low toned, very quiet, and for all that very insistent and stern. Just outside of the front door, dim in the pale moonlight, barely touched by the faltering rays from the dirty lamp, a man with a heavy six-shooter in each hand leaned slightly forward, peering in upon them, his attitude alert and determined. A wide soft black hat was low over his eyes, a red handkerchief knotted about the forehead falling over the face and below the throat, his eyes looking upon them through slits in the mask.

Yvonne, still dreaming, noted that he fitted into the landscape picturesquely, that he was a harmonious part of the new world into which her wandering fancies had made pilgrimage. Mrs. Estabrook ceased rocking her body back and forth, and sat wide-eyed and still, save for the little shivers running spasmodically from head to foot. Mr. Dabner got to his feet with such promptness that in jumping up he came dangerously near swallowing his cigar. Mr. Cushing in one and the same instant opened his eyes, closed his mouth, stifled his incipient snore, and shot his short arms high above his head. And Sibyl murmured to herself:

"So our Outlaw has turned highwayman!"

"I hate to seem rude," went on the man outside quietly. "An' I sure hate to make you folks rush. But I ain't got much time. You ladies set right still. An' you gents can walk this way when I slip you the word. Get your money ready, an' if you got much sense you won't try none to hold out on me. All right, Fatty. You're the first one across. Step lively."

Mr. Cushing, his puffy hands still high above his head, came forward so promptly, albeit so tremblingly, that he stumbled in so doing.

"I — I *beg* pardon," he gasped. "I —"

65

"That's all right, Fatty. You can cut it short. You can also take your han's down long enough to dig. An' dig fas'."

Mr. Cushing's right hand shot into his pocket, coming out with a handful of greenbacks which he proffered eagerly. His left hand dived into his breast pocket and thrust forth a fat, red-leather wallet.

"Put 'em on the floor," commanded the quiet voice.

Mr. Cushing dropped them as though they were hot.

"My watch —" he volunteered, nervously anxious to please, his fat fingers trembling up in the chain across his little fat stomach.

The hold-up man laughed shortly.

"You can keep it, Fatty. Now back up an' give the res' a show. Come ahead, you with the cigar."

Mr. Cushing fell back as from the presence of royalty and sank weakly into his chair, his fingers still lifted high. Dabner, almost as white as Cushing, came forward slowly, really less fear in his heart than shame that that fear should have been manifested in the presence of the Estabrook women. The revolver gripped in the highwayman's right hand dropped its nose until it pointed at Mr. Dabner's hesitant feet.

"You'll step livelier, young feller, or git a hole through that hind foot of yourn. Which is it?"

Dabner's fear grew at a bound greater than his shame, and he hurried forward.

"Now dig."

Like Cushing, he pulled a handful of small bills from his pocket. These he tossed to the floor and began to move back.

66

"No, you don't!" There was an ugly snarl in the steady voice which had not been there before. "You come across proper an' do it fas'. Come across with the rest."

"That's all I have," grumbled Mr. Dabner.

"You lie!" The words fairly slapped him in the face, and his head went back as though a hand had struck him. "An' 'anyway, it ain't enough. Anybody gits alive out'n this if he has enough money to pay his fare. If you ain't got the coin, an' if I don't git it damn quick, I'll shoot you up for bein' broke an' wastin' my time. I'm countin' three. One — two —"

But Dabner's hand, like Cushing's before him, shot into his coat pocket and drew forth a wallet which was cast hurriedly at the threshold with the other loot. Then again like Mr. Cushing, he stepped backward, hands up-lifted, and took his place near the wall.

Crofton and Bates were called. They stepped quietly up to the door, emptied their pockets, and stepped as quietly back. The hold-up man nodded approvingly.

"Which is actin' like two real sports should," he muttered. "I reckon you're the two real gents, an' that old Fatty an' the guy with the cigar is your hired men, huh? Well, folks, that'll be about all to-night. No, I ain't troublin' the ladies. An' I guess they ain't got much cash aroun', anyway."

Mr. Dabner had flushed red at the stranger's diagnosis, Mr. Cushing had grown a trifle paler, Crofton and Bates had merely looked deferential and apologetic, Yvonne had smiled faintly out into the darkness. In the bar-room a faint creaking of boards under cautious tiptoes was lost in the noise of the falling chair which Crofton's foot had toppled over. There was no light in the bar-room now; perhaps the oil lamp had burned down and flickered out unnoticed, perhaps a gust of wind had swept out the little flame.

The door was just ajar. Slowly, so slowly that the moving was imperceptible, the door had opened a little, enough to allow a man to look in, to fire in if he desired. But all faces in the room were intent upon the face of the man out in the moonlight, and he in turn had eyes only for the men and women whom he was swiftly robbing.

"Now," he was saying crisply, "I got to be goin'. You folks can turn your faces to the wall while I pick this mazuma up. An' don't turn back till I tell you you can."

His command was obeyed swiftly. Shoving one of the guns into its holster at his hip he stooped and with the free hand swept up the loose bills on the floor, beginning to stuff them into his pocket. As he lowered his head the bar-room door suddenly swung wide open.

"Han's up!"

Hal's voice — as cool, as indifferent, as steady and quiet and determined as the other's had been. Hal himself standing in the doorway, his hat pushed far back upon his head, his lips smiling, his eyes stern, his left hand upon his hip, his right hand outstretched with a revolver trained upon the man at the threshold.

Yvonne, near the door, started up, a little cry that sounded like fear whipped from her lips. The man stooping so near her lifted his head with a quick jerk and leaped back, dropping the two wallets and leaving

68

the loose greenbacks, strewn over the floor. As he leaped, he jerked up the gun in his hand.

"Cut that out, pal!" Hal's voice again ringing ominously stern. "You know me. I'll drop you dead in your shoes if you try to use that gun. Han's up!"

The masked man paused quickly, dropped the gun, and lifted his hands. And although his face was still hidden under the red handkerchief, fluttering now in the evening breeze, there was that in his bearing, in the very droop of his shoulders and quick upfling of his hands, which bespoke a gripping fear.

"Now," went on Hal, his lips twitching again into a smile, his eyes none the less steady upon the man whom his gun covered, "I reckon we'll finish this little show. Don't you know as how these folks is Easterners?" There was a deal of contempt in the epithet. "Don't you know as how they might get a shock an' die when you go an' play bad man like this? *You'd* ought to know better'n that!" There was a certain strange emphasis upon the pronoun. And the man to whom it was applied started perceptibly. "Well, we'll let it pass. You c'n drop your lef' han' an' dig that rag money out'n your pocket. Don't make no mistakes an' go browsin' aroun' for your gun! Dig out the money an' jus' drop it on the floor."

There was hesitation in the other's attitude for a brief second. Then the left hand, as commanded, went swiftly to his pocket, the few greenbacks were jerked out and dropped to the floor, the hand was again uplifted.

"Much obliged ol' timer," grinned Hal. "You'd ought to apologise for pickin' the feathers out'n my birds. But we'll let that slide too. Now you c'n back up, an' git out'n the house. *An' keep on goin'*! Don't take all night gittin' out'n the country right aroun' here. So long."

The man stepped back swiftly. They could hear his great sigh of relief. He passed out of the door and into the darkness.

Sibyl had sprung to her feet, her eyes flashing. There was a little smile upon Yvonne's lips.

"Why did you let him go?" cried Sibyl hotly. "He's a robber, a thief, a murderer in his heart! Why did you let him go?"

Hal shoved his gun back into his holster with a short laugh and turned to leave the room. Sibyl stamped her foot angrily.

"You know who he is!" she called after him. "He's a friend of yours. You are trying to shield him."

Hal turned slowly, looking straight into her eyes.

"You purty near called the turn," he said shortly. "He *was* a sort of frien' of mine."

For a moment he stood, looking at her, a curious light in his eyes. Then with a second laugh he turned again and strode into the bar-room.

"You see," moaned Mrs. Estabrook, and there was a something triumphant in the shudder with which she accompanied her words, "they're friends. This Hal person is a dangerous, treacherous criminal!"

"Who carried himself," murmured Yvonne under her breath, "like a gentleman loyal to his friends."

70

CHAPTER
SIX

The Bear Track

He's got one of his silent streaks on, I notice," Swayne offered to young Dick Sperry as the two men cut and dealt at "crib." To be more explicit, he jerked his head at the tall, lithe form leaning in the front doorway, thumbs hooked in belt, hat low drawn over his brows, eyes lost in the shadows. Sperry nodded and discarded.

"He's always that way after a jag," he returned in the same low monotone. "I've knowed him to go a week without openin' his face excep' for grub an' tobacco. An' it's a fair bet the lady was right, an' he does know who the jasper was."

Yes, Hal had "one of his silent streaks on." He had shaken his head when Swayne demanded particulars, when Dick Sperry had asked if he was crazy to let the man go. He had shaken his head when they asked him to make it a three-handed game of poker. He had said no word when Swayne suggested whisky, but had tossed off his brim-filled glass and strode to the door, to stare moodily out across the little lake. The excited visitors had had many things to say, and he had shrugged his shoulders at the volley of exclamations and questions. Now they had gone wearily to bed, reminded by Dick that they would "hit the road about sun-up," and he stood in the half-light of the doorway, hearing but not hearkening to the indistinct hum of Swayne's and Dick's voices from the bar-room.

There was some one near him who had not been there a moment ago. He had heard no board creak, the footfall was too light a thing to be counted a sound. But he sensed what he did not hear, and his head turned slightly. It was a girl, Yvonne Estabrook.

In the weak rays of the kerosene lamp trailing across the bigger front room from the bar he could see that there was a little flush upon her cheeks, that her eyes were very bright. He made no second movement, but stood looking steadily at her.

She was prettier than he had noticed to-day. There was about her a refined delicacy, a daintiness which seemed to him to emanate from her, to float out about her as the fragrance does from a violet. He regarded her coolly, critically, almost insolently, as was his way. He noted the warm white curve of the throat, the soft brown of the hair at her forehead and cheek, the frank, grey eyes like a child's. And as she paused and came a step nearer he frowned at the slight limp which he had seen to-day. She was so like a flower, and a flower should be all beauty, with no flaw.

"I had to come back." Her face was upturned, her eyes questing his, her voice as gentle as her eyes. "I wanted to thank you."

"What for?" as bluntly as he knew how to say it.

"For what you did a little while ago" — a look flashing in her eyes which made him wonder if she had

72

felt some twinge of physical pain. "You see, I understood."

He made no answer, but waited for her to speak again or to go.

"And," with a quick little smile which, too, had something of pain in it, "I wanted to say good night."

"Good night."

She turned and was gone through the side door leading to the stairs. He stared after her a moment, listened to the patter of her feet as she ran up to her room, and turned back to the lake.

"I wonder," and he drew out his tobacco and papers, "what she meant?"

Swayne's heavy voice called something to him, and Hal, rather than answer, went outside and down to the lake. He found a flat-topped rock and sat down upon it, smoking slowly, frowning at the reflected stars dancing in the water. And when the game of "crib "was done and Dick Sperry and Swayne had had their parting drinks and had gone to bed, he sat and smoked and stared at the flickering points of light.

"No," he told himself as he flipped a burning cigarette out into the water, "I ain't made a mistake. I'd 'a' knowed him any time. But what in hell he's turned hold-up man for —" He broke off into a soft, wondering oath and got to his feet. And then he jerked viciously at his neck-handkerchief, drove his hands deep info his pockets, and strode off to his own bed.

The last man to sleep, Hal was the first to wake. Half an hour before his charges had come down to the call of a clamorous iron spoon against the bottom of a tin pan, he had taken his hasty breakfast, had called to Dick Sperry, and was out in the barn with his horses. And then, when he had allowed the Estabrook party a bare twenty minutes to eat, he drove up to the door for them, slammed on his brake, and shouted shortly, "All aboard!"

As they filed out to his summons — Sibyl Estabrook at their head radiant in her chatter with Mr. Louis Dabner, Mrs. Estabrook complaining and being comforted by Mr. Cushing, Fern Winston and Yvonne sleepy-eyed and gleeful, Crofton and Bates and Mimi mere struggling heaps of baskets and suit-cases — the cowboy lifted his hat perfunctorily, spoke a curt "Mornin'," and gave his attention to his horses. Yet he did not need to be told when the last one of his party had been seated. He loosened his reins a very little, threw off the brake, and swung his horses out toward the south-east. The springs whined under the sudden jerk, Mrs. Estabrook groaned, Mr. Cushing dropped his fresh cigar, the dust puffed up underfoot, and in a moment Swayne's Road-house was lost behind a clump of oaks.

Nor did the Bear Track man's taciturnity thaw under the running fire of talk from his passengers. His replies to the few questions which were put to him in the early morning were curt monosyllables, and in a little all remarks to him ceased. He spoke quietly to his horses now and then, but far more often he made his will known to them by an impatient hand upon the reins or by a sharp cut with his whip. Their way ran through a narrow valley where a dim dusk brooded long after the

74

sun had flared out across the mountain-tops, winding under the outflung branches of live oaks and white oaks in whose shadows little "blue" rabbits nibbled and scampered with bobbing tails as the wagon rocked by, through ragged hedges of vine-tangled brush into which bands of quail slipped with their suspicious pit-pit-pit. All these things called for exclamations from his passengers, but brought no turning of the driver's frowning eyes from the jingling harness and the road-bed ahead.

By nine o'clock the horses' hides were growing black with the sweat of their pounding trot, then grey with the settling dust. They swept down a curving slope at a gallop, leaping forward at the sound of the brake flung off, raced across a dry creek-bed, and took the uphill climb of Gold Mountain grade on a run. The grade steepened and narrowed, the pace slackened to a straining walk, and the wagon creaked dismally in dry-voiced protest. At a spring trickling from the clay bank across the road the driver stopped his horses for water and "to blow a spell." When they went on, still upward, the cliffs were falling straight and steep at the side not a yard from the wheels.

For an hour they were upon the grade, and Sibyl and Dabner, who had entered a spirited discussion concerning what would happen if two teams met here where there was scarcely room for one, had no way of securing an answer to their question. At a little after ten the horses were racing again, the country opening out before them as they dropped swiftly down toward the cattle land. They passed through the last steep-sided canyon, under the last of the thick-foliaged live oaks, and out upon a road which ran as straight as a string over a flat, dry, treeless country. Far ahead of them they saw the blue line of another range of mountains, with only the level, brush-covered brown and grey country intervening, and here and there across the miles made out the moving dots which spelt cattle and horses.

"Yes." Hal had answered Sibyl's question, with a deep breath of relief. "That's the Bear Track ahead. Runs along the foothills over yonder. The range-house is in them trees you see jes' this side that V-shaped cut. We'll be there for dinner."

Sibyl peeped at her watch. "But it's only ten o'clock," she protested. "And it can't be more than six or eight miles."

But he was answering no more questions. That it was close enough to twenty miles to make a couple of hours necessary to reach it was nobody's concern but the driver's.

She turned laughing to Louis.

"It doesn't look very inviting, does it? And for a summer vacation spot —"

"'A loaf of bread, a jug of wine,'" he retorted cheerfully.

Yvonne was pressing Fern Winston's hand under the lap robe.

"You are glad, Fern?" she whispered teasingly. "And you don't care if it isn't filled with flowers and bird song, do you?"

76

Whereupon a warm red crept up under Fern's dusky skin, her eyes grew very soft and very bright, and her hand tightened upon Yvonne's.

They dipped into a long hollow, unseen in the flatness of the country until they came upon it, and for a little the clump of trees, where Hal had said the range-house was, was lost to them. When they came up out of it the mountains and the scattered dots of cattle were no nearer, looking the same distance away they had seemed from the rim of the level lands behind them. But the mountains had lost their blueness and were growing from grey to brown and black. In a little their eager eyes made out the difference in cattle and horses wandering along the slopes, and presently picked out the forms of two riders among the herds.

Then, from a little knoll, they saw the range-house, its freshly whitewashed walls showing very bright and neat and inviting against the live oaks. For a moment the house shone and glistened into their eyes, the long, low bunk-house stood out clearly outlined, the corrals and barns standing a little to the south. Then again the wagon had dropped down into a hollow in this flowing sea of gently swelling earth, and the brush-crested billows shut out the still distant range headquarters. Suddenly Sibyl was waving her handkerchief, Yvonne was pressing Fern's hand tighter than ever, and Miss Fern herself, with sparkling eyes and flushed cheeks, was trying to look as though she was not the very happiest girl in all the world.

It was Oscar Estabrook, and he rode swiftly to meet them, his hat waving a wide welcome, his smile growing broader and broader as he drew rapidly nearer.

"Hello, cowboy!" Sibyl cried gaily to him as Hal brought his horses to a sudden halt. And, "Hello, big brother!" cried Yvonne. Fern, breathing deeply and quickly, said nothing, merely looking her greeting to the young, boyish, sun-browned fellow. And after the way of brothers — and lovers — Oscar Estabrook saw none of them, heard none of them, until his eyes had found out Fern's flushed, happy face, and had flashed back his greeting, and his answer to hers.

Hal over his cigarette-making watched his employer with a curious smile as he kissed his two sisters carelessly, and Fern Winston carefully, and gripped Dabner warmly by the hand. He nodded briefly to Hal, turning back quickly to Fern. Hal returned Estabrook's nod as carelessly, his eyes a bit thoughtful, and Oscar jerked his horse around to the side of the wagon and rode near Fern as they started again toward the range-house.

"There's your mother and Mr. Cushing in the wagon behind us," Fern suggested. Oscar laughed.

"The mater will be cross until she's had something to eat," he chuckled up into her face as he cantered along in the dust. "So I'll have to ride with you and see that there's something ready for her."

Since he had not seen his sisters and Dabner for something like two years, and Fern for exactly twenty-six months and twelve days, there were a thousand fragmentary things to say, to ask, to go unanswered. The few miles before them grew short, and it seemed that the clutter of buildings and corrals ran forward to meet them as the range's "boss" had done.

They came to the first fence they had seen since leaving Queen City. Oscar galloped ahead, and bending in his saddle jerked a gate open, and they swept up the knoll, through the grove of big oaks and to the house. There were many cries of delight, there was the look in Fern's eyes which Oscar looked quickly to see there . . . He had had this house built nearly two years ago, when he had first come out to the West to take charge of his father's range, and before Mrs. Winston's last long sickness . . . They caught their first glimpse of the deep windows about which he had coaxed climbing roses to grow, roses brought a hundred miles; they saw the little courtyard about which the house was built, with its natural spring playing that it was a fountain, with its flowering shrubs taken from the mountain canyons, with rude stone chimneys rising through the low roof and bespeaking wide-mouthed fire-places within. And Fern, who alone had had, long ago, all the details in long, joyous letters, recognised before she had got down from the wagon the out-jutting room yonder with the many windows, and knew that there one would find such things as a dainty lady loves in her own little sitting-room.

"I drove every nail in it myself," Oscar whispered to her under cover of helping her down. "And no one else has ever been in it. I want you to run ahead — to go in first!"

So Fern picked up her skirts and ran. She was sitting in her own little rocker, and had had time to cry over it and dry her eyes and laugh over it before the others came trooping in. When the second wagon had come, and Oscar had kissed his mother and laughed at her woebegone face and had assured her that there really was a bathroom in the house, and though no hardwood floors and rugs there was a spick-and-span linoleum, and that a white man did the cooking, and that she could have Mimi bring her meals up to her room if desirable, and that his tan was only skin deep and would come off when he went "back home," and that even the hardened skin upon his hands would yield to gentle usage and manicuring — when he had hurriedly done all of these things, and had called to the cook to put lunch on, and had sent his guests to prepare for it, he knew where to find Fern Winston. And she was both crying and laughing as she put her arms about him and held up her lips to be kissed again.

"It is wonderful, wonderful, Oscar," she whispered, holding him tight. "Everywhere I can see that you didn't forget me once and — Oh, I love you so hard! And now — I am never going to go away from it! It is going to be home!"

He laughed happily. "Home for a little, Fern. And then, when you begin to get tired of the humdrum of the life out here —"

"But I'll never get tired of it," she cried quickly. "Never! And —" She broke off suddenly, and held herself a little away from him, looking steadily into his face. "You have changed, Oscar. Did you know it? You have grown up and are a man! A big, strong, good man. I can see it in your eyes. And I love your hands, all hard and brown and strong. Oh, I am glad your father knew and understood and sent you out here. And we can go on living here, always, together, just you and I. Don't you want to?"

"Oh, Dad knew what he was doing all right." He frowned a little and then laughed again. "I kicked like a bay steer at first, but I guess it did do me a lot of good. Stay here always?" He gathered her to him quickly, hungrily. "Just as long as you want, dear. Where Eve was, there was Eden,'" he quoted softly.

"Then it is going to be Eden for us as long as we live," she told him impetuously. "We'll keep good watch together that the serpent doesn't get in. And we'll take long horseback rides into the mountains, to the Valley of the Waterfalls you wrote about, and over the long sweep of level country, and we'll go fishing and hunting, and maybe" — she blushed a little but held her eyes upon his and went on swiftly — "for our honeymoon we'll go to Swayne's Road-house where the little lake is. And we'll have wonderful days in the wooded country, and nights out under the stars, and all the time in the world to read and dream and be happy!"

There was a little mist in her eyes, the tender mist of dreams. They stood in silence, looking into each other's eyes and trying to look into the future. And maybe the girl knew that the life she was building up for them to enter together was more golden and glorious than the reality. For in the end she sighed a little.

"And here lunch is served," Sibyl's voice came to them through the shrubbery about the spring-fountain, "and the guests are hungry, and the host has forgotten all about them!"

"Which is the plain, unvarnished truth," Oscar laughed back. And then, for Fern alone, "Come on — little hostess!"

CHAPTER
SEVEN

A Man and a Horse

Hal and Dick Sperry had driven down to the corrals where they unharnessed and turned their horses out to roll in the little pasture. Then while Sperry hastened to the bunk-house for the meal which should now be hot on the long table, Hal turned into the stable. The heavy door which he jerked open had not ceased its creaking upon its rusty hinges before the eager whinnying of a horse greeted him. The sober set of his countenance was suddenly lost in a wide, pleased grin.

"You ol' son-of-a-gun!" he cried genially, a great deal more pleasantly and fraternally than he had spoken to any one since he had parted with Ches in Queen City. "You sure got a nose for a frien', ain't you? How they been treatin' you?"

He came to the stall where the horse was tied and was greeted by an out-thrust muzzle with bared teeth, and the gleam of evil eyes whose whites showed wickedly. A tall, rangy, black horse with no spot upon his satiny skin except where the little white saddle-marks told that some one had mastered the big brute's spirit, jerked at his halter chain until his whirling body was tight pressed to the manger and

83

snapped viciously with the big teeth from which the lips were drawn back in an ugly, threatening leer. Hal laughed softly and went to the horse's head.

"You damn' ol' bluff, you!" he chuckled as his calloused hand wandered over the soft, twitching nose. "Makin' out like that that you ain't glad to see me!" He ran his hand over the horse's side and back, touched the flank, laughed again when the animal snorted and snapped, saw the leg half lifted as though ready to kick, and slapped it resoundingly.

"Feelin' good, huh, Colonel? An' sorta sore 'cause I went off an' left you that-away?" He passed about the horse's heels and back to his head. "An' makin' out you ain't glad to see me none? Now, you jes' cut out your nonsense, an' don't go to tryin' to make me think you've gone an' forgot your sex! You ain't no lady hoss, an' them flirtatious ways ain't befittin' a gentleman hoss, an' you'd oughta know it, Colonel! So put up your-paw an' shake, or I'll jes' nacherally pull your ol' tail out an' spank you with it!"

The Colonel snorted his disgust, but none the less lifted his right fore leg and shook hands. And he snapped again, his nose fairly in Hal's face, with the sharp click of teeth — and the quivering lips brushed the bronzed cheek softly. Hal grinned delightedly.

"Lay back your ears an' snort, you ol' four flusher," he sympathised, as he unfastened the halter chain from the staple in the manger. "You an' me is goin' to git out an' tear some ground up this afternoon. Come ahead; let's go git a drink."

84

He led the way out of the stable, and the Colonel, head lifted high upon his long neck, the tips of his slender ears pointing skyward, followed close upon the heels of his master. A young deerhound that had been playing with a piece of rawhide in the corral came bounding up with a superabundance of playful good will and a youthful lack of caution, and retreated as hastily as he had come, carrying with him a memory of the Colonel's snapping teeth and of a slender shapely leg that had barely missed ending the pup's joyous career.

"They won't leave you alone, will they, Colonel?" Hal said, as his eyes rested upon the pup, sitting at a safe distance with cocked ears and a puzzled frown wrinkling its forehead. "Four legs or two," he mused, shaking his head; "most of 'em is like that. Let's drink, Colonel."

The man stooped to the faucet which poured its clear, cool water into the trough, the horse thrust its nose into the trough. Hal drank thirstily, wiped his mouth upon the back of his hand, and turned to watch the horse. And as he turned the good nature left his eyes and the old, frowning, almost sullen look came back. For the Colonel was wont to do all things daintily, as a thoroughbred should, although often viciously. It was the Colonel's way barely to touch the water with twitching lips which thrust aside little bits of straw or dead leaves or other things which gather upon the surface of standing water, and to drink slowly, leisurely, "like a man as knows how to enjoy his licker." But now he had driven his muzzle deep down and was drinking as a horse drinks, be he thoroughbred or of mixed range blood, when he is very, very thirsty.

For a little Hal said nothing. His eyes, for a while steadily upon the Colonel's, went at last toward the bunk-house and remained upon the doorway, seeming to grow blacker moment by moment. Finally they came back to the Colonel, and then dropped to the making of a cigarette. Only when he had drawn the first deep lungful of smoke did he speak gently:

"Some day, Colonel, ol' pardner, I'm jes' nacherally goin' to kill Club Jordan. An' now you come away from that! It ain't considered wise to drink too much all at once when you ain't been drinkin' for a spell."

The Colonel did not want to leave his drink yet, but gave over with ears laid back against his head, and, contenting himself with glaring at the still curious but suddenly cautious pup, went back to his stall. Hal climbed over the manger and threw down a handful of hay. Then, when he had already gone to the door, he came back suddenly. He went to the box nailed to the wall in which was kept the barley he had put out for his horse before he had gone to Queen City. He lifted the lid, stood a moment gazing into the box, and then turning shortly went slowly back to the door and went to the bunk-house.

The Bear Track bunk-house was what all bunk-houses are upon the big western cattle ranges, a rough, one-room shack where a score of men can eat and sleep. A dozen men were here now, Dick Sperry with them, being served at the long, oilcloth-covered table by the big, upstanding cook.

Club Jordan, the foreman of the Bear Track under Oscar Estabrook, had come in a moment before Hal and was hanging his hat upon a nail in the wall preparatory to joining his men at table. He was a big man, lean in the flanks, heavy and round in the shoulders, with a little droop at the left corner of his wide mouth and with something of the same sort of a droop at the corner of his left eye. His face was broad and smooth and usually quite expressionless. His left foot was deformed and gave him his name of "Club," a name by which he was known over many hundred miles of cattle country, and which perhaps he did not even know had been bestowed upon him.

Jordan glanced casually at Hal, and without nodding, went on to the table, his eyes resting upon a man at the farther end, at Dick Sperry's side.

"I want to talk to you, Jerry," he said in a blunt, unpleasant voice. "Right after dinner."

Jerry looked at him curiously, making no sign that he had heard. Nor did Jordan look for answer or expect it. Instead, he jerked out his chair, flung himself into it, and let his eyes run hungrily over the table.

"An' I want to talk to you, Jordan," Hal said quietly as he too jerked out his chair and sat down. "Right after dinner."

"What is it?" Jordan's eyes came away from the platter stacked high with dripping steaks, and met Hal's steadily. "You c'n talk now, can't you?"

"I guess so. I wanted to know about the Colonel. Has anybody give him water an' grub while I was away?"

Club Jordan laughed. "So that's worryin' you, is it, young feller? What did you go away an' leave him tied up in the barn for then?"

"You know I been lookin' for him, off an' on, for more'n two weeks back in the mountains. You might rec'lec' as how I jes' got my rope on him the day before you says I'm to go to Queen City." Hal was explaining very calmly, very carefully. "An' if I'd a-turned him loose he'd a been back in the hills somewheres an' there'd a been another two weeks lookin' for him. That's why I left him in the barn. I tol' Mr. Estabrook, an' he said he'd have you look after him."

"The hell he did!" exploded Jordan derisively. "Then you c'n take this here an' lay it by where you won't forgit it none: Any time I'm a-dancin' roun' feeding' any of your locoed hosses you c'n have my job an' I'm quittin' the cow business for sheep!"

"Then," persisted Hal, as quietly as before, but with a little dusky flush creeping up in his dark cheeks, "the Colonel ain't had no water at all since I lef'? For about four days?"

Jordan shrugged his shoulders. "The Ol' Man tol' me about him," he admitted after a moment. "An' I tol' one of the boys to water him the day you lef'. I'd forgot about the onery mustang . . ."

"He ain't no mustang," Hal cut in sharply, the colour rising a little higher in his cheeks. "The Colonel's a thoroughbred, an' I'm bettin' all I got with any man as says he ain't. An' he can do a mile or a hundred mile in quicker time than any hoss on the range. Which I'm bettin' also."

Again Jordan laughed, making no further answer. The other men about the table seemed to have taken scant interest in the conversation, and now suddenly both Jordan and Hal himself dropped it, and one would have said that the whole thing was forgotten. When the meal was finished the men got up from the table one by one and went about the afternoon's work. Dick Sperry, one of the last to go out, found Hal loitering outside near the doorway.

"Wait a minute, Dick," Hal said softly. "Have you got a bet what Jordan wants with Jerry?"

Sperry opened his blue eyes frankly and shook his head.

"Then listen to my bet: Jerry has been on the Bear Track for about eleven years, ain't he? He was here a long time before Club Jordan ever pulled his freight out of Wyoming. Now you wait a minute an' see if he don't get fired right now!"

"Fired!" snapped Sperry. "What are you talkin' about? We need all the good men we got, an' more, an' you know it. An' Jerry's as good a cowman as ever shoved his boot in a stirrup! What would Jordan want to fire him for?"

Hal shook his head and did not lift his eyes from his cigarette-making.

"I'm makin' my guess," he responded colourlessly. "You see if I ain't called the turn right."

From the bunk-house came to them the low jumble of words, Club Jordan's voice sharp and angry, Jerry's blank with surprise. In a moment the big foreman came swiftly out of the door, glared from under bunching brows at the two loitering forms, and strode off toward the corral. Jerry, too, came to the door, where for a little he stood hesitant. Then jerking angrily at the belt of his sagging overalls he passed Hal and Sperry and hurried away toward the range-house.

"He's mad," frowned Sperry. "An' mos' likely he's going up to see Mr. Estabrook."

"Mos' likely."

Five minutes later Jerry had returned from the range-house, his face red, his hands at his sides doubled into fists with whitening knuckles. He went wordlessly into the bunk-house, and through the open door they could see him jerking his blankets out of his bunk, rummaging for the odds and ends which a cow-puncher carries with him from range to range when he is giving up a home upon one to search it upon another.

"He's got the hooks proper," admitted Sperry wonderingly. "With us short-handed now! An' Estabrook's backed up Club's play. What I want to know is, why did they can him?"

"What I can't answer," laughed Hal shortly, as he turned away to the stables and the Colonel, "is why you an' me ain't been fired yet! We're due to go nex', Dick, an' real soon. Only when Club Jordan gits aroun' to me he's goin' to ketch a awful big surprise"

CHAPTER
EIGHT

Moon Madness and Music

The days which followed were busy days upon the Bear Track. And they were gay days for the men and women who were placed for the first time in their bored lives where they could watch the workings of a big cattle range. Oscar Estabrook, in their honour and for their amusement, had arranged that the big round-up came the first week after the arrival of his guests. Always the gentlest of the saddle horses were kept in the little pasture where they might be had when Sibyl and Yvonne and Fern, Louis Dabner and the slow-moving Mr. Cushing wanted them. There were rides at dawn and by moonlight across the gently swelling meadow lands or back into the mountains, along steep winding trailsthrough the pines. And always Louis Dabner followed Sibyl Estabrook like a shadow, and Oscar rode with Fern, and Yvonne watched them with eyes that were deep and very thoughtful, and sometimes dancing with amusement.

Of Hal they saw little those first few days. They knew that the Bear Track embraced some seventy-five thousand acres, and that Bear Track cattle grazed over twice that area of Government acreage. They knew that from edge to edge of the great, scattered band of cattle and horses entrusted to the care of Oscar Estabrook by his father, Pompey Estabrook, there stretched many miles of mountain and meadow. And they knew that Hal had ridden away upon the Colonel upon the afternoon of his arrival at the range, and somewhere was doing his day's work.

Then came the round-up, and with it fifty new faces to the Bear Track. Punchers from the Bar Circle Cross in the south, from the Warm Springs outfit, from the Diamond Bar and the Double Tree, lean, brown, soft-spoken, quick-eyed men upon range business, each alert at the cutting out and branding, each watchful for strays from the home range. And there was "the Judge" from Split Horn with his comfortable-looking little wife and two bright-eyed girls, come to spend the week with the Estabrooks. There was the whole Jolliper family from Hill Town, father and mother, girls and boys, come in their big camp wagon. There were the Kelseys from the mining camp a hundred miles to the south-west, and there were the Brightons from another camp seventy-five miles to the north-west. And there was the "string band" all the way from Kennebec, beyond the valley of the Waterfalls, the whole band, José with his violin, Michael with his guitar, and Little Rooney with his flute.

Each day there was a barbecue and picnic out under the big oaks in the little pasture, and each day sixty or seventy men, women and children, most of them men, to be sure, but with a sprinkling of bright ribbons in the assemblage, and gay calico dresses and rosy cheeks, made mirth out of the day's work. When that work was done and the violin and guitar and flute called to the rough board platform under the oaks, there was the scurry of feet and the titter of laughter, bespeaking the careless, bubbling happiness of these people upon the "rim of the world."

And there came certain people from Queen City. There was a gentleman who wore diamonds, whose air was the air of a great gentleman, whose bow to the ladies was all grace, and whom they called Prince Victor. There came a big man who rode a big mule, a man whose voice boomed out often in heart-laughter, whom the little children captured and kept as their very own property, perching high upon his back or swinging to his coat-tails, and whom they called Big John Brent.

In the afternoons there were the games and races which Oscar Estabrook arranged largely for the amusement of his guests. There was the eternal greased pig to be chased by small boys with five dollars as prize to the lucky urchin who could take and hold the elusive squealing porker. There was the ancient greased pole to climb. There were sack races and egg races. And, for the men there were races upon saddle horses.

The days came and went merrily, and the merry guests of the Bear Track feasted and frolicked and had a good time. In the evening, while the violin and guitar and flute played Virginia reels and waltzes, two-steps and quadrilles, certain of the men withdrew from the rough board dance floor and met about a table in Oscar Estabrook's room at the range-house.

They were Oscar, Prince Victor, Club Jordan, and now and then Hal. For Hal had come back upon the full tide of the round-up.

To-night was the last night of the merry-making. At noon the work of the round-up had been finished, and the afternoon had been given over to horse-racing and "bronco-busting." Hal had kept pretty well in the background during the week, his "silent streak" being still upon him. But to-day he had said that he would enter the free-for-all race, and he had ridden the Colonel and had laughed impudently into the scowling face of Club Jordan as he swept by the big foreman in the home stretch. He had pocketed the fifty dollars which went to the winner, and now, to-night, his fifty dollars lay on the table in front of him, and with his hat low drawn over his eyes he watched Club Jordan and Victor Dufresne and Oscar Estabrook as they cut and dealt and bet.

Outside, the guitar and violin and flute were making the night tinkle and ring with the "Blue Danube", and the laughing voices of men and women came floating in, mingled with music. Prince Victor sighed, toyed with the diamond in his shirt-front, and wished that he were ten years younger. And he looked at Oscar Estabrook curiously. It was only the third deal. There came a gentle rap at the door. Estabrook put down his cards hastily and went out.

"You, Fern?" they could hear him say, as he closed the door behind him. "What is it? What's the matter?"

"Is anything the matter, Oscar?"

"Why," he hesitated. "Your face looks white and worried. And you looked flushed and so happy a minute ago —"

"Oscar." She put her hand upon his arm, and stood in the half light, looking up into his eyes. "Why aren't you out there? With the rest? Don't you want to come and dance?"

"I told you —" he began, only to be interrupted by Fern saying swiftly:

"— That you had a little business with Mr. Jordan, Oscar," pleadingly. "It has happened before, more than once during the week. You are gambling again, aren't you, Oscar?"

"Well?" he demanded a trifle irritably. "What if I am? If the boys want a little game of cards, does it hurt any one?"

"No one," she answered quietly. "Unless it hurts you. You are the one to know that. But I thought that you had promised your father when you came West —"

"What right had he to make me promise anything?" — bitterly. "After he jerked me out of college the way he did and packed me off into this wilderness? And —"

"And," she ended in the same quiet tone, "I thought that you had promised me."

"It's only a little game, Fern dear," he pleaded. "And Dufresne is a guest, too. I am under obligations to him, very heavy obligations. If I can give him a pleasant evening . . . there's a dear girl. I'll be out in an hour. Then we'll have all evening to dance in, and I can tell you all about it."

Fern laughed a little and assured him that it really didn't matter the least bit in the world, and went back to the others. Oscar Estabrook returned to the card-table.

There were two men who played poker in that room for the sake of the lure of the game. And there were two who played for money, making a business of it. Hal lost his fifty dollars in a good deal less than fifty minutes, and went outside to smoke and go to bed. Oscar Estabrook lost two hundred and fifty dollars in a very little more time, wrote an IOU which he handed to Prince Victor, and in a very ill-humour went to seek Fern Winston. When he found that she had slipped away and had gone to bed, his ill-humour was not lessened by the fact.

The dance floor had been built upon a log foundation, just off the ground. At one end were chairs for the musicians, about the sides ran long benches for the women and children. Hal, standing back a little in the shadow of the oak, watched them as the couples went by him, swirling to the fast beat of the music. He could see Sibyl, as in the arms of the adoring Louis Dabner her lithe body swayed, yielding to the waltz. He could see Yvonne as Dick Sperry sought her out and as she gave him her hand, laughing. And, drawing thoughtfully upon his cigarette, his losses of a moment ago already forgotten, he watched the two girls, following them through the maze of the dance, comparing them with each other and with the country girls who bounced joyously about them.

96

"There's a difference," he muttered. "An' it ain't altogether bein' raised diff'rent. It's bein' born diff'rent. Take them Jolliper girls, all the raisin' in the world wouldn't make 'em like Miss Sibyl an' Miss Yvonne."

A heavy hand fell upon his shoulder, startling him. He whirled quickly and looked up into the face of Big John Brent.

"Howdy, Brother." The voice was a hearty roar, as abrupt as his heavy hand had been. "Why hold aloof with cloudy brow when soft music and beautiful ladies invite to the dance?"

Hal did not seem to have moved, and yet his shoulder had slipped out from under John Brent's broad hand. Now, hardly seeming to have returned the preacher's glance, he saw that there was the thickness as of some sort of bandaged padding under the big man's shirt between the left shoulder and collar bone, and that the shoulder was carried a trifle stiffly. He flushed a little and frowned. He had not spoken with John Brent since that wild night in Queen City, had avoided him here at the Bear Track, and certainly had no wish to speak with him to-night. But if the Disciple of Jesus realised these things, he in no manner showed that he felt them.

"Verily," John Brent ran on, his smile broad and unconcerned, his eyes twinkling, "never since my two feet have been set in the path which is the path leading straight to the Most High has such temptation come to turn them aside from dusty righteousness to the more flowery fields of pleasure! Pretty girls and music!" and he laughed genially, his full-throated boyish laugh.

97

"Why, a man wants to swing the pretty girl away in his arms to the beat of the music and forget all other lesser — and greater! — considerations by the way."

Hal turned so that his shoulder was upon the big man, drew his hat a little lower over his eyes which followed Sibyl and Louis Dabner back and forth across the floor.

"There's a fine woman, a glorious woman!" John Brent's eyes had gone with the cowboy's; in some way John Brent had sensed that this particular figure had drawn Hal's gaze. "As wonderful to look upon as anything the great God ever set His seal upon. And yet," — and he sighed and shook his head, — "not the great God alone has set His seal there!"

"What do you mean?" For the first time Hal spoke, whirling upon him suddenly.

"I mean, Brother, that a temple may be builded by righteous hands and given over to the worship of little gods that are ungodly. I mean that in Sibyl Estabrook simplicity and sincerity are hidden by vanity and arrogance, that although she is beautiful to look upon she is less beautiful than the maiden she sees in her own glass, that she is selfish, that she has been spoiled by flattery, that her nature has been warped by it until —"

"A man," cut in Hal shortly, his anger leaping out at the preacher like a sharp flame, "as talks that away about a woman, is a damn poor man. If that's church talk, I don't want none of it."

"A man, Brother," returned John Brent gently, "should tell the truth, without fear or favour of man or

98

of woman. It would be better for women like Sibyl Estabrook if there were more truth spoken, bluntly. Now, mind you, I am not saying she is without good. But I am saying that while she queens it out here, ruling with a high hand and the beauty of her body, she is less the woman, yes, and less of an actual power than her sister, Yvonne. There is a difference between those two girls," — unconscious that he had dropped into the train of thought that had been Hal's a moment ago, — "a vast difference. Yvonne is quieter, gentler, less self-assertive in character, just as she is less self-assertive in her way of beauty. But she is the more womanly woman."

"Two things I don't like," said the cowboy curtly. "One is to have you call me Brother. If you was a real man inside like you look to be outside, you'd remember what I done to you the other night, an' there wouldn't be any sof' talkin' between you an' me. The other is that there ain't no reason for you to say things like that about a lady, an' special' behind her back. If you got any remarks to make, go make 'em to her or to her brother."

John Brent laughed easily. "What I've said to you I have said to her already. And I shall say it over again. And I'm sorry that you don't want to be friends with me. Maybe it is because I am a man inside that I don't choose to remember what you did the other night. Well, well, the ways of the Lord are hidden until His good time for them to be known. And I had an object in coming to you here."

"Well?" — ill-humouredly — "what is it? If you want money for your damned church —"

John Brent chuckled. "I don't. If it pleases you, let my damned church be damned for the present. I am bringing you a message. The young woman of whom we were speaking, I so disrespectfully, you so gallantly, wants to see you."

"Me?" Hal looked his astonishment from under lifted eyebrows. "What for?"

"For the sake of her womanly interest in your manly beauty!" smiled Brent. "I fancy the ladies find you a handsome young dog, with just enough of the spice of the devil in you to make you fascinating. Anyway, I think that Miss Sibyl would be glad to give you a waltz."

Hal flushed under the bantering tones no less than under the words themselves, and his hands clenched without his knowing it. And John Brent, who saw the flush, who felt the spurt of anger in it, knew that there was a surge of youthful gladness in it too.

"I don't dance," snapped Hal, when he found words. "An' I'd be glad to have you 'tend to your own business."

"I believe," grinned John Brent, "that my Bad Man is afraid of a woman!"

Hal, muttering angrily to himself, turned and strode through the strollers coming down from the platform at the end of the dance. Before he had gone ten steps he met Louis Dabner.

"I say," cried that young man, laying a detaining hand upon Hal's arm; "Miss Estabrook wants to speak with you."

Hal glared at him, jerked away, and strode on, turning toward the bunk-house and bed. And then Sibyl, seeing his tall form among the others, a little spirit of recklessness upon her from the night under the stars and from the music, left the Judge and Mr. Cushing, and came to meet him. He stopped suddenly, slowly lifted his hat, and stood looking steadily into her shining eyes.

"Good evening," she was saying, her hand held out to him. "I have not seen you all night."

"Good evenin', miss," he answered quietly. "No, I ain't been aroun' much."

"We have seen almost nothing of you since you brought us out from Queen City," she ran on graciously. He had taken her proffered hand a moment, firmly in his own, and now was again turning his hat in his fingers. "And I had wanted to see you again."

"What for?" he demanded, frowning a little, feeling a little uncomfortable, knowing that the Judge and Mr. Cushing and many others were watching them.

For a little she was at a loss for an answer to his straightforward question. And then, remembering who and what she was, who and what he, she laughed lightly.

"You don't seem a bit glad to talk with me," she replied. "You see, the other night, at Swayne's Road-house, I was frightened and nervous I suppose. And I accused you of something which I knew was not true. I have wanted to apologise."

"That's all right," he told her colourlessly. "It was true. I knew who the man was, an' he was a frien' of mine."

101

"Oh!" Instead of looking angry, as he had supposed she would do, she merely looked delighted. "Won't you tell me about it?"

He shook his head. "I can't, miss. There ain't anything to tell."

The violinist had tuned and scraped, and now, with a nod to his fellow-musicians, flung himself into a new waltz. Sibyl Estabrook, looking curiously upon the Bear Track man, for a little hesitating, suddenly leaned nearer to him and said gently:

"You haven't asked me for a dance! If you have really forgiven me —"

His quick refusal, curt and ungracious, was upon the tip of his tongue. Then he saw beyond her the odd smile upon John Brent's face, remembered his "I believe that my Bad Man is afraid of a woman!" saw the amusement in Dabner's eyes, and said shortly:

"I'd be glad!"

It was just an impulse, the impulse of a coquette, that had made Sibyl Estabrook seek him out. She had laughingly admitted to the Judge that she ought to be ashamed to fling herself at a man's head this way, that never before in all her life had she ever dreamed of forcing herself upon a man in a dance. But she had seen that he had danced with no one else, she had seen that he had not more than lifted his hat to any woman there, and it was not her way to go unnoticed. She had invested him with a certain romance, had built an outlaw out of him, had been quick to see that no other man there had this one's natural beauty or slow-moving grace; while she did not intend to forget that he was but a cowboy, a being beyond the pale of her set, none the less he was a man, and a woman might play with him. She was a bit tired of Mr. Dabner's monotonous graceful platitudes, and a bit reckless with something in the open air. And now, as Hal put his arm about her, and they caught the beat of the music, there was a flush of triumph in her cheeks, a quick light of satisfaction in her eyes.

She sought to speak further of the affair at Swayne's Road-house for a little, but Hal made no answer. Then she grew silent with him. She felt his arm about her, holding her close to him, and suddenly forgot all else than the dance as they swept out to the middle of the floor. For this man did not dance as did Mr. Dabner, as did any one with whom Sibyl had ever gone through the steps of a waltz. The music crept into him until its rhythm was one with the rhythm of his supple body, until the waltz was what a waltz should be — the soul of the poetry of motion. With a little gasp of surprise that this cowboy could dance as she had never known a dancing-master dance, she gave herself over to his guidance, gave her soul over to the keen enjoyment of the moment.

She sighed a little as she felt his arm tighten about her, knowing that she had not really danced until now. She forgot to note the effect they were making, she with her gauzy white gown and fair skin, he with his holiday chaps and red knotted handkerchief, and swarthy, tanned bronze of cheek and throat. She just remembered that after all he was a man, she a woman, that they both were young, that the music and the night

103

and the stars made one of the two of them. When she looked up into his face the blood ran red into hers. For there was a smile in his eyes, and back of the smile were the flattering things which many men had said to her but which none had said with the eloquence with which they were being said wordlessly to her now.

At her seat she made room for him, drawing her skirts aside. He stood for a moment, looking down at her very gravely.

"No," he said quietly though a bit unsteadily, "I'm going to bed now. Good night."

He put on his hat and left her abruptly, going across the platform and dropping down into the shadows. And he didn't see the men and women among whom he moved.

CHAPTER
NINE

Distrust and Suspicion

Hal had seen little enough of woman in his life, and especially of young, pretty, well-dressed women. And he was young. Therefore there was nothing strange or novel in the situation which resulted from his seeing Sibyl Estabrook, from his dancing with her. He did not go to bed as he had told her he was going to do, but instead went down to the stable, saddled the Colonel, and rode far out across the flat lands lying bright in the starlight. He gave the Colonel his head and rode mile after mile, head down, frowning. After a long time he drew his horse down to a walk, and sat straight in the saddle, his eyes upon the stars.

His quick fancies told him that at last the impossible had happened and he was in love. He did not see clearly, did not analyse. He took the woman that was Sibyl Estabrook and invested her with those attributes for which his heart yearned. Knowing less than nothing of the actual woman, he made of her a creature as glorious in soul as she was in body. He bestowed upon her the generosity which was a part of himself, the frankness, the honesty and straightforwardness. He made of her the Perfect Woman, all truth and

105

tenderness and unselfishness and sympathy and love. And that thing which he himself had made he worshipped.

Only when love, real or fancied, comes to a man does he for the first time measure himself. Almost before he lets his soul seek for the glories of the woman does he turn it inward upon himself. Now in the first flush of the dawning passion does he ask himself what manner of Man he is who dares lift his eyes to the Incomparable Woman. And with the joy of the shock at discovering Her comes the sickening shock of finding himself.

To the cowboy, Sibyl Estabrook spelt culture, education, refinement, all of the things that come to the true woman in the world which was her world. For a little his face grew very dark, his eyes very black with the pain in them, when he realised how little he had to offer. He knew that his scanty schooling had been forgotten long ago, that the language he used was crude, full of the wrong words, of mispronunciations, of crimes against grammar. He knew that he was without the social refinements of Mr. Dabner, of Mr. Cushing. He knew that these people could speak together and in his presence of many things intelligible to them of which he would understand no word. He saw a thousand points in which he fell far, far below her and her kind. And, because he had made of her in his thoughts the True Woman, he did not see the one great thing, the thing which made his plane so far removed from hers; he did not think of it even. That Sibyl Estabrook was used to the things which wealth brings,

106

and that he had nothing but his horse and his pitiful day's wage, did not come to him to widen the gulf between them.

The thing which he saw in the end — and then the frown left his face and a look of quiet determination crept into his eyes — was that she was a Woman, he a Man. In many things he was unworthy, but he would force himself upward from his plane to hers. He had, in his boyish way, been proud of his evil reputation, of his drinking and brawling. Now he was ashamed, and the shame of it dyed his face a stinging red. He would not drink again, he would choke down all desire for such wild nights as had earned him his title of the Outlaw.

For the first time in his life he thanked God that he was young. He had time to do the things which must be done. He could read and write, and he would learn to read and write better. He had avoided the society of the Easterners; now he would cultivate it. He would listen to their talk, he would learn to speak as they did. He would begin to work his way upward to her, and he would begin *now*. And, such is the assurance of youth, such the confidence of such a man, when Hal turned the Colonel's head back toward the bunk-house he saw a long, uphill road ahead of him, but at the end of it a crown for his endeavour.

In the days which followed Hal avoided Sibyl Estabrook as he had never before avoided any one. Keenly conscious of his shortcomings, ashamed that he had grown to a man and was more ignorant than the boys whom she knew at home, his one desire was to improve himself all that he could before he came to her

107

again. He wanted books, and books were very scarce upon the Bear Track. In the bunk-house he found a couple of old magazines, a couple of backless, torn novels, and these things he carried away with him, taking them when no one was looking, hiding them about his clothes. He felt that if the cowboys saw him looking at a book they would all guess his secret and laugh at him. And other things also he took like a thief, his heart tripping and pounding at the thought of discovery.

These things which, little by little, disappeared from the bunk-house and from the range-house itself, were a few books, one of them a geography, one an ancient history, the others novels, a bit of lead pencil, some stray scraps of paper, a lantern. They went with Hal after dark to his "studio."

Close behind the Bear Track range-house stood the mountains, their sides cut into straight, bare cliffs on each side of the pass which led away from the flat lands and into the broken country where there was much summer feeding for the cattle upon Government land. If one went through the pass and along the trail which led into the mountains, he came after two or three miles of steep climb to a little valley. Here the cliffs stood straight up all about, and it seemed hardly as though a man could work his way up them on foot. And here was Hal's "studio."

He had found the place two years before when looking for strayed cattle. Then he had left his horse tethered in the little valley, and had climbed up one of the walls of rock that he might come to the top and look far out across the other little valleys. He had wormed his way along a spine of rock, slanting upward from the creek bed, from it had drawn himself up upon a ledge, and little by little had climbed the rock wall towering above him, finding that it was not the unbroken surface it had seemed from below, but cut with many grass-filled seams and cracks. Then, unexpectedly, he had come to a wider shelf and the mouth of a cave. The cave itself ran back twenty feet into the cliff-side, widening out so that a man could stand upright and not touch the rock above. Since it was placed so high here above the trail, and its mouth was hidden with man-zanita bushes, the thing had not been found before and was not found since. And here, leaving the Colonel in the valley below, Hal brought his books, his paper and pencil and lantern.

He had even sought out a place to leave the Colonel where no chance-passing cowboy would find him. There was a narrow canyon entering the little valley up which he had worked his way one night on horseback, making his own trail, pushing the interlacing laurel branches aside as he rode through them. This canyon was too narrow, too steep and rocky for cattle to wander into its barren bed, and when he came to a little level space, shut in with bushes, he knew that he had found the place here he could tie the Colonel, give him his barley, and have him as securely hidden as though he too were in the cave.

In this solitude, more than two miles from the bunk-house, Hal took up his studies night after night, striving that he might shake off the rude shell into which cattlemen grow, seeking to become a "gentle-man." To the middle of his rough floor he had dragged a boulder, and upon this he set his lantern, a lot of cut bush piled high between it and the mouth of the cave. Beside the boulder he had placed a soap box taken from the cook's heap of kindling wood, and this was his writing-table. A cracker-box was his study chair. A dictionary, a geography, a battered copy of *David Copperfield*, volume two, and some half-dozen disreputable magazines was his library. Farther back in the cave, near the rock wall and upon some dry leaves, were a couple of ragged blankets. For there were nights when the Colonel fidgeted all night in his hiding-place and his master did not go back to the bunk-house.

When the lantern was newly filled from the bottle which had been brought in Hal's hip pocket, and its wick trimmed, the yellow light found out a spot on the wall of the cave where two bits of cardboard had been fastened by twigs pressed into cracks in the rock. And Hal nightly, before he picked up the book from the soap box or took up pencil and paper, sat for a little looking steadfastly at the cardboards which had once been top and bottom of a shoe box and which now were essential parts of the workshop. They bore big black letters, carefully and plainly printed, and were numbered at the tops, CHART 1 and CHART 2. Across the top of CHART 1 was written in large characters:

THINGS TO CUT OUT

And below, carefully tabulated, followed:

110

1. *Cussing.*
2. *Getting Drunk.*
3. *Playing Poker.*
4. *Saying:* THERE AIN'T NOTHING, DON'T KNOW NOTHING, *and such-like.*
5. *Saying* DAMN *when* VERY *will do as good.*

Then followed a column of numerals from 6 to 15 with blank spaces left opposite each number for the entry of some new thing to "cut out" when it should suggest itself to the student.

CHART 2 was labelled:

THINGS TO DO.

As far as Hal had yet gone with them they were:
1. *Read some Dickens and Shakespeare and Robert Chambers.* (He had seen a late novel with Sibyl Estabrook's name upon the flyleaf.)
2. *Read some History and Geography.*
3. *Study Grammar and Spelling.*
4. *Practise talking proper.*
5. *Learn some fancy new words every day.*
6. *Talk a good deal with L. Dabner.*

These were days during which it seemed upon the surface of things that life flowed smooth and untroubled upon the Bear Track. The cowboys working under Club Jordan came and went upon their accustomed duties, easily slipping back into the old régime which had been for a little disturbed by the round-up. Oscar Estabrook saw a great deal more of Fern Winston than he did of his father's cattle, leaving the management of the range in the hands of his foreman. And to Fern Winston's eyes came back the look of gladness which had left them a little during the round-up.

And yet, under the surface of things, there was a certain vague unrest, known at first only to Hal, sensed little by little by Dick Sperry, grasped almost fully by Jerry. But Jerry had gone; for no reason that appeared he had been discharged when the outfit was short-handed. That in itself had stirred certain quick suspicions in the minds of Hal and Sperry.

The great herds of cattle belonging to Pompey Estabrook carried the Bear Track brand over considerably more than a hundred thousand acres. They strayed from end to end of the unfenced range, they pushed back into the rich feeding-grounds of the mountains skirting the range, they came and went, and no man could have said what was the number of them. The Bear Track cowboys, under the instructions which came to them from Club Jordan, rode far out along the broken line of the borders of the scattered herds, always watching that they should not stray beyond the encircling imaginary dead-line. Now and again big ranging steers, interloped from the neighbouring ranges, were driven back, and perhaps straying Bear Trackers were brought homeward. There were no fences, and only the brand upon the hip and man's honesty to take the place of fenced fields.

112

In such a condition of things it was natural enough that there should be some losses, that now and then a few head of cattle should disappear, and perhaps never be missed. That was but a part of the game, a part of profit and loss, and to be reckoned with. Such a thing had happened upon the Bear Track two months ago, and little mention had been made of it. And yet it was that incident which first stirred Hal's suspicions, and which now made them quick to fire again.

Three months before there had come three men to the Bear Track riding from the south and asking for work. Club Jordan had taken them on and had sent them to ride line where the range slipped into the mountain passes. And Hal, because he was a loyal Bear Track man, and because he knew two of these men, went promptly to the foreman with what he knew.

"One of them jaspers is Yellow Jim Gates, an' one is Shifty Ward, an' both of 'em got run out'n Colorado for crooked cattle work. I happen to know 'em both, an' a man oughta keep his hoss tied up while they are aroun'. There's some good men from the Diamond Bar lookin' for a job if you want more men —"

Club Jordan had looked at him curiously.

"You're a real nice boy, Hal," he had answered with leisurely insolence, "an' real nice lookin'. If I was you I wouldn't let them boys hear you talkin' like that. One of 'em might spoil the looks of your face for you. An' you listen to me: When I'm wantin' your advice I'm askin' you for it. Them men might be straight an' they might be crooked, an' I don't give a damn which it is. They're all good cowmen, an' I need good cowmen.

113

An' there ain't nobody goin' to pull off anything on this here range I don't know all about."

Hal had shrugged his shoulders and had gone his way. And his way had been straight to the range-house and to Oscar Estabrook. It was not the custom of Hal to interfere in another man's affairs, and yet it was not his way to see trouble coming to a friend and remain silent. In a way he felt something of sympathy, much of pity, and a sort of friendship for young Estabrook. He had been on the range when Oscar came West; he knew why the son of the Eastern millionaire had suddenly left his old trails in the cities of the East for a new trail here in the cattle country. He knew, as men knew for a hundred miles north, south, east and west of the Bear Track, that Oscar Estabrook had been taken out of college, where he had made a dismal failure of things, that his father had paid his gambling debts, and had sent him out here with a man's responsibilities, hoping that they might make a man of him. He knew that there was a girl in young Estabrook's story, for he had seen the letters which came so regularly, and he had sensed the young fellow was trying to make his stand, trying to grasp the manhood that had always been beyond him, trying to make good, trying to keep his feet steadily in the new trail. For these things, because of his frank smile and hearty laugh and open good nature, the cowboy had felt at once liking and sympathy for his employer. Now, seeing that all might not be well with men like Yellow Jim Gates and Shifty Ward in a position of extreme responsibility for the mountain herds upon the border, knowing that if they wished to do the thing it would be a very simple matter for them to rush very many cattle across into the next county and into the hands of accomplices, Hal did what he had never thought of doing before, and passing his foreman went up to the "boss".

Oscar Estabrook had heard him, and smiled, and thanked him, and had said that he would look into the matter and take it up with Jordan. There had been the end of it. Then, only four weeks after the coming of Yellow Jim Gates and Shifty Ward, one of the old hands — it had been the same Jerry whom Jordan had recently discharged — had reported that a band of fifty young steers, which he had seen one day in the Valley of the Waterfalls, had suddenly dropped out of sight, as though the earth had swallowed them. For Yellow Jim Gates and Shifty Ward were emphatic in denying that the particular band had ever passed through their territory. And yet the steers had never been seen since.

Now there was no faintest doubt in the mind of Hal as to what was going on under his very eyes. He had long distrusted and disliked Club Jordan. But he had known all along that there was not a better cattleman in the West. Hal saw one after another of the old hands discharged, saw new men put into their places, and sensed rather than knew that all was not well upon the Bear Track. He had no way of telling if cattle were being lost, but he knew what might happen with men like Yellow Jim and Shifty Ward upon the border lines. Since Club Jordan was a good cowman, he too must realise this. So while Hal spent his days upon the duties allotted him, and many hours of the nights at his work

115

in his studio, he watched and waited and wondered. For there was nothing further to do after the one warning to young Estabrook, nothing further to say until he had proof. He told himself grimly that when he found the proof he wanted it would mean the end of Club Jordan's reign.

"That man could 'a' put away ten thousan' dollars in them two years," he thought, frowning. "An' men like Yellow Jim and Shifty don't hold on to a real job this long unless there's something crooked in it somewhere. An' " — as an after thought which settled matters entirely in his mind — "a man as'll treat a hoss like Club treated the Colonel won't stop at cattle-rustlin'."

Now there was something else which added fuel to the smouldering fires of his suspicion. The round-up was over and the visitors and cowboys from the neighbouring ranges had gone. Still Prince Victor Dufresne stayed on, still he loitered in the shade with the ladies, still he and Oscar now and then had their little game of poker. And, what was a great deal more to the point, Prince Victor seemed to have formed a great friendship for Club Jordan. The two were much together about the range-house and out among the herds. Hal, knowing the gambler as well as he did, began to think that he saw the brains, the head of the whole "stick-up game".

"That man," reasoned Hal each time he saw the dark, handsome, smiling face and immaculate frock-coat, "can make big money every day in the week in a dozen of towns playing crooked cards. What does he stick here for unless there's money in it? It isn't just his

116

winnings off'n Estabrook, 'cause the games ain't big enough." He shook his head, forgot his CHART 1, and swore softly to himself. "They must be gittin' awful sure, for their work's gittin' mighty raw. An' I'm a big Swede if I don't git the dead-wood on the bunch of 'em before snow flies."

CHAPTER
TEN

Schooldays Again

If, in his adoration for what he chose to see in Sibyl
Estabrook, Hal shunned her until the day when he
might be less ashamed to stand in her presence, there
was no reason why he should avoid her grey-eyed sister.
So within a week, the secret which he hugged to his
bosom was no secret to Yvonne. She was quick to see
the look in his eyes when Sibyl passed gaily on
horseback with the attentive Louis Dabner, quick to
understand why he grew silent in Sibyl's presence, why
he even withdrew from it. And she was quicker than the
rest to see some of the things which lay under the
surface in this man.

"If he has set himself to it," she mused, when first the
thing dawned upon her, "he will do it. He will make her
love him."

Hal, seeking about him for stepping-stones, had
found first Mr. Dabner. He had been with the dapper
young man all that he could, had invited him to ride
where there was hunting and fishing, had drawn him
out to talk, to talk about anything in the world, and had
listened to each word, making mental notes of
constructions, of the proper way of saying little

118

nothings. While he had grown to rather like the polished young gentleman, he had seen to the bottom of him and had had no great fear of him as a rival. But he had not been able to bring himself to the point of asking the thousand questions which clamoured for answer.

But with Yvonne, in some strange, subtle fashion it was different. He found that the shyness which he felt before the others was gone when he was alone with her. It seemed that she understood him, that she was in some incomprehensible way more "his kind," that she would not laugh at him, that she would help him as a friend helps a friend. And one day, when he had been detailed as guide for the party, showing them through the picturesque country about Death Trap mine, he and she had dropped behind the others, and he had found himself suddenly coming very near opening his heart to her. True, he did not mention Sibyl. But he confessed simply, and without the flush which would have rushed into his cheeks had he been speaking with any of the others, that he was trying to better himself intellectually, that he wanted to read, to study, to learn to be such a man externally as the men she knew at home.

"I understand," she said, smiling upon him encouragingly. "When one is very young — it is especially true of a man, I think — he doesn't see the use of books and the things that books mean. And then when he begins to grow a little older, and his chance for schooling has gone by, he realises what he has lost. That is it, isn't it?"

119

He nodded. "You see, Miss Yvonne, I went to school just about long enough to learn to read an' figger a little. An' then I went punchin' cows. If I only knowed how to go at it now I'd like to work nights an' try to learn something. Do you think" — hesitating a little, his eyes searching hers with a vague hint of trouble in them — "that its too late?"

She laughed, and then very seriously told him of the men who, through their own efforts and with many difficulties confronting them, had mastered an education and who had risen to prominence through it.

"It just takes work," she ended. "And if I could help you any way —"

"Would you?" — quickly. "It wouldn't be stupid-like for you?"

So, neither looking ahead to where the roads led, they formed a compact. Heart-hungry for companionship — for Fern was with Oscar; Sibyl was either galloping across the fields with Louis Dabner, or listening to the soft speeches of Mr. Cushing, or day-dreaming over her novel; Mrs. Estabrook was either complaining of the ingratitude of one's children, or quarrelling with John Brent, or napping in the shade — Yvonne found a keen interest in watching the unfolding of a man's soul. She confided much to Hal, simply, in return for his confidence.

She limped a little when she walked, he had noticed it? She smiled at his embarrassment, and ran on to tell him about it. It was her ankle; she had hurt it last year, twisted it in stepping down from a slippery sidewalk, and it had never got strong. Yes, doctors had been called in, but they simply named the names of muscles and bones and looked wise and did nothing. And she was going to cure it herself.

"It is natural for one to be strong and well, you know," she had told him quietly. "It is not nature for one to limp, is it? Why, you men out here who live the way God meant us all to live don't know how strong you are! I have never been strong, because I have lived very foolishly, wickedly, as though I were in a hothouse. I have never had the surplus strength to mend a sick ankle, even. Now I am going to live outdoors, to ride out in the open all I can, to walk a little, more and more, and to let Nature do for me what the poor, foolish doctors cannot do. Do you see? Is it a bargain? If you will ride with me, if you will teach me to catch my own horse, to saddle him, to find my way about through the mountains, I'll try to pay you for it by helping you with your studies."

That night she began helping him by slipping to him, under cover of the darkness, a little bundle of books, and by writing a letter to a bookman in the East, sending for more. The letter Hal carried twenty miles that same night to give to a man on the Diamond Bar who was going to town within the week.

They rode on that day to Death Trap mine, the whole party, Hal guiding them, since Oscar Estabrook could not get away. The cowboy had frowned when Jordan had told him briefly that he was to ride with them, thinking that he saw the reason why, little by little, he was being given duties which kept him from knowing what happened to the herds along the border.

But now, as he galloped along at Yvonne's side, catching glimpses of the frank, open sincerity of her nature, which there was no reason for her hiding from him, he grew very content. For in a new endeavour a man always wants encouragement, needs encouragement, and she gave it to him freely.

He told her of the country through which they passed, speaking slowly, choosing his words, trying to speak correctly. And she, never losing the thread of what he was saying, stopped him now and then, smilingly, and told him of a word mispronounced or misused, and explained to him why he should not use double negatives. He thanked her and grinned at her like a boy, calling her "Teacher," and he remembered. She noted that he did not make the same mistake twice when once she had corrected him.

"Yonder," he said, lifting himself in his stirrups and pointing beyond his horse's bobbing ears to a great ragged gash in the barren mountain ahead of them, "is ol' Death Trap. There was right smart minin' there once. Gold. They took the ore out on hosses an' mules across the mountains an' to Hang Town. That's forty mile. From there they took it in wagons clean across the country to the railroad."

"They don't work it any more?" she asked, her eyes coming back from the site of the mine to rest upon his. "Why? Did they get all the gold out?"

"No, m'am," he explained. "I reckon they lef' a heep sight more than they ever dug. An' I reckon it's there yet, if a man could find it. You see, it was like this: Winter come on 'em awful quick an' unexpected. There was a cloud-burst or something, an' a lan'slide on top of it. The whole side of the mountain above seemed to have give way, an' come down on 'em before they knew it. It caught 'em right there with their picks an' shovels an' things — twenty of 'em — an' covered 'em up an' the mine too. It's funny what a winter like that will do. It was more'n a month before men could get in, an' by that time no man could say just where Death Trap mine was — they used to call it the Yellow Boy until them pore jaspers got covered up in it."

Yvonne shivered a little, and her eyes went back to the mountain towering calm, stern, and, it seemed to her, still threateningly above them.

"They were all killed?" she asked softly. "Every one of them?"

"Every one. If one of 'em even had got out maybe he could 'a' helped relocate the mine. There was a whole two miles along the mountain where the lan'slide come down, an' the diggings might be any place along them two miles. Right over yonder, on that cliff" — again pointing it out to her — "is a cabin. See it? Some lone prospector, lookin' for the ol' Death Trap, made it. We're goin' up there. There's a spring there, an' we'll have lunch by it an' res' before startin' home."

A quarter of a mile ahead of them they could see Sibyl and Mr. Dabner, Fern and Mr. Cushing, as they rode around a turn in the trail and appeared upon the lower slope of the mountain.

"Do you want to let your hoss out a little?" he asked. "They think they're beatin' us to it. We can take a short trail an' head 'em off."

123

So they shook out their reins, gave their horses their heads, and galloped down into the canyon, losing sight of the others as they went. In the rocky bed of the ravine he showed Yvonne a dimly defined cattle trail leading to the left of the main trail the others had taken, and they turned into this. They had to bend low in their saddles now, passing under the low-flung branches of the scrub oaks and cedars, and must ride slowly again. But in a little they came out upon a bench of the mountain, and found a steep trail leading straight upward to the base of the cliffs.

"We can ride aroun' that way," he explained, as he drew rein and she came to his side, her face rose-flushed, her eyes bright with the rugged beauty of the country about her. "When your ankle gits — gets stronger — I beat you that time, didn't I, Teacher?" — before she could correct him — "we can climb up here an' make it in five minutes —"

He had hardly finished when she had swung down from the saddle.

"I can do it now," she told him positively. "There is nothing like knowing you can do a thing, is there? And besides, I haven't walked a bit to-day."

So they left their horses with dragging reins, and Hal showed her the way up. There was a cut in the face of the cliffs, and into it bits of rock had fallen, wedging themselves so that they made rude steps. He climbed a little ahead very slowly, and stopped often to hold out his hand to her, helping her over the harder places. He marvelled at the strong, steady grip of the little brown fingers, and when they had got to the top and stood

124

close together, panting, their faces flushed, he said nothing, but she saw the look of approval in his eyes and her flush deepened.

"Look," he laughed softly, "there come the others."

She clung to his hand a moment, dizzily. They stood now upon the very edge of the cliffs, which fell away like a steep wall below them. Far below, following a winding trail across the uneven slopes, came the others. Yvonne saw them, opened her lips to cry out to them, and grew suddenly silent as the panorama of view opened out before her.

There below, dotted with cattle, lay the valley through which they had ridden, with a glinting ribbon of water through it. About it rose the mountains steeply, but yonder not so high as the cliffs upon which they stood. As one looked across the lower hills the vast level lands of the range swam mistily into view, mile after mile of them, until far away against the horizon rose the faint blue blur of those other mountains where Swayne's Road-house was. And yonder, ten miles away by airline, fifteen miles as they had come, was the Bear Track range-house and corrals in the half-moon curve of the hills.

"Isn't it wonderful!" she whispered, drinking deep of the glory of the world about her. "It is like medicine to the tired body, like a sermon to the tired soul." She turned from the broadening view to him, and said simply, "I should like to live here always!"

"It's the only place," he replied simply, feeling something of the same thing that had rushed up from the low-lands into her soul. "I ain't never — I haven't

125

ever saw — *seen* much of the other thing; cities you know. But I couldn't live in 'em. I know what you mean about it's bein' sermon an' medicine." He nodded gravely, his eyes upon the luminous grey depths of hers. "Maybe I know better than you do. When a man hasn't done the right thing, when he's gone a long way out'n the trail he knows he oughta keep his feet in, when he's done things a man oughta be ashamed of, why, he can come here an' somehow he can see things straight. That's sorta what you mean but, of course," — hurriedly, — "you haven't side-stepped that way."

"I don't know." She shook her head and sighed a little. "I rather think that we are all pretty much the same about things like that. We all have our little rules about right-doing, and we all have our weak spells or stubborn spells and — sidestep."

"But you are so good," he said with quiet positiveness.

She laughed at him, and again shook her head and sighed.

"Am I? And you? Are you then so wicked?" — again laughingly.

He had a sudden boyish desire to tell her something of himself, intimately. He guessed already what her friendship would mean to him, and he wanted it, yearned for it more than he knew. And he felt that in some way it would be unfair to her if they grew to be friends and she did not know the sort he was, the sort he had been foolishly proud of being until very, very recently. Upon the impulse he blurted out, forgetful of grammar:

126

"I ain't been a good man, Miss Yvonne. I ain't sure as you'd like to talk to me if you knowed. Jes' the night before I firs' saw you I shot a man as wasn't even heeled, as hadn't never done nothing to me — an'" — running his hand across a moist brow, his eyes steadfastly upon the far-off plains — "it's jes' plain miracle I didn't kill him."

For a little she didn't answer, and he couldn't bring himself to look at her. Then, as the moment of silence grew longer, unbearably long, he turned to her — and saw that she was smiling faintly.

"Why did you do it?" she asked gently.

"Because I was a coward, mos' likely," he returned bitterly. "A man as shoots another as ain't got a gun on him is always a coward. An' secon', because — because — I was drunk, crazy drunk."

He saw the smile die from her eyes, saw the flush go from her cheeks, leaving them pale.

"I am sorry." There was only a sad sort of pity in her tone. Her hand for a second lay upon his arm. "But you are sorry, too, and you wouldn't do it again."

"An'," he went on moodily, "you ain't ashamed to be with me? Knowin' as I am that sort?"

"You are not that sort! You — why, you haven't had a chance! There is good in all of us, and there is bad. And — *Look* at me!" she broke off quickly. He turned his eyes upon hers, frankly, steadily, unflinchingly. "Do you want me to tell you what I see in your eyes? You have made yourself a reputation. They call you the Outlaw, don't they? And yet, have you ever done a mean thing in your life? Have you ever really done a cowardly

127

thing? Have you ever done a dishonest thing? Have you ever set out wilfully to harm any one in all the world — except yourself? I will tell you what I see in your eyes, Hal, the Bad Man! I see that you are a great big boy — and that you are growing into a great big man! And there is my hand, if you want it, and my friendship as long as you care for it. And," — again smiling suddenly through the little mist in her eyes — "I think that we both understand about the medicine and the sermon!"

CHAPTER
ELEVEN

Tragedy and Premonition

Now at last the undercurrent of trouble running through life on the Bear Track began to ruffle the surface: When there is corruption in the blood it will, soon or late, show in the skin. The things which were happening in the darkness were too big not to throw their shadows across the sky in the daytime.

Fern Winston had come to feel that all was not well. For her eyes were the eyes which love sharpens and does not blind, and events of which she could know nothing were settling their brand upon the man she loved. Again and again there came swiftly into the eyes of Oscar Estabrook a look which was like the look of haunting fear. Through the thick tan of his cheeks there came to glow fitfully feverish spots, and he grew restless, laughed little, and when he did laugh Fern frowned at the false note.

Prince Victor was still at the range-house, a welcome guest like the others, and despite his great courtesy, his extreme deference to the ladies, Fern came to hate the man with his smooth smile and gentle manner, and felt instinctively that in some way he was the cause of Oscar Estabrook's trouble. And yet there had been no poker games of late, and Dufresne seemed to have only the best of goodwill for his host.

What Fern noticed first soon enough ran on to the others, to Yvonne and Sibyl, even to Dabner and Cushing. Oscar Estabrook was little more than a boy, and the West had not been able to put into him the strength of character, the lack of which had made a failure of him in the Eastern university. That he was deeply distressed now showed to them all in his anxious eyes. What the worry was, he did not confide in them, and yet he could not hide that it existed. He ate little, and they all knew that his sleep was broken, that often in the middle of the night he got out of bed and went outside to smoke and wander up and down.

It was as though the atmosphere of the range were electrically charged. The genial, rollicking spirit had gone utterly. Mr. Cushing worried through a few days of it and finally said good-bye, and with his man was driven back to Queen City and the train. Louis Dabner stayed on, but he pleaded each day with Sibyl to set the day, and to hasten with him back to New York. But the Estabrooks had planned to stay upon the range during the summer, until the coming of Pompey Estabrook, and Sibyl shook her head and promised nothing. Yvonne watched her brother with puzzled, troubled eyes and said nothing, knowing that he would confide in Fern Winston if in any one.

Only Mrs. Estabrook seemed to feel nothing of it all. Sibyl's French maid waited upon her almost continually; she dozed in comfortable arm-chairs and complained of all things, — especially of the ingratitude

130

of one's children when Yvonne was in earshot, — and was quite contented for Mrs. Estabrook. But the others, looking into each other's eyes, saw there the same question:

"What is it? What has happened? What is happening? What is Oscar afraid is going to happen?"

And, since everywhere there was the same question, there could be no answer.

It was Sunday evening. Rather for the sake of its cheeriness than because of the faint chill in the night air, there blazed a great log fire in the deep rock fire-place in the sitting-room of the range-house. Big John Brent had returned only this afternoon from a two weeks' visit to the churchless lands lying to the south, and only now, as he closed the Bible upon his knee, did the roaring fire have it all its own way in the quiet room. He had read to them a few chapters in his fine, rich voice, and had, all unsolicited, preached them their Sunday sermon — such a sermon as they had never heard before and which shocked Mrs. Estabrook very much. He had not employed the conventional pulpit voice and phraseology. He had spoken sternly and bluntly and frankly, telling them for the most part what he thought of them. He had scored Louis Dabner for being a dandy and a do-nothing, he had accused Sibyl of vanity and selfishness and uselessness, he had scolded Mrs. Estabrook in the name of the Lord as though she had been a small and naughty, whining little girl. And then he had prayed.

"God Almighty," he had cried impetuously, his voice ringing out so that it carried to the men in the bunk-house, "help us to get out of ourselves for a little. Help us to forget our own narrow lives, our own petty cares, our own snivelling souls! Teach us that there is much in the world for us all, and that there is much for other men and women, and that there are other men and women who are better and more deserving than we. Lead us where we may put out our hands and help another. Knock the eternal conceit and vanity and egotism out of us, and put a little glow of hope and helpfulness and love into us. Make us *be* something, make us *do* something. Make men and women out of us. And pray God, that is not asking Thee to make fine, silken purses out of sows' ears!"

Whereupon, in the sudden silence falling in the room, Mrs. Estabrook's shudder was almost an audible thing.

Miss Sibyl sat smiling upon a couch in the firelight, Mr. Dabner sprawling on some cushions at her feet. Mrs. Estabrook, her hands folded properly in her lap, lending by her apppearance and grave face what she could of the proper Sabbath air to the proceeding, sat erect near the table, her head lowered at the conventional, religious angle. Yvonne and Fern, who had been watching the pictures in the coals upon the hearth, had not moved while John Brent read and prayed. Now that there came a step in the hallway they both looked up quickly. It was Oscar Estabrook. They heard him drop his spurs at the door of his own room and come on to the sitting-room.

"Just too late," thundered John Brent jovially. "I have preached at these people and prayed at them until they are all chafed and raw in spirit. And you time your arrival, Brother, so that I cannot include you in my tirade and chide you for the wickedness of which you have been guilty during the day."

"What do you mean?" demanded Oscar quickly.

The preacher laughed, and laid a heavy hand lightly upon his host's shoulder.

"You start as though you were a Macbeth and there were a dead Duncan somewhere in the house," he chaffed. "My boy, you are working too hard, you are getting nervous."

Oscar laughed with him, the forced laugh which jarred so on Fern Winston's nerves, nodded to the others, and went to Fern's side, dropping down wearily upon the rug at her feet.

"I am tired," he said, staring moodily into the fire, all unconscious of the soft hand wandering through his hair. "Tired out. And I am sick of the whole thing here where a man spends his days with bawling cattle and boorish, uneducated, ignorant workmen. When Dad comes I'm going to chuck the whole business and go home."

For a moment Fern's fingers stopped, Fern's face clouded at the whine in her lover's voice. Then her love made excuses, and her fingers were softer than ever on his hot brow.

"Oscar is right, I'm sure," chimed in his mother, glad to find some one else complaining. "I don't know why his father ever sent him out here."

"Because, madam," thundered John Brent, whirling upon her so suddenly that the poor little woman shrank back in her chair and cowed like a very small mouse under the glare of a very large cat, "because he knew what he was doing! Because he believed that his son was breaking all records down the merry toboggan slide to hell where he was, because he hoped that rubbing up against the raw edge of life out here might make a man of him! He knew the West, madam! He knew that if there was man-stuff in his son it would manifest itself sooner than in your hothouses at home. And if there were not man-stuff — why, then, the road here to hell is just a bit shorter and straighter than elsewhere, and it's just as well to get the thing over and done with."

"How can you say such things!" shivered Mrs. Estabrook.

"I know, I know what I am talking about and I say what I mean! Life here is just a touchstone, that's all. Sling your untried man up against it and it tests him and shows him up for what he is. And if he is merely weak, why, then it smashes him. And if he is strong for good or for evil, it hardens his muscles and makes him stronger. It makes men like Victor Dufresne, who is a gambler and a thief and —"

"Stop!" Oscar had lifted his head suddenly, his face flushed, and had thrown out his hand. "He is my guest, you will remember, Mr. Brent!"

"Your guest!" roared John Brent. "And so shall I still my tongue to the truth because the man with whom I would point my moral happens to sleep and eat under your roof? The man they call Prince Victor is an unprincipled rascal, and you know it as well as he does and as well as I do. And still he is a *man*. He is not a

134

coward, he is not a weakling. The life 'that runs large' out here took him and made a man of him." Oscar sank back, muttering a little, and John Brent ran on, heeding him not at all. "There is the man they call Club Jordan, the foreman here. He is another man, and the country hereabouts made him. God knows what of good and of bad there is in him, but any one who looks him in the eyes knows that he is a strong, purposeful, self-reliant man. And" — his eyes very bright — "it is a great, wonderful thing just to be a man — and it is a horrible, pitiful, damnable thing to be a Tomlinson! Then, there is our friend, the Outlaw Hal . . ."

"What of him?" asked Yvonne quickly. Sibyl too turned from the enraptured gaze of Louis Dabner to watch the big man. John Brent threw out his two arms widely and let them drop to his side, his deep chest rising and falling with the gesture.

"There is one in the retort of Life's experimental laboratory!" he said slowly. "There is one who is tugged two ways, who is seeking for expansion and expression, who is even now being tried and tested at the great touchstone. And watch, watch!" — his voice again gathering volume, his face graver, more earnest than it had been before. "He has in him the making of a man, the biggest, truest man of us all! He doesn't know himself, but then, Mother of God, he is only a boy! And he is finding himself fast. He is a gambler and a brawler and a spendthrift — he gets blind drunk, and he forgets his God who is his Father — and yet, I should be proud to have a son like him, and I should be hopeful of the ultimate outcome. A Woman is what he needs, and

135

when she comes, if she is the right woman, she is going to make a good man of him — he will always be a strong man — and if she is the wrong sort —"

There came a sudden loud knocking at the front door, and, without waiting, the one who had knocked flung it open and came rapidly down the hallway and to the sitting-room. There was something in the short, hurried stride as well as in the quick, impetuous blows that made them all turn curious, half-anxious eyes to the newcomer. Oscar got hurriedly to his feet. And there on the threshold, his spurs catching the winking firelight, his face showing very grave as he swept his broad hat from his head, stood the man of whom John Brent had been speaking.

"What is it?" demanded young Estabrook sharply.

Hal's eyes roved from one to another of the faces which were turned to him before he answered.

"There's been trouble," he said very quietly, as though speaking of a matter of no moment. And yet the glow from the fireplace showed the suppressed excitement in his eyes. "The stage has been held up at the Bear Creek Crossing. The express agent is half a mile behind me. He wants Mr. Estabrook to git the boys out an' help corral the man as did it."

They were all on their feet now, crowding close up to the newsbearer, a-flutter with excited interest.

"Did — did he get away with anything?" asked Oscar out of a short silence.

"Yes. Got the box with the five thousand dollars as was goin' to the mines."

"Was any one hurt?" asked Yvonne quickly.

136

"The driver," grunted Hal, a little spurt of anger flaring up through his short-spoken words. "Bill Cutter. An' Bill had his hands up, too. It was cold-blooded murder an' no use for it."

Fern cried out and clutched at Oscar's arm. But Oscar was running to his room for his rifle.

"Where's Club Jordan?" he cried back at Hal. "Have you told him?"

"Where's Club Jordan?" repeated Hal dryly. "Nobody can't find him! That's what I want to know. Where's Club Jordan?"

John Brent spoke for the first time.

"You don't mean —"

Hal laughed, and it wasn't a pretty laugh to hear.

"I mean," he said gently — and Mrs. Estabrook got up quickly from her chair and drew away from him — "I mean that Bill Cutter was a frien' of mine, an' somebody's goin' to pay for a dirty deal!"

They heard his spurs clank and jingle down the hall. And a sudden chill fell over the room which the leaping fire could not thaw.

CHAPTER
TWELVE

A Chance Spark in the Darkness

Hal closed the new grammar which Yvonne had bought and pencil-marked for him, laid it carefully upon his soap-box, trimmed the wick of his lantern, and sighed deeply. He made a cigarette with slow-moving fingers, rolling the brown tube of paper over and over and over, frowning at his own wavering shadow upon the rock floor. And he was not thinking of his new book, in which he realised he had made little enough progress to-night.

"They're all liars," he muttered heavily. "Club Jordan an' Yellow Jim an' Shifty Ward. Every one of 'em is a damn liar; an I know it. They'd lie for a drink an' they'd lie to save a pal's neck. But jes' the same —"

He broke off where he had broken off many times before. They *would* lie, yes. But how could a man be certain that they had lied in this particular case? How could a man be absolutely positive? One must be very sure of his ground before he accused another man of murder.

"But," he went on in a little, "if Club Jordan didn't do it, *who did?*" He shook his head, and at last lighted his cigarette. "I ain't quit, Club Jordan, an' I'll get the deadwood on you yet. Poor ol' Bill. An' with his hands up, too!"

There had been a wild night of haste and search after the word of the Bear Creek Crossing tragedy had been brought to the range-house, but haste and search had been alike profitless. The Crossing was full ten miles from the range-house, close to the broken mountain country, and the man who had held up the stage had had ample time to make his escape before the cowboys got to horse after him. Hal had made no attempt to hide his suspicion, and all ears waited for Club Jordan's explanation of his absence. But the explanation came smoothly enough when the foreman was at last located near morning, in camp with Yellow Jim Gates and Shifty Ward upon the south-eastern border. Jordan spent many nights away from the bunk-house, and every one knew it — knew that his duties as foreman carried him hither and thither, and that he spent the night wherever it came upon him. Besides, both Yellow Jim and Shifty had told that he had been with them all the late afternoon and evening.

In the range-lands, cut by the sharp feet of many browsing herds, and in the rocky mountain passes there had been little use in looking for the tracks which the murderer had left behind him. There followed days of speculation, of suspicion, of watchfulness. Now that the weeks had run on, the green grass of forgetfulness was growing over the wrong done in the night, a new driver had taken Bill Cutter's place on the stage, and the Bear Creek Crossing hold-up seemed to be sinking rapidly into the misty veil of mystery which covers so many stage robberies. There were a score cowboys upon the Bear Track and upon the borders of the ranges at the north, each one of whom might have been guilty of the thing; and no one knew what men might have come down from the mountains to commit their crime here and then draw back the way they had come.

But Hal, to whom the combined oaths of Yellow Jim and Shifty Ward and Club Jordan meant less than nothing, who thought that he saw in the killing of the driver a bit of sheer hatred, since the thing was unnecessary, and who knew that Bill Cutter and Club Jordan had had trouble before, did not for a moment lose his first swift suspicion. But, as he told himself over and over, a man must be very certain in a case like this.

So, to-night, in his study-cave, he learned little grammar. Bill Cutter's dead face had a way of getting into the pages of his book and looking out at him reproachfully; Club Jordan's sharp eyes seemed to stare at him full of mocking, jeering lights. He got to his feet and went to the mouth of his cave, looking out across the valley below and at the heavy black clouds scurrying before the wind across the scattered stars. He walked up and down, paced back and forth from end to end of the cave, even threw himself for a little upon his blanket, and with his hands clasped behind his head stared upward at the shadows clinging to the rocks above him. At last, with a strange restlessness upon him, he flung himself to his feet again and once more strode up and down, seeking to know the thing that perplexed him.

"The only way," he puzzled out, "is to wait an' watch. An' when one of them jaspers flashes a fistful of money, make him show where it come from."

He picked up his book again, settled himself upon his cracker-box, and turned to a page that Yvonne had marked. Here were sentences with glaring errors in them which he was to correct, write out, and hand to her to-morrow. He took up his pencil and paper — and threw them down, muttering angrily.

"What's the matter with me?" he grumbled. "I ain't never been like this before."

He went back to the cave's entrance and sat down cross-legged, staring down into the shadows of the valley, watching the thickening clouds, listening to the moan of the night wind in the pine trees. The minutes dragged by and he did not move, did not even light the cigarette dangling from his lips.

Suddenly he jerked his head up, his listless body grew tense, and he leaned forward, peering out over the cliff's edge. For he had seen a spurt of light, a quick, short-lived glow through the darkness below him, and had known that the shod hoof of a horse had struck a spark from a bit of flinty rock on the trail. Because shod horses were not running loose on the range, because ranging stock rarely came here, because he knew no reason why a man should be riding here and now on honest business, because chiefly of the things of which he had been thinking, that tiny, chance spark, chance seen, fired a quick hope in him that here was the beginning of an explanation.

141

He strode swiftly to his lantern and put out the flame, for fear that a pale yellow ray might leak through the brush across his doorway. And then he came back to the mouth of the cave and crouched there in the thick shadow, watching, listening.

But there was nothing to see, and in the swish of the wind through the pines all other sounds were lost to him. And yet he felt that a man was moving down there below him, moving guardedly, cautiously. Now he knew every foot of the narrow trails hereabout, knew that if a man were riding toward the Bear Track headquarters he must pass through a little clearing, where he could see him if he watched carefully and unless the clouds thickened too fast for him. And the man, even if his horse walked, and walked very slowly, must reach the open place in five minutes.

But the five minutes passed, another five followed them, and he knew that the man, if man it were, must have ridden from the Bear Track and must follow the trail winding about the base of the cliffs.

"An' I'll see him against the sky when he rides over the ridge," he told himself confidently. "An' then I c'n follow him an' we'll see what he's up to."

But the minutes passed, and no shadowy outline of horse and rider stood out against the patch of sky where the trail ran out of the little valley. So long was the silence and no sign that the man who watched began to wonder if he had seen what he had seen, or if he had been misled by a glow-worm. Then his body stiffened again, and he thrust his head out, scarcely breathing. For he had heard the rattle of stones and knew that some one was climbing the cliffs.

"He's coming up here!" he muttered wonderingly. "Up here!"

Again there was silence, again there came to his straining ears the noise of slipping earth and stones, and in a little he made out a moving object clinging to the rocks below him — not twenty feet below — and little more than that distance to the right.

"It looks like he knows about my cave," he told himself. "Like I was goin' to have company. An' — There's two of 'em!"

He could see them plainly enough now, although he could not see the faces, could not make out who they were. They were drawing steadily, although slowly, nearer to him. Now they were but ten feet below him, and he lay flat, peering down at them. And then, one after the other, they stepped out upon a ledge and began edging off to the right. Hal wanted to laugh aloud. For he could see them now more plainly as the wind drove apart the clouds above, making a great rift for the stars to shine through. The man who went ahead was Victor Dufresne, and the man who followed panting, whose deformed foot made the climbing doubly difficult for him, was Club Jordan!

"It's a fool thing," cursed Jordan, as for a little he rested and clung to a rugged knob of rock. "It's the devil's own work, an' it's takin' too many chances."

Dufresne laughed softly.

"It's the last time, Jordan," he consoled. "The last but one, and then damn the chances. Come on!"

143

Again they moved on. Hal saw that they had passed out of sight along the ledge of rock. At least they were not coming to his cave. His decision swiftly made, he worked his way down the old way he knew until he came to a great cut in the cliffs, very much like the one up which he and Yvonne had gone that day when they had visited Death Trap mine. Now he hurried, climbing upwards again until he came to the top of the cliffs and just above his cave. Here he crept forward slowly, stopping often to listen, to try and see through the darkness into which Jordan and Dufresne had gone. When he saw nothing, heard nothing, he moved on again, climbing over boulders, slipping down great piles of rocks, and always to the right, in the direction they had taken.

Suddenly he stopped and crouched down in the shadows. There before him was a great cup, twenty feet across, ringed about with flinty spires of rock, a hollow of which a man could not guess from below, into which he could not see unless he came upon it from above, as Hal was coming now. In the hollow he made out the glowing ends of two burning cigarettes. He wedged himself between two upstanding boulders and watched, a little puzzled that Jordan and Dufresne could have come here so much ahead of him as to have made their cigarettes. Then he saw that they were not the men he had followed, saw both Jordan and Dufresne pull themselves up over the edge of the cliff and drop down into the rock-rimmed basin.

"Four of 'em," he muttered. "Who's the other two? Yellow Jim an' Shifty, mos' likely."

144

"You fools," grunted Club Jordan, as he limped across the narrow hollow and stopped before the two men who were smoking. "Ain't we takin' enough chances without you two burnin' tobacco? You'd oughta know better'n that, Andy."

Andy! So Andy Holloway, the young fellow whom they had taken on only two months before, was one of them? Andy laughed a little insolently.

"What's eatin' you, Club?" he scoffed. "Scared the sheriff's goin' to smell it down to Queen City? You're gittin' nerves, you are."

"Nerves, hell," grunted Jordan sourly. "I got sense, that's all. You young pups think it's smart to show off, an' take chances. God!" he ran his hand across his forehead and sat down heavily. "You're a fool if you run into any danger as ain't in the game. Maybe I am gittin' nerves. Anyway, I'll be mighty glad when this thing is over with."

Dufresne had followed him and now stood leaning against a boulder, looking down at them.

"There's always danger in taking a kid like Andy in," he said gently. "But this thing is too big for us to worry about a chance here and there. And since the others are smoking — have a cigar, Jordan?"

Jordan grunted, and turned to the man who had not yet spoken.

"That you, Jim?" he asked.

"Yes" — shortly. "I been here an hour, too, an' I want to clean out. I didn't sleep none las' night. What's the word?"

"Did Ward send anything?"

Yellow Jim untied something from his belt and dropped it at Jordan's feet. As it struck against a stone it gave out the unmistakable jingle of minted gold. Jordan picked it up, weighed it in his hands, and then passed it on to Dufresne.

"Look a here," put in Andy suddenly. "I'm gettin' tired of this business. I want to see the colour of mine."

Dufresne tied the strings of the buckskin bag to his own belt. Then, very carefully, he lighted his cigar. In the flare of the match which he held cupped in his hands his face looked placid and unconcerned. Only when he had drawn two or three puffs at his cigar and had looked to see that it was burning evenly did he speak.

"You want to see the colour of yours?" he asked softly, as though he was not quite certain that he had heard rightly.

"Yes," snapped young Holloway. "I do. I'm gettin' damn' tired doin' a big share of the work an' havin' you fellows play treasurer with the coin. How do I know —"

"Well?" — quietly. "Go on and finish. How do you know what?"

"How, do I know," Andy blurted out, "that I'm ever going to get anything out'n it? If you guys was to hold out on me, an' try to double-cross me, what show would I have? I want mine now, an' before you're all ready to cut an' run for it!"

"So," repeated Dufresne slowly, "you want yours now. Well?"

"Yes," cried Andy, emboldened by the quiet way in which Dufresne took his words. "An' jes' talkin' don't

146

help none. There's been too much talkin' an' promisin' already."

"You are right," nodded Dufresne. "There has been a whole lot too much talking. If there hadn't been you would have been an honest boy now, Andy, punching cattle and knowing nothing about what was going on. But you were quick, weren't you, to pick up things and put them together and see the truth? And then you demanded your share, and you've been demanding your rights ever since, haven't you?"

"Yes, I have, damn you. An' I mean to have 'em. An' I'll take my share of that money now."

"And what will you do with it?" — the tone of the words hinting at a tolerant smile back of them.

"Whose business is it what I do with it?" challenged Andy hotly. "Ain't it mine? Ain't I worked for it? Can't I do as I please with it?"

"Andy," went on the gambler in the same serene, untroubled tone, "we haven't finished this thing yet. We're just about half through; we've turned just about half the money there is in it. Jordan here hasn't got his yet. He's willing to wait. So is Jim, so is Shifty, so are the other boys. We've got to be careful, don't you see it?" — his voice almost pleading. "If you get your money the other boys will have a right to theirs. Then some one of you is going to spend his, he is going to get drunk and talk, and before you know it the whole kettle of fat will be kicked in the fire and we'll all have to run for it. It's only a month longer now. We'll put the last big deal across then, and then you can take your money in a lump and do as you please with it. It would be better to wait, Andy."

"I won't wait," cried Holloway stubbornly. "I want what's comin' to me."

Dufresne sat silent, drawing thoughtfully at his cigar. Both Yellow Jim and Jordan were leaning forward tensely, watching him. Hal, who knew this man so well, wondered a little, and leaned a little nearer, trying to see his face. At last, after a long silence, in which Andy moved restlessly once or twice, Dufresne took his cigar from his mouth and spoke.

"Holloway," he said gently, his voice just a trifle softer than it had been before, "you're young, and young men are apt to be hot-headed. But I can't reason with you all night. Now listen; you are going to do just exactly as the others are doing, and you are going to get your money just when they get theirs. Remember that if you are doing a good bit of the risky work I am running this game. And I say that I don't want and won't have anymore talk from you. Understand?"

"Understand?" cried Andy, on his feet in an instant. "You bet I understand! I know you, Dufresne, for a damned, dirty scoundrel that would double-cross his best friend if he got the chance. An' let me tell you something: I am going to have my money and have it now, or I'll fill your carcass so full of holes that you can't crawl away."

As he spoke his hand jerked forward, and the starlight ran down the barrel of a heavy six-shooter. Dufresne shrugged his shoulders.

148

"Young," he said, as though making excuses. "Very young. Well, Andy, have it your way. Here's your money."

He took the cigar from his mouth, and with Andy's gun trained full upon him laid it very carefully upon the rock against which he was been leaning.

Andy took a step forward, eyeing Dufresne suspiciously. The gambler untied the bag from his belt and tossed it to the ground.

"Count it. Count out your share," he said lightly. "You're a fool, Andy."

Andy stooped, his fingers closed on the heavy buckskin bag. He never lifted it an inch from the ground. For Dufresne had sprung forward suddenly, and as he sprang had whipped high above his head the knife which he always wore under his vest. Panting audibly with the exertion he put into the blow, he drove the long, keen blade deep into young Holloway's neck. Again he lifted it, again, as poor Andy was falling, drove it into the writhing body, then stepped quickly back, wiping the sharp blade upon the grass, taking up his cigar with steady fingers.

His back was to the rock, his eyes running back and forth between Jordan and Yellow Jim. They had leaped to their feet. Yellow Jim had cried out hoarsely, Jordan had made no sound. And already Andy Holloway lay still, his face in the hollow of his arm, one hand touching the buckskin bag.

"He was a fool, and I told him so," Dufresne said as he slipped the knife back into its sheath. "I was afraid

I'd have to do that all along. If you've got anything to say, Jim, and you too, Jordan, say it now."

He paused, and Hal could see his head turn as he looked again from one to the other of them.

"I — I don't like it," muttered Yellow Jim after a little. "To rustle cattle is one thing, to murder a man —"

"Murder!" For the first time there was an ugly snarl in Dufresne's low tone. "After he drew a gun on me? Murder? And if I had let him shoot, who knows what one of those damned deputies that are still filling the canyons looking for the Bear Creek Crossing man might have heard and found us here? Why, you fool, I've saved your life for you as well as mine for me — and twenty thousand dollars for us all!"

"He had it comin'," muttered Jordan throatily. "Victor's right, Jim. An' we better move him, an' quick, too. There's no use everybody knowing about it."

Hal, feeling sick as he watched them, drew back a little when Dufresne and Jordan took up the quiet body and moved laboriously with it to the far edge of the hollow, putting it in the thick shadows there and throwing a little brush over it. Then he drew nearer again as the three men resumed their places.

"We'll attend to him later," Dufresne was saying, once more as nonchalantly unconcerned as ever. "Now listen to me, Jim. Jordan will have five hundred big steers pushed up Bear Creek from the plains some time next week, and moved back into the hills. Ward will know and he'll pass the word to you. Within two or three weeks the whole herd will be in your territory.

You're to keep them pretty well bunched, where you can get every hoof of them on the run at an hour's notice. As soon as the coast is clear on the other side, they'll let you know, and you'll push the cattle on to the edge of the Double Triangle. I'll join you there. Willoughby will pay cash, and as soon as the cows are within fifty miles of the railroad. Then we're through. You are to pass the word on to the other boys, and to tell them that as soon as this deal is pulled off they will get their money, and it will be up to each one of them to keep his neck whole. And now for details . . ."

Hal could have cried out in amazement. These men were speaking, not of running off ten, fifteen, a score of cattle, but of five hundred in a bunch! Why, at that rate, there would soon be nothing left of the Bear Track brand! It seemed incredible, impossible. And yet was it even difficult if they had it so planned that there were men ready to buy, to pay for the stolen cattle, to rush them away on the railroad? If Willoughby of the Double Triangle were in with them — and he did not believe Willoughby to be above it — where was the difficulty? For long ago had Club Jordan let most of the old men go, long ago had he put men of his own in their places, so that now there was only Hal left, and Dick Sperry, and perhaps two or three of the others who were loyal to the Bear Track and to the Estabrook interests. And these men had been kept busy about the range-house, or out in the level lands, and knew nothing whatever of what was happening in the mountains.

"At last," he thought grimly, "I know something. At last I can show the cards. I can go to young Estabrook an' show him the kind of man his foreman is. An' there's goin' to be a squarin' of accounts for Andy an' poor Bill Cutter."

He saw that the three men had stopped speaking, that they had turned watchfully toward the edge of the cliff. And in a little he saw another man climb upward and drop down into the hollow. As he came forward Dufresne picked up the buckskin bag and jingled it before him.

"Luck's running high!" he cried lightly. "One more whirl and we can all pay our debts and take a fresh start!"

And then — Hal felt as though a man had struck him across the face. The man who had come forward to join them was young Oscar Estabrook!

CHAPTER
THIRTEEN

A Shattered Idol

Oscar was one of the gang stealing his own cattle! That was the one thing that stood out clearest of all, and that was the one thing which Hal could not fully grasp. For he knew that Pompey Estabrook had entrusted all things pertaining to the management of the range to his son, and that Oscar could drive what cattle he pleased to market and in broad daylight. So why should he consort with thieves to rob his own father, to rob himself?

No word of what passed between the four men in the hollow was lost to Hal. He heard how they had driven off other herds, how they were now preparing to rush the band of five hundred steers across the border and into the hands of Willoughby on the Double Triangle, how Willoughby would have them in cattle cars and on the way to Chicago within forty-eight hours after they were turned over to him. He learned that these things were planned very largely by Victor Dufresne, and that it was Dufresne and not Jordan who in reality was managing the colossal steal. He heard how it was Dufresne's plan to wait a little for the turning of this last trick, to move slowly and cautiously, to have the steers along the border at the time of the first rains. For it would not be long now, four or six weeks at most, when the season would break in the mountains and there would come the heavy downpour which in a few hours' time would wipe out all signs that a large herd of cattle had passed that way.

And Oscar Estabrook was standing among them, asking nervously of this and of that, where Andy was, why he had not come, if Shifty Ward was doing his part and keeping his mouth shut, if Willoughby could be trusted to have the cash ready when the time came!

A little further they talked, and for the most part it was Jordan or Dufresne who directed Yellow Jim, who took his orders in silence or with quick, sharp questions, Oscar Estabrook who moved up and down restlessly and said little. Directions were plain enough, each man of them — and the names of five other Bear Track cowboys, all new men, were mentioned — having his duties to perform. Yellow Jim was entrusted with it all, and was to report before morning to Shifty Ward with the details.

At last Oscar Estabrook and Victor Dufresne and Club Jordan and Yellow Jim Gates, one after the other, had climbed out of sight. Hal, with only a backward glance at the shadows where a heap of brush had been piled over all that was left of young Andy Holloway, slipped away through the darkness and went slowly back to the cave. Sitting in the darkness there upon his cracker-box, forgetting to smoke, he tried to work the thing out, tried to explain to himself why Oscar

154

Estabrook should be one of a crowd stealing Bear Track cattle.

The remark with which Prince Victor had greeted Estabrook helped Hal to the explanation he sought. "One more whirl," he had said, "and we can all pay our debts and take a fresh start!" Which one of them was in debt? Jordan? Positively not. For Jordan was a close-fisted man, who gambled little and drank not at all, and he had been making money and saving it. It was not the man's nature to run into debt. Dufresne? Again no. For Dufresne wore to-night all his diamonds — the stone in his shirt-front, the one upon his finger, the one in his tie. And when Dufresne ran out of money, as he did often enough when luck was against him, his diamonds were invariably pawned to relieve the stress and to give him a new start. Men who knew the gambler knew that when he wore the three stones at the same time he had plenty of money. Yellow Jim then? Who would trust him far enough for him to get into debt?

It only left Oscar Estabrook. And Oscar must be heavily in debt. His poker games alone with Dufresne, games in which he lost over and over, winning now and then just enough to make him hope to win largely, must have put him deeply in Dufresne's debt. Hal knew that the other night when he had lost to Dufresne he had paid, not in cash, but with an I O U for two hundred and fifty dollars. There was no way of telling how deeply in debt he was to Dufresne, or what other gambling debts he owed. But one thing was obvious. If Oscar did have heavy debts, especially gambling debts, he would not want his father to know. For gambling was one of the things that the stern old man would not tolerate, and gambling in college had been one of the causes of Oscar's being sent West.

"If," Hal worked it out finally — "if he's in the hole deep, he's got to git the money without the ol' man knowin'. An' if he sol' cattle the regular way his dad would know an' the money would have to be turned over to his dad. An' the chances is they've snaked him into this, an' he's takin' the one chance he sees to git out'n Dufresne's claws, an' before Dufresne goes to his ol' man with a fist full of notes. The poor, deluded young fool!"

And there was a great deal more of pity than of censure in his tone. For long ago he had come to know his employer as a weak man, not a bad man, and he knew that his integrity had had little chance with men like Dufresne and Jordan.

Now, what to do? He could not do the thing he wanted to do, could not go to Estabrook and expose Jordan and Dufresne and the rest, for Estabrook knew more of the whole thing than he did. He could not go to Jordan and Dufresne and accuse them of the thing, as they were now in a position where they could laugh at him. For who would believe that Oscar Estabrook was stealing his own cattle? And it would be so easy for them to show that what they had done had been done with his sanction and approval. He could not go to any one and tell what he knew, for then he would be branding *her brother* as a cattle thief, and in the West a cattle thief is a grade lower in the scale than a rattlesnake. He groaned inwardly over the hopelessness of the situation, and in the end decided to wait, to watch, to do nothing for a little, and to hope to see the way before the rains came.

Now more than ever he shunned Sibyl Estabrook, and, seeing her only from a distance, he raised her higher and higher upon the altar he had built for her, and strove manfully to lift himself after her. During the long days in which he was sent about the routine of work — always to some point upon the level lands, or on some errand to a neighbouring range, never back into the mountains where the real work was — he carried his book with him. At night he slipped away to his cave and sat up late, preparing the lessons which Yvonne was to correct for him. And he knew that if he were making little progress in finding a solution to the trouble which every day cast its shadow blacker and blacker over the range and over its young manager, still was he making great strides toward being that thing which he had set out to make himself. He had touched no drop of whisky, he had played no game of cards, he had dropped many of the faulty, ungrammatical expressions which he had used all his life. And he had flushed with pleasure when Yvonne had told him that he was doing veritable wonders.

Now Oscar seemed feverishly anxious that his guests should be amused. Often he himself rode with them, taking them miles away from the range-house to camp over night, to hunt and fish and wander through the more beautiful spots of the mountains. Generally Hal, and often Dick Sperry, went with them. For Club

157

Jordan had no use for them in the work he was doing, and was obviously glad of an excuse to send them far afield.

So the weeks passed and there came a second visit to the country about Death Trap mine, and the colour of the world was suddenly changed for Hal. This time the party had consisted of Sibyl, Yvonne, Fern, Louis Dabner, Victor Dufresne, John Brent, and Oscar himself. They had gone for a "week end" in the mountains, following the big camp wagon, to hunt and camp out. In the afternoon it happened that the party had separated in this way: Yvonne had wanted to climb again to the cabin on the cliffs to take advantage of the clear day and the wide expanse of view, and Sibyl had coaxed Louis Dabner into post-poning his hunting until the following day, and going to the mine. So these four, Hal riding with the others, had gone up the cliffs, and the rest of the party had ridden on to camp, half a dozen miles farther in the canyons.

Little things grow into big things, and a tiny black cloud in the southern sky carried with it a tremendous influence over human destiny. They came to the cliffs in the late afternoon, and in the west the sun was weaving a tumult of colours into a wondetful sunset, red and golden and splashed across with soft wavering tints and shades. It was the glorious curtain that the Master Artist was painting to drop over the end of the summer, and it seemed that He was making strange, new, unheard-of colours to do justice to an *opus major*. They stood silent, touched with the magic and mystery of it, listening to the rising breeeze through the tree

158

tops far below them. Then, since there should be a moon later, and since they had their lunches with them, it was Sibyl's suggestion that they make their evening meal in the old deserted cabin, watch the moon rise, and join their companions after nightfall.

So they built a fire in the old stone chimney and made their coffee and dined merrily, even Hal's silence melting in the warm glow of companionship which fell over them. He found himself telling them stories of the old mine, talking slowly, choosing his words carefully, feeling that Yvonne's eyes were bright upon her "pupil", and that he was not disgracing himself.

"Then the place is haunted!" cried Sibyl delightedly. "Think of it, a whole haunted mountain! It must be. And, positively, I am not going a step until I see a real ghost."

They fell in with her mood and told ghost stories. The darkness gathered in the cabin, with only the fitful fire-light playing with the shadows, the wind rose and wailed about them like the lost spirit of the mountain, and the atmosphere of the night was already one that had set its seal upon their memories. Then, suddenly, there came the patter of big raindrops.

Hal got up swiftly and went to the door. Rain already! The, first rains were to be the signal for the moving of the herd of five hundred steers — and he had done nothing! He had not looked for a storm for another two weeks yet, at earliest. But surely this was but a passing shower, and in fifteen minutes would blow over. Dabner came to the door to join him.

"It isn't going to storm much, is it?" he queried a bit anxiously. "The girls — we've got at least three hours' ride to camp, haven't we?"

Hal didn't answer for a little. While they had talked the rain-clouds had piled high and black in the sky, shutting out every star. There was no sign of moonrise, it was already night-black in the canyons.

"I don't know," he said slowly. "It may rain half the night. Maybe we'd better hurry on."

As if in answer there came a mighty gust of wind under, which the cabin rocked and groaned. The rain fell faster, heavier, with a little hail beginning to bound and rattle against the shake roof. Here and there the water was already running through rifts in the shakes and forming black pools on the floor. Sibyl and Yvonne came to where the men were standing. The wind caught a sheet of rain, swirled it about the corner of the cabin, and drove it into their faces, forcing them back.

"Isn't it great?" cried Sibyl, wiping the moisture from her face. "Isn't it fun?" And then, quickly, "It isn't going to last long, is it?"

No one answered for a little, and then Dabner, speaking lightly, said:

"It can't last long. These mountain storms come up out of nothing like this, in a second, and are gone as quickly as they come. Anyway we'll have to wait until it's over. We'd be soaked to the skin out there before we had got to our horses."

Hal stepped outside and brought in an armful of wood from the heap of brushwood that had jammed against the higher side of the cabin. What he had seen in the black sky sent him out twice again for fuel.

Instead of lessening, the downpour increased steadily, the wind rising until it seemed that it would sweep the cabin from its foundation and hurl it over the edge of the cliffs. And now there came crash after crash of thunder, and the sky was cut from horizon to horizon by sharp, jagged streaks of lightning under which the mountains about them stood out as clearly outlined as though it were bright noonday, quivered an instant, and were sucked back by the darkness. It seemed as though the forked lightning had ripped open the bursting clouds above them, and the rain fell about them in one mighty, steady down-pour.

"A cloud-burst," muttered the cowboy, slamming the door shut and standing with his back to it to keep the wind from flinging it open again. "If it keeps up an hour at this rate we can't get across the creek to camp to-night."

"What shall we do?" asked Sibyl, her tone showing a vague alarm. "We can't stay here all night!"

He shook his head. "I don't know. We can't go out in this storm. With the dark and the wind and the trails all slippery underfoot it would be dangerous trying to make it. Bein' as this is the first rain of the year, it oughtn't to amount to much. And at the same time," he told himself, doubting, "you can't gamble on the weather at any time. Anyway" — aloud and cheerfully — "we've got a roof over us and a fire. Which is something."

161

"It's little enough," complained Sibyl, her gaiety at the frolic of a moment ago gone suddenly. She moved a little, and stepped into a pool of the gathering water. "Ugh!" she cried. "We were fools to come at all."

"It's not so bad," laughed Yvonne, setting a tin can which they had found in the cabin where it would catch the dripping rain. "And we *have* shelter and fire. And pretty soon we'll have coffee again, and — listen to the wind! Can't you imagine you are at sea and in a storm?"

Dabner threw more wood on the fire, heaping it high, and filled his pipe. Hal opened the door long enough to dart through, slammed it behind him, and went for more wood. As the wind beat in his face, all but forcing him back, and he felt the pounding rain and saw the heavens cut in twain by the crackling lightning, he knew that there was little hope of riding that night.

"And," came the thought consoling him, "there'll be precious little cattle-rustling in this storm. Besides, Dufresne is at camp with the others."

It was a long, wretched night. Hal fought his way down the cliffs to where the horses were, removed the saddles, and thrust them into a sheltered spot under outjutting crags, tied the animals, and brought the saddle blankets back to the cabin.

"There's something to sit on," he said quietly, as he spread them out upon two dry spots on the floor. "You ladies had better lie down too, after a while, and get a little sleep. There won't be any ridin' to-night."

"But," cried Sibyl again, petulantly, "we can't stay here like this."

162

"What are we goin' to do?" he asked gently. "We've got to stay."

"But," she exclaimed, "I'm cold and wet and — and miserable already. And I can't sleep on the floor like — like a cowboy. And I'll catch cold —"

"I'm sorry" — he spoke as though the whole thing were his fault; "but it would be plumb mad to try to move on now."

Still the storm doubled and redoubled its gusty fury, still the rain fell in slanting torrents, now and then frozen into big, rattling hailstones, and the cabin rocked and shuddered under the battering of the wind. One by one came new leaks in the old roof, until the water stood everywhere upon the floor and ran in quick, black streams to the door. An hour it continued, and there came no lull in rain or wind. Hal had seen great storms in the mountains, and yet he had never seen one like this. It was as though the skies were emptying in one great flood all the moisture they had drunk up thirstily during the long summer. Upon the floor stood an inch of water that had beaten through the roof or seeped through from the slope against which the cabin stood. Sibyl and Yvonne were standing upon the old bunk to keep their feet dry, and had about their shoulders the saddle blankets which Hal had brought. There was water even in the fireplace, hissing about the logs, threatening to extinguish the smoking coals. And the night was growing colder, so cold that now, fully half of the time, it was hail and not rain that fell.

Dabner for a little attempted to be gay, to keep up the sodden spirits of his companions with bantering remarks and scraps of stories, but since for the most part, as usual, his remarks were addressed to Sibyl, and since that young lady's mood was in no way responsive, he too fell into a moody silence. And Hal, musing over his cigarette as he sat in a corner upon a log, was very busy with his own thoughts, very busy making excuses for the woman whom he idolised.

For he was seeing now a bit of her nature that had been no part of the character of the being he had worshipped from afar. He saw that as the night wore on, heaping higher upon them its bleak discomfort, Sibyl's irritation grew with it. There came no cheery word from her, no attempt to accept philosophically an unpleasant situation. She called crossly upon Dabner to put wood on the fire, she found fault because the rain ran in upon her, she cried out that the smoke from the fireplace was stifling her. And always it was of herself that she spoke, and of her own discomfort, seeming to have forgotten that the rest were, in the same plight.

"She's not used to this sort of thing," he told himself, standing loyal to his faith in her perfection. "It's hard on a man — it's hell on a woman."

And yet — and it made him frown and gnaw at his lip — no single word of complaint came all that night from Yvonne. She too was wet and cold, she too felt the sting of the acrid smoke in her eyes, she too suffered all the inconvenience of the wild night. And when she spoke, it was brightly and cheerfully. It was Yvonne who busied herself with the coffee-pot, and set a little lunch before them, and laughed at it all, saying what a lark it was.

Yes, there was a difference between the two girls, and he had known it all along. But it was not this difference, not the thing that the fiendish night made it seem. Sibyl was tired and nervous, that was all. She was not selfish, petty, weak, and cowardly. So while the storm crashed against their frail shelter, and the aroma of coffee stole out to mingle with the sharp smell of damp burning wood, Hal sought to find excuses, to blind himself to the real nature of the woman he had elected to love.

These were small things, he told himself. They meant nothing. And yet, to him, they meant a great deal, and he could not keep them from meaning a great deal. As hard as he fought with himself, he realised that he had never known Sibyl, the woman he had known was a dream woman, and that he himself had created her to fill the want of her in his heart. Now, the first time that he had seen her intimately, the first time that it had been given to him to glimpse anything at all under the surface of her, he had found a flaw.

He started to find that it had been nearly two hours since the storm had opened upon them, and that suddenly the rain had ceased falling. He flung a great armful of wood upon the fire and went to the door. As he opened it he felt a fluffy, feathery something cold against his face, and knew that if the rain were gone the storm had not ended. It was snowing heavily. The great flakes fell vertically through the air, which had abruptly quieted, and as it fell, caught and held to bush and tree. In a little the whole would would be white with it.

Yvonne had joined him at the door and cried out softly, her cry one of delight at the new beauty of the big out-doors.

"We can go out now, can't we?" she asked breathlessly. "We can ride through the snow?"

"Snow?" cried Sibyl sharply, and she too came hurrying to the door, pushing by Yvonne to stand upon the threshold.

"Yes," Hal answered, his eyes steadily upon the whitening ground about them. "It's snowin' heavily, and looks like it would snow all night."

"Then we can go at last," sighed Sibyl, with a little shiver at the draught of cold air. "Thank Heaven we can go. Let's hurry."

"Wait a minute." Hal shook his head, and hesitated. "We better stay where we are until mornin'."

"But why?" demanded Sibyl impatiently. "It won't hurt us to ride in the snow. And how do we know that it will stop in the morning?"

"Maybe it won't." But anyway we'll have light. I'd be afraid to try to make it now."

"Afraid?" she challenged rebelliously. "Why? Afraid of what?"

"If we try to join the others," he told her, "or if we try to make it back to the Bear Track, it'll be the same thing. One way we got two fords to make, the other way it's three. The water'll be up higher than you'd think."

Sibyl laughed at him, and he winced a little under the note in her voice.

"Those crossings!" she scoffed. "Why, we could take off our shoes and stockings and wade them!"

166

This afternoon, when they had twice crossed the winding creek following their trail through the canyons, the water had had been little above their horses' knees.

"You don't understand," he expostulated gently, still making allowances for her. "You see, it's been rainin' unusual heavy for a couple of hours. And there's about a thousand little creeks running into the Bear Creek all along, down the steep canyons. The water'll be up now, and raisin' fas' every minute. It'll be jes' like a big dam had busted somewhere up in the hills. In the daytime it'd be diff'rent. Now it would be plumb dangerous tryin' to get a horse across —"

She laughed at him again, and again the blood raced into his cheeks.

"If you're afraid," she jeered at him, "I'm not. And I'm going to go on to camp if I have to go alone. Will you get my horse for me?"

"Sibyl!" said Yvonne gently, putting her hand on her sister's arm. "Surely he knows more about this than we do? And if he says there is danger —"

"It's because he's a coward!" cried Sibyl, shaking the hand away. And, swinging upon Hal arrogantly, "My brother is paying you to work for him, and he has sent you with us. And I tell you that I am not going to stay in this wretched hole any longer. Will you saddle my horse for me?"

Yvonne drew back a step from her and stood looking anxiously at Hal. He, biting his lips, stood for a moment without answering. At last, when he did speak, it was calmly, his voice very low.

"I'm sorry, Miss Sibyl," he said firmly. "It would be like murder if I did it. We've got to stay here until day-light anyway."

"You refuse?" she cried hotly, as though she could not believe her ears.

"Yes'm."

"Then I will go myself. And I'll tell Oscar what a coward you are!"

She pressed by him, and was hurrying through the falling snow toward the cliffs. Hal turned helplessly to Yvonne.

"Stop her," he said swiftly. "She'll never make it. I couldn't help her any. Stop her."

"Sibyl!" cried Yvonne in distress, running out after her. "Come back —"

But her pleading was lost in a new crashing roar. It was as though peal after peal of thunder, merged into one long-drawn-out mighty volley, were tearing the night to bits about them. And with the shock of sound came a sudden quiver and jar of the earth under them, until it seemed that the solid mountain were rocking upon its base, Everywhere the night rumbled and grumbled about them, strange noises echoing hollowly through the canyons, the ground shivering and trembling underfoot. Sibyl had heard, had felt that the world was going to pieces about her, and turning, came running back, crying out aloud in sharp, sudden fear. Yvonne too turned, but as she did so something struck against her ankle and she fell.

"It's an earthquake!" cried Dabner excitedly, seizing Hal's arm.

The cowboy, sensing what the thing was, shook him off snarling, and leaped forward to where Yvonne was rising upon her knees.

"Back to the cabin!" he cried sharply to Sibyl. "Get inside. Quick!"

Seizing Yvonne's lithe young body up in his arms he turned and ran with her. As he ran, the dirt and stones were rattling about him, and he fell once, and staggered on, stumbled, and rose again.

"What is it?" cried Sibyl, clutching at his arm.

As he put Yvonne down lightly upon the bunk, he stared at the white faces about him and answered:

"It's a landslide — like the one that covered up the old Death Trap and all the men in it. And our one chance is right here!"

Even as he spoke the rumbling roar about them gathered in volume, and the cabin shook under it like a frightened animal. A great stream of earth and broken boulders, leaping down the steep mountainside, struck against the logs of one side of the cabin, and the logs snapped under the blow like rotten sticks. There, where a moment ago had been a wall, was now a great hole torn so that the snow floated in through it. The cabin tottered and settled a little, and stood on its three walls. They drew back until their bodies were tight pressed against the farther wall. Standing there, waiting for the death which it seemed could not pass without striking, they saw the rocks and uprooted bushes flung in upon them like wreckage upon some fierce, storm-swept sea. Hal found time to pray God that at least the cabin

169

stand firm on its foundation, and not go swirling along in the mad dance of hell and over the cliffs.

Even then, as a chance gust of wind caught at the fire in the stone chimney and sent a flash of light over them, he caught a quick glimpse of Sibyl's face and of Yvonne's — and sought to make excuses!

CHAPTER
FOURTEEN

The End of a Dream

It was such a night of terror flung down upon them without warning as no one of the four persons in the wreck of the cabin had ever thought to live through. Again and again it seemed a sheer impossibility that any one of them should see the dawn, but a few hours off. The landslide shot hissing and screaming by them, the flank of it tearing at the wall of their shelter, and they heard the thunder and thud of leaping rocks flung far out over the cliffs below them. But the cabin stood back against a ridge of the mountain that was crowned with dwarfed pines and clothed with thick chaparral, and above them, directly above, the ground held, and only a few loose stones came bounding down at them. To right and left they heard the rush of the strange flood, saw hurtling stones and crashing, uprooted trees go racing by in a frenzied chaos, and, looking into one another's drawn faces, waited for the end.

But the thing passed, passed with incredible swiftness, and once more the deep stillness of the night dropped down about them. The snow fell steadily, thickly, and in a little while the rocks and sticks that had been strewn across the level space on which the cabin stood were furry-white with it. Where in the early evening there had been a narrow, dry cut down the mountain-slope, to be seen from the cabin door, now there ran a swirling, black torrent edged with white spume, growing rapidly, steadily, carrying much dead brush and dry sticks down with it to whirl them over the edge of the cliff. Everywhere the night was noisy with the waters which had run from the steep slopes and down into the sheer-sided ravines. Even Sibyl could see now the utter foolhardiness of attempting to cross Bear Creek to-night. So they kept the fire blazing in the chimney and drew close about it, watching the snow heap and swirl and drift about them, waiting for morning.

Twice again through the dark hours did they hear the crash and roar of slipping earth, and they shivered with tense nerves, expecting each second to have the avalanche of soil hurled against them. But the lone prospector who had built the cabin had chosen his site wisely, and the rocky side of the mountain behind it held firm, only the treacherous ground to north and south of them yielding to the flood of waters and weight of fast accumulating snow. In the weird, softly diffused light which came at last to follow the pitch-blackness, trees and shrubs and boulders stood out spotlessly white, as though in reality they were the dead that another night like this had buried here many years ago coming back as sheeted ghosts.

It was such a storm as had not visited the Bear Track country since Hal could remember, and yet again and again he found himself forgetting that it was raging

172

outside. For, after all, it was only a battle of the elements, and the battle in a man's soul is a greater, more fearful thing. He saw Sibyl's face drawn and terror-stricken; he saw Yvonne's calm and bright and hopeful even when the night shrieked and threatened at the top of its fury. He heard Sibyl's voice complaining, finding fault, querulously demanding that some one dry the blanket she had drawn about her shoulders, growing strident over her own bodily discomfort; and he heard Yvonne's voice, always gentle, always cheerful, saw Yvonne always seeking to find light instead of making shadows deeper and blacker. He saw that as Sibyl grew more and more fretful Yvonne grew like a mother comforting a little child. And it seemed to him when the fire flared up and he could see their two faces for a little, that the Sibyl he had thought he had known had worn a mask, and that now the mask had slipped a little, that the face beneath it was not gloriously beautiful, that there were hard lines about the mouth, that the eyes were cold, that the fear in them was the selfish fear which forgot all of them but herself.

Hard he fought then and loyally, telling himself over and over that a night like this was enough to shake a strong man, that she was tired and wet and cold and nervous — that she was a woman. And yet there was Yvonne, Yvonne who was slighter and less strong physically, and whose face in the same fitful flash of light startled him with the pure, transcendent loveliness of it, the calmness and faith and soft gentleness.

It was as though the merciless night had ripped all wrappings from about their souls, and one shrank back

173

cold and weak and selfish, while the other stood forth strong and fine, sweet and womanly. This thing he saw all night along, and all night long he went on telling himself that he did not see it, that he was unjust, that he had no right to measure her by these little things.

Then morning came. In front of the cabin the snow was piled up three feet deep. Yonder on the flat it lay ten inches, fourteen inches deep. Where the wind had swirled it into hollows, where it had drifted, it was heaped until the chaparral beneath it was hidden under the smooth whiteness of it. And the snow still fell silently, steadily, in great feathery flakes.

Again Yvonne was making coffee, the last grains from the little bag going into the blackened pot. While the water was boiling upon the stones of the hearth she came to where Hal stood in the doorway, looking out.

"We have only a little bit of our lunch left," she told him softly. "Shall we have it for our breakfast? Or had we better save it?"

He turned and looked at her curiously. And she smiled at him as she went on, her voice lowered so that Sibyl and Dabner, crouching by the fire, could not hear.

"I mean shall we be able to go now? Or is there danger of our having to stand siege until the creeks go down?"

So she had thought of that, and had said nothing! He turned suddenly away from her and began making a cigarette. She watched him, and waited until he spoke.

"I'm goin' to make a try of it now, Miss Yvonne. I'm goin' to the cliffs to — to take a look. And maybe" —

hesitating, and keeping his eyes away from her — "you better just give 'em coffee until I come back."

She nodded to show that she understood, and he went out abruptly. For a little he ploughed easily through the snow, with it rising only a few inches above his ankles. Then he struck a drift, and grew hot floundering through snow which was already to his waist, and growing higher as he went on. Now he had lost the trail, and must fight hard for each inch that he went forward, his feet catching in the brush which the snow had covered. He shook his head savagely, drew his hat lower over his brows to shut out the blinding flakes, and at last, after twenty minutes of battling, came to the edge of the cliff.

He looked over eagerly, straight down into the hollow at the base of the precipice where last night he had tethered the horses. In spite of him he groaned at what he saw. The hollow was no longer a hollow, but a great, irregular, snow-capped mound, a heap of brush and earth and boulders that the landslide of last night had hurled down into it. The horses were gone. For a little he thought that the tons of earth that had fallen had rushed down upon them unawares and had buried them. But, on the whole, it seemed more likely that the animals had heard the onrushing avalanche, had been stricken with sudden, blind terror, had broken their ropes and had run from it. The one thing certain was that it was fifteen miles by rail to the Bear Creek, and the horses were gone.

"They'll head straight back to the range-house," he told himself thoughtfully. "Two of 'em will, anyway, seein' they've been kep' up and fed hay so much. And the boys will look us up."

As he turned and looked down the canyon where the creek ran, the frown gathered and deepened upon his brow. He could hear the rush and roar of the water down there, through an open space could see its muddy, racing surface, could even make out the trunk of a dead pine being borne along like a straw upon a mill stream.

"They'll 'ave to come quick," he muttered. "She's raisin' all the time, and raisin' fas'."

Slowly he made his way back to the cabin. Although he found the trail this time and kept it, he was breathing heavily, and the muscles of his legs and back were aching from the unaccustomed work, when he stamped the snow off his feet at the door.

Yvonne was drying a dripping blanket before the fire, and turned to look at him quickly, questioningly. Sibyl, seated upon the floor close to the hearth, had just finished her cup of coffee, and was rocking her body back and forth, moaning in a low monotone. Dabner, walking up and down, his hands in his pockets, jerked his head up and demanded sharply:

"Well? Are the horses saddled?"

Hal felt a sudden pity for them, even for Dabner. They were so unused to this sort of thing, to hardship and danger. So, he spoke lightly, as though the matter were of no great moment, as he answered:

"I'm afraid we're goin' to be a little up against it for a spell yet. The hosses musta broke away in the storm las' night. Anyway, they're gone this mornin'."

"Gone!" exclaimed Dabner. "Then how are we going to get away from here, man?"

"Gone?" Sibyl ceased rocking back and forth and turned widening eyes upon him. "Didn't you tie them last night?"

"Yes'm. But the racket of the landslide musta scared 'em. And when a hoss is real scared it takes a mighty strong rope to hold him."

"What are we going to do then? We can't stay here another day! Oh, I told you, *I told you* we ought to have gone on last night!"

"I don't know jes' yet what we are goin' to do. I ain't had time to figger it out." He took the steaming tin cup of coffee that Yvonne had brought to him and drank slowly, without looking up. "I guess the best thing is for you ladies to try and git a little sleep. You didn't sleep much las' night, and —"

Sibyl laughed at him, her laugh sounding nervous and hysterical.

"Sleep! Sleep when we're cold and hungry and wet! And stay here always?"

"No'm. Not always," he reminded her gently. "No longer than we got to."

"Why don't you *do* something?" She was upon her feet, and had snatched up the blanket which Yvonne had dried, wrapping it about her shoulders. "We have been in this wretched place twelve hours already and you want us to lie down and sleep!"

"Oscar will send for us," said Yvonne a little hurriedly.

"Look here." Hal put his cup down carefully at the side of the hearth and stood back, confronting the three of them gravely. "There's no use monkeyin' at a time like this, and there's no use lookin' at things crooked. It won't help none. Now, I thought of Oscar. He'll sen' for us, and sen' quick — if he can! But if he got caught the same way we did, and chances is he did, he's bottled up with three crossin's to make before he can come to the Bear Track. And he won't know but what we've got back already, beatin' the storm to it. So we can't count on him too much. Now, if the storm breaks this mornin' the water in the creeks will go down as fas' as it come up, and we can laugh at the whole business. But if the storm don't break — we got to look out, that's all. We got precious little grub, and we got to make it las'. And the safes', warmes', dries' place I know of is right here."

The new alarm showed in their white faces. Dabner went hurriedly to the corner where Yvonne had put what was left of their scanty lunch.

"There's not enough here for one meal!" he said anxiously. "If we don't get out soon —"

He broke off with a little shiver.

"It's got to make a meal, more'n one meal," Hal told him shortly. "And them old coffee-grounds can be boiled over. One good thing" — with an attempt at levity — "there's sure plenty of water."

"And we're just going to sit here and wait — and maybe starve to death!" cried Sibyl rebelliously. "Is that it? And what if Oscar doesn't send for us, and the storm doesn't break?"

"We ain't goin' to take any chances." Again he drove himself to speak pleasantly, cheerfully. "I'm goin' to start right now for the Bear Track. I'll bring grub and warm clothes back here, some way, to-night or in the mornin'."

Sibyl looked up quickly, her eyes brightening.

"I knew there was *some* way," she cried. "And if you start now, right away, you can be back before dark, can't you?"

Yvonne came swiftly to him, laid her hand upon his arm, and looked up at him with troubled eyes.

"Can you do it?" she asked, and there was a little tremor in her voice. "The snow is so deep in the canyons already, and it's getting deeper all the time! How will you do it?"

"There's tough rawhide strings on the saddles," he answered lightly. "I can cut some branches off'n some manzanita bushes, and make some sort of snow-shoes as'll hold me up, I reckon. It's only ten mile the way I'll go across the hills. I'll make it, Miss Yvonne."

"But," she persisted, "the crossings!"

"They ain't very wide, and goin' the way I'm goin', I won't have but one ford to make. If the hosses left some of the tie-rope I guess I can manage to get across all right."

Yvonne looked for a little into his eyes, and when she saw the calm determination there she turned and went back to the corner where the scanty provisions were.

Sibyl came forward and put her hand in Hal's.

"It's brave of you," she said softly. "I knew you would find a way out for us! And you will hurry, won't you?"

179

He took her hand awkwardly, flushed a little, and turned away.

"It ain't nothin'," he told he jerkily. "And I better be startin'."

Yvonne — for it seemed to be always Yvonne who did the little thoughtful things — had made a bundle of half of what food was left to them, and forced it into his hand.

"If you have made up your mind to go, you will go," she said softly. "And you must take this with you. All we have to do is just sit and wait, and you have a terribly hard day ahead of you."

"No," he said huskily. "No, Miss Yvonne. I don't need it. I'm used to goin' hungry now and then. And you —"

"You must take it," she insisted, and there was a note of determination in her low-pitched voice which was almost like stubbornness.

"Don't be stupid, Yvonne," said Sibyl sharply. "This is no time for foolishness. Goodness knows he must be hungry, but we all are. And he will be at the Bear Track where he can eat a long time before we get anything."

For the first time since he had known her Hal saw Yvonne stung into quick, hot anger. She whirled about upon Sibyl with flashing eyes, and Sibyl drew back, staring.

"Do you know that he is risking his life for us? Do you know that he knows he will court death a dozen times before he can ever hope to come to the Bear Track? Oh, Sibyl, you don't think!"

"You little fool!" cried Sibyl shrilly. "You sentimental little fool!"

Hal laughed, and his laugh grated harsh and unnatural in his own ears. Laughing, he put aside Yvonne's hand with the little lunch she had made for him, and swinging about strode out into the storm. But before he had gone ten steps he stopped dead in his tracks, jerking up his head to peer through the thickly falling snow. For he had heard a shout, a mighty shout which rose and echoed and thundered like a great war trumpet.

Before him, upon the cliff top, coming to meet him, all furry-white with the flakes which held to his clothes, looking a monster of a man as he floundered and struggled with the shifting snowy Pactolus about him, shouting lustily, cheerily, manfully, was Big John Brent.

CHAPTER
FIFTEEN

The Work of God, Nicodemus, and John Brent

"The Lord was my shepherd and He guided me!" laughed the big man, stamping up and down the cabin floor, smiting his hands together to get the chilled blood running. "The Lord pointed the way and smoothed the path, and Nicodemus brought me to the door of my hungering children!"

He had flung to the floor near the fireplace a great bundle which he had borne upon his back in a barley sack, and now, as he strode up and down, laughing jovially, he beamed upon them brightly, one after the other.

"How'd you get here?" demanded Hal wonderingly. "You ain't got any snow-shoes . . ."

"Didn't I say that the Lord smoothed the path and Nicodemus brought me?" He stopped still long enough to put his head back and laugh again, until they all brightened under his thunderous mirth. "You have heard of the Lord, Brother, but perhaps you don't know. Nicodemus, Brother, is my mount whenever there is a day's riding to do. He's a mule, a great big Texas mule, a raw-boned, evil-eyed, vicious-heeled brute of a mule. For the horse hasn't been foaled yet that can carry John Brent day in and day out . . . Have you breakfasted yet?"

Their looks answered him as well as their voices could do. He stamped across the room, snatched up the barley sack, and poured its contents out upon the floor. There was a whole side of bacon, there was flour, there was a bit of fresh venison, coffee, sugar, butter, salt, a small bag of rice, and several packs of cigarette tobacco.

"Presented by the good Lord, Nicodemus, and John Brent," he chuckled. "Nor have I yet broken my fast. Let us eat, children. But first let us pray."

He dropped suddenly upon his knees, his enormous bands clasped, his head bowed upon them.

"O Lord our God," he spoke lustily, and although the old cheeriness was still in his tone there was a note that spoke of a deep sincerity of reverence, "we thank Thee for all things. We thank Thee that this glorious morning we are well and happy, and that we are hungry and that Thou hast provided food for us. We pray Thee that our brothers and sisters, wherever they be this morning, may be as blest as we are. We thank Thee that Thou hast put out Thine hand over us in loving protection this night that is passed and this morning that has dawned. We thank Thee for the shelter over our heads, for the fire upon our hearth. But most of all we thank Thee for the warmth that is in our hearts. Be with us, God, for we need Thee now and always. Amen."

He rose abruptly, and with the broad-bladed knife which he drew from his pocket set himself to cutting strips from the side of bacon. Yvonne ran to his side

183

and began to open and arrange the smaller packages upon the hearth.

"How'd you make it across the ford?" Hal asked, still wondering. He knew that the crossing was a thing fraught with danger for any man, and this was a preacher! John Brent sat upon the floor, looking up at him, for a little ceasing to ply his knife.

"I would that you had been there, Brother! We came to the ford, Nicodemus and I, and I was singing lustily, filled with the majesty of the night and the glory of the Lord. It was as black-dark as your hat. And in Nicodemus there was little reverence, little appreciation of the most wonderful electric storm I ever saw. There was only in the breast of Nicodemus a spirit of mutiny and rebellion. I brought him to the bank, and he set his front legs out, stiff as iron staffs, and refused to go a step further. I remonstrated with him, I pleaded with him, I threatened him with all the things which are fearful to a mule's heart. And still he would have none of the hissing waters.

"Once I too was a Texan, Brother," he continued his tale whimsically, the rare, oddly sweet smile of him making his face look like a boy's. "That was before I heard the call and became a Christian! And suddenly — the Lord has forgiven me, I know, for He knew that I meant no harm by it — I forgot that I was a Christian, and became a good Texan again! I lifted my voice to Nicodemus in words that he could understand! There is but one thing in the world that will reach through a mule's skull and put reason into him, and that is fluent, sulphurous swearing. I swore at that

184

mule, Brother, and all the wicked words that I had used in my unregenerate days or heard used came back to me in my hour of need, and Nicodemus hearkened and heeded! Last night was the first time in fifteen years that I had taken the name of the Lord in vain, and" — his smile broadening — "I didn't take it in vain then! For, verily, the spirit of Nicodemus was softened and chastened. I drove him close to the edge of the bank, and got down from the saddle, and — then do you guess what I did? I put my shoulder against the side of my Nicodemus and threw my weight against him suddenly and pushed him off into the stream! Ho, ho! You should have heard him snort! And then I had him by the tail, and he couldn't kick for once in his life, and he swam, swam like a glorious old duck with John Brent clinging to his tail and swearing at him! And so the good Lord brought us across in safety."

For a moment Hal stared at him, speechless in his amazement. Then he came suddenly forward.

"If you don't mind," he said bluntly, "I'd like to shake hands — Brother Brent!"

"Brother John, Brother John!" laughed the preacher, grasping the proffered hand in his warmly, his eyes bright and twinkling. "And now for breakfast. We'll drink Nicodemus' health in a cup of coffee."

A little warmth came back into the pinched features of Dabner; and Sibyl, now that day had come and the world was quiet about her and there was a hot breakfast steaming and hissing on the coals, lost a little of her ill-humour. Yvonne came and went busily, spreading bits of paper she had smoothed out from the wrappings

185

about the parcels in John Brent's sack upon the bunk which Hal dragged out for their table. Before she had done, John Brent and Hal were working side by side upon the battered wall of the cabin, replacing the broken logs as best they could, and fastening the saddle blankets across the holes to shut out the swirling snow. Then they all stood about the improvised table, drank black coffee from the two tin cups, took up strips of bacon in their fingers, and ate hungrily of the blackened, charred things which Yvonne told them were biscuits! Altogether it was a merry meal, and the cabin seemed a warmer, brighter place when it was done.

"The good Lord put the thought in me that we might be forced to stand seige here for a little," said Brent, when at last they had finished. "And I didn't know but that my Brother Hal might run out of tobacco. Once I too leaned heavily upon the weed, and I know what it means to be without it. Hence the Durham, Brother."

Another little thing, surely. But little things seemed so big here and now. Hal, who had already begun to save his cigarette stubs, turned away flushing, and made no reply. This was the man whom, a few short weeks before, he had sought to kill!

"You have not told us," said Yvonne, sensing an awkward silence, "how you happened to come to us?"

He told them how the storm had caught the others as they were making camp, how for a little their thoughts were only of themselves as they sought shelter in their camp wagon, how, when the time passed and the storm grew in fury and the four who had turned aside to the Death Trap did not come, he began to worry about them. Oscar had maintained that with Hal to guide them they were all right, that perhaps they had turned back to the range-house. But Brent was not satisfied, and when the night came upon them and he heard the waters rising in the creek upon which they had camped, he had feared that what had happened would happen, that they might be caught there upon the mountain-side, and if the storm continued it might well be a matter of days before they could work their way back to the lower lands.

"And I knew," he concluded, "that you had no provisions, that when morning came our Brother Hal would see that he had to try to get out and bring help. I knew that in the morning the creeks would be harder to ford than during the night, for the water has been rising steadily for hours. So, just as soon as I realised all these things, I saddled Nicodemus and came. It seems I came just in time, too, for no man who lives could hope to make the crossing now on foot." He looked at Hal gravely a moment and then at the others, smiling again. "It was a man's part to try it, though."

"And Oscar?" asked Yvonne quickly. "Did he agree with you? Did he want you to come?"

"He didn't know," chuckled the big man. "I waited until they were all asleep. Then I stuck a note in the coffee-pot and came. And now, Brother, shall we fetch in some more firewood?"

The morning wore on and the snow continued to fall heavily, showing no sign of ever ceasing. John Brent climbed down the cliffs and saw that Nicodemus was made as comfortable as he could be in a sheltered spot, gave him a little of the barley which he had not forgotten to bring, and worked his way back to the cabin, declaiming joyously of the beauty of the world in her white furs. His cheeriness, the sunny gaiety of Yvonne, and the calm unconcern of the cowboy had their influence, and the prisoners of the storm were not unhappy in their cramped quarters. At noon it was still snowing, the trees were bending under their heavy loaded branches, and the drifts were piled deep. Then, in the late afternoon, the storm was gone with the same suddenness that had marked its coming. The sky went swiftly clear and blue and smiling, the sun burst out as warmly and brightly as he had been shining all summer, and were it not for the dazzling white mantle cast over earth and rock and tree, it were hard to believe that last night had not been a nightmare.

As far as they could see the world was white, pure white save for the black cliffs standing out here and there in bleak relief, and the black-green of the pines where the snow had not clung to them. The mountain-slopes ran away, smooth and brilliant and glistening, to the level lands where there was no sign of grey or black or brown. The farther range of mountains, where Swayne's Road-house was, stood out snow-capped and shining, and very, very near in the clear, crisp air. It was a veritable home of Christmas studded with ten thousand Christmas-trees ready for the things from the toy-shop windows.

"It is a wonderful world!" John Brent was standing, his hands upon his hips, towering above the others in the doorway. "And a wonderful Mother Nature. Man might strive a hundred years to change the face of the earth here about us, and do nothing. She has done it in a night!"

"Thank Heaven she has contented herself with what she has already done," laughed Sibyl, all of her old gaiety returned. "Surely we can go soon? For you have Nicodomus and can ride back to the range for our horses —"

"Young woman," said the preacher sternly, "if you thought a little of the other fellow now and then, and not eternally of yourself, you'd be a little nearer what God meant woman to be! Do you think I'd so much as venture Nicodemus' life trying to cross Bear Creek this afternoon, and when there's no use in it? Go get on your knees and thank God that we are all alive and well, and pray Him to set something besides a mirror in front of your eyes."

Sibyl bit her lips and reddened. But she returned his gaze scornfully, insolently.

"When I want religious advice, I'll ask for it, Mr. Brent," she told him curtly. "And I'd not go to a minister who boasts of his ability to swear at mules!"

He only laughed at her, and told her that if wicked men made swear words, at least God made mules, and the two must go together.

"And," he ended rather gently for him, "it has been a hard night, enough to fray any one's nerves. The storm is over, the creeks will go down as fast as they rose, and,

189

at latest, by morning, Nicodemus and I shall fare forth again. In the meantime, what say you all to such a snow-man as never was thought of before?"

Sibyl very naturally withdrew and as naturally took the devoted Dabner with her. John Brent and Yvonne like two children let out of school, set themselves to play in the soft snow, making their huge, malformed snow-man. Hal, into whose soul there had entered a wide, deep blackness, stood apart and smoked the tobacco the preacher had brought, and no longer sought to make excuses. The one thing that he wanted was to get away from them all, and to bury the thing which had died in his heart. For he knew that it was dead. And in the swift darkness which fell upon his spirit he did not yet see the new light which already was shedding its soft, warm radiance over him.

CHAPTER
SIXTEEN

Black Days

For Hal there came black days. Ever was it his nature to rush into things, to follow this way and that the impulse which came upon him, to dwell upon the heights, to plunge into the depths. The whole tenor of his life had changed because there had come a woman and he had glorified her. The old life had been dying behind him, he was choking it to death with strong, purposeful fingers. And now? Now he was one who had dreamed dreams, who had been awakened by a rude hand, whose dreams haunted him and mocked him.

For the nature his mother and father had given him, and which his life in the open had nurtured in him, was one of a wide, albeit reckless, generosity. His soul was hurt at the petty, narrow, selfish thing which he now so clearly saw his dream-woman to be. He felt something shrink up within him and harden and grow bitter. It was not the things that Sibyl had done, not the words she had said, that hurt him. It was what he had seen when he had looked into her eyes, what he had sensed, what he had known when there was given to him the first opportunity to know anything of her. He knew, with the clear knowledge which at last had come to him, that the beauty he had seen in her was all surface beauty, and that that thing which a man clings to in a "pardner," loves in a woman, was lacking. And now, with a suddenness which stunned him for a little, even that outer, physical beauty seemed dimmed and lessened. He was like a man who, deeply, devoutly religious, has his faith killed. Being the man he was — or the boy — as his idol dissolved before him into mere clay and cheap gilt, and his hold upon all things loosened, his old recklessness surged back, and he slipped swiftly down from the heights to which he had been climbing.

He went no more to his cave at night, sought no longer to work at the books which Yvonne had given him. For all incentive was gone. When he thought of his charts he laughed bitterly, and told himself that he was a fool. He thought at first of leaving the range, of riding far out to north or south to see what the world had for him, to shut out of his eyes all things that might remind him of his folly. Let the thieving go on, it was none of his affair. Let Oscar Estabrook play the fool or the rascal, it was none of his concern. And he would have gone, with no word to any one, had it not been that Bill Cutter had been his friend, and that it was not his way to forget a friend, dead or living. He would stay until he had proved to himself what man had killed the stage-driver. Then that man should pay for his crime, pay to the uttermost, and Hal could go back to the old life, and to things which had put their sombre colours into it.

So he stayed on, silent, moody, a man without companions. Already was he back in the old life, already had the old, false gods smoothed the way and opened their arms to him. The cook came back from his annual spree in Queen City and brought with him a goodly supply of bad whisky. It had happened that he returned to the range in the middle of the afternoon one day, and that Hal was working in the corrals as the cook's buckboard came weaving its way homeward. To be sure Charley was only a Chinaman, but in drink he was very human. He waved a bottle at the cowboy, and called out gleefully to him in his broken English, inviting him to drink. Nor did Hal hesitate. He helped Charley to unhitch his sweating horses, helped him to carry his bottles to the bunk-house. And then, availing himself of the generosity of the drunken cook, he took a fresh bottle, sat himself upon the edge of his bunk, and drank.

The raw, fiery whisky burned in his throat, but it quenched a crueller fire within his soul. It was the first that he had tasted in months, and as it ran down his throat the blood ran up into his cheeks and his eyes grew unusually bright, Charley laughed at him shakily, patted him on the shoulder, and launched into the tale of his doings in town and his winnings at the wheel and bank. Hal heard his incoherent mutterings as from a distance, laughed back at him, and drank again. He felt the fire racing throughout his whole body now, felt it throbbing through his blood, rising to his head. He knew that his work in the corrals was unfinished, but he could not see that it mattered. He knew that the only thing that did matter was that he had long fought this very thing, his burning thirst within him, and that a man is a fool who does not drink when he wants to.

Little by little as he poured the stinging liquor into his empty stomach he grew greedy and cunning. He knew that Charley's supply of whisky was limited, that Charley was in generous mood, that when the boys came trooping in for supper they would make short work of the many bottles. So he bartered with the cook, promising for two other bottles twice what they had cost in Queen City, and, taking his purchases in his hands, went to the stable with them. He climbed up into the loft with them, hiding them carefully in the hay. Then he went back down into the corral and to work.

Already he walked unsteadily, laughed unsteadily when he found that he could not strike the nail he was driving with the hammer which acted strangely in his hands. He felt a rising tide of happiness within him, and told himself that this very tide was bearing away for all time the fool thoughts which a woman had put into him. He made a cigarette, merely amused at the clumsiness of his fingers. And again and again he went back to the loft, watching that no one saw him, to drink thirstily, deeply.

Once, in the late afternoon, he stood with a bottle in his hand, swaying a little, frowning and muttering. And not yet had he forgotten the thing which he drank to forget, for he spoke aloud, slowly and thickly:

"Fallin' in love with her was jes' like gittin' fond an' foolish for a bottle of red-eye on account of it's havin' a

194

bright, purty label outside . . . an' that's a damn' poor way to jedge goods! Fallin' in love?" He shook his head and his frown deepened. "It wasn't that — it never was! It was jes' like a man lookin' so hard at the sun he goes blind an' can't see what he's lookin' at. Hell!" He drank a little, slowly, as was his wont, started to put the bottle away, and then, humorously, again lifting it to his lips, "Here's to Dabner. Pore little damn fool Louis!"

The hour for the evening meal came, and through force of habit rather than because he was hungry he went up to the bunk-house. There was a little blur about him, and through it, as he looked toward the range-house, he saw that the girls were loitering there — one in the hammock, two upon the steps. He even saw the flutter of a white handkerchief, but as he lowered his head and lurched on he did not know who had waved, and he was not sure that she had waved to him.

That night was one of the many nights that Club Jordan did not spend at the bunk-house. So there was no wrathful hand to descend upon Charley's shoulder because he had not immediately resumed his duties. There was no hot supper upon the tables, and the fire had not been kindled in the stove. But Charley, very drunkenly and very generously, proffered them his bottles, and with his slant-eyed, Oriental grin bade the house drink on him. There was no man of them who refused. Those that cared to eat went to the cupboard and rummaged among the cold victuals. They all drank.

Even now Hal held aloof from them. There was no man there save young Dick Sperry whom he trusted, whom he did not at least suspect of being hand and glove with the cattle-rustlers, and he was in no mood to talk with even Sperry to-night.

The hundred-proof whisky ran into empty stomachs that had not known the sting of alcohol for many weeks. The men began to talk loudly, to laugh the strident, boisterous laugh of intoxication. One of them with a marked proclivity for song broke into a rollicking cattle-land chant which others took up. The bunk-house grew noisy, noisier. A falling chair, the rattle of tin dishes, told when some one's feet grew mutinous of his will and he toppled over the object he had sought to circumnavigate. And, finally, they found cards, produced small sums of money from their banking-places in old socks or under straw mattresses, and played poker.

When the night grew late upon them, when Charley was in a stupor where he had sunk from his chair to the floor and Charley's whisky was gone, they went to bed. But Hal, his brain burning, his heart bitterer within him than it had been before, left them and went back to the stable. He had drunk heavily, but not heavily enough, only enough to distort and twist his fancies, not to kill them. There he sat alone, brutishly sullen, fighting the demons within him with alcohol.

When morning came, the men in the bunk-house kicked Charley into wakefulness and drove him to his breakfast-making. They had gone about their work, and Charley was again asleep when Hal, his eyes evil and red, staggered into the bunk-house. No one had remembered to wind the alarm clock upon the shelf, but the sun told him that he had slept away half of the morning. He drank a couple of cups of the luke-warm coffee, made a wry face at the half-burned bacon, and went back to his work in the corrals. Before noon he made many trips to the stable, and when noon came he did not go to the bunk-house.

Again it was late afternoon. When he moved, no longer caring whether the work were done or not, he held to the fence to steady himself and moved jerkily and uncertainly, his hat very low over his eyes. He cursed often and thickly as he stumbled, or as the young deerhound grew playful and got between his legs. He worked his way laboriously around the corral fence until he came to the corner where the oak tree was. Then, as he sank down there, feeling the world reel drunkenly about him, he was dimly aware that some one was standing over him. He merely pulled his hat a little lower over his eyes without looking to see who it was.

"Brother" — and he knew who it was now as the deep, rich voice was lowered in wonderful gentleness, with only a sorrowful pity in it that caused the scowl to deepen on Hal's drawn brows — "Brother, what is it?"

Hal's laugh was ugly and harsh and false, and there was very little mirth in it.

"I'm drunk!" He strove hard with his words. "Go 'head — preach, damn you! I can't — git away!" And again he laughed, sneeringly.

"Poor boy!" That was the sermon that Big John Brent preached. For a little his face was very soft as he looked down upon the man for whom he had hoped

197

much during these last few weeks. Then he turned, and his eyes ran to the range-house, and his face grew hard, as hard as rock. "If she had only been a *woman!* Good God, if You had only let her be a real woman!"

Hal stirred a little and looked up, his bloodshot eyes glaring suspiciously.

"What do you want here?" he demanded savagely. "I ain't — your kind — of man."

Big John Brent's deep chest rose to a sigh, which was like the rustle of a breeze in the tree-tops.

"Not my kind, Brother! You don't know. You are my kind, and, drunk or sober, I wouldn't swap you for any two men on the range! Yes, you're drunk, but there are times when it looks to a man as though there were nothing to do but get drunk. I have been drunk myself, God forgive us both! And now — is there anything I can do for you?"

"You've — been drunk?" — curiously.

"Blind, roaring drunk. And" — in a whisper, as again his eyes ran to the range-house — "with half your excuse . . . Is there anything you want?"

Hal put his hand to his head, and then, staring up with leering eyes, he muttered:

"I want a — nother drink! I had three bottles — broke one — 's all gone."

There came no change in the preacher's face save that it softened a little and the pity upon it deepened. He was praying softly, under his breath, as he turned and walked slowly away. And in a little he was back, and had brought a glass of whisky with him from the range-house.

"I know how it feels," he said gently, as he put aside the cowboy's shaking fingers and held the glass to his lips. "And this is all, mind. You can take John Brent's word for that."

Hal gulped it down and straightened up a little against the fence, wondering. He wondered more when he saw John Brent turn suddenly, and run, his great body ducking and dodging behind the stable. Then he saw Yvonne coming down to the corrals, singing as she swung her riding-whip against her skirt, and sank back, hoping that she would not see him.

"Pray God" — John Brent was down upon his knees behind the stable, his voice shaking, his clasped hands tight pressed against his eyes — "that Thou art sending the Right Woman to him now."

Yvonne had come on into the corral to saddle her own horse as Hal had long ago taught her, and now she stopped very still, and her song died, and a sudden fear surged up into her eyes. Then she came on slowly, straight to where her "pupil" was huddled.

"Hal! Oh, Hal!" She went down upon her knees at his side, and her hand was on his shoulder. "I'm so sorry."

He drew back a little from her, his eyes dropping before hers, the hot blood of shame in his cheeks. He strove hard to make his voice cold, cruelly, brutally cold when he spoke.

"There ain't nothin' — to be — sorry for. I ain't hurt, an' — I ain't sick. I'm jes' plain drunk!"

That surely would drive her back, would send her away from him so that she would never speak to him

199

again. He could not see that it merely drove the tears into her eyes.

"I know, I know," she whispered, and her eyes, like John Brent's, went to the range-house, and came back to him, full of pity. "And I'm sorry for you, oh, I am sorry for you!"

He tried to look at her and could not. He realised that this was the first time in his life he could not look the other fellow in the eye.

"Don't feel bad, Miss Yvonne," he said clumsily. "This ain't the firs' time. I told you — that day on the cliffs — I wasn't no good."

"And I told you then," she cut in swiftly, "that you could have my friendship as long as you wanted it. And I meant it!"

"Not now," he said heavily. By a mighty effort he pulled himself to his feet, and dragged the hat from his tousled head. "Not now. Not when I'm — like this."

"What's a friend for?" she cried softly. "Yes, now and all the time if you want me for a friend. But maybe," — and as he glanced at her he had a confused impression that a little look of hurt had leaped into her troubled eyes — "maybe you don't want to be friends?"

"I — I —" He shook his head. "I ain't the sort for you to know," he broke off.

"Listen," she cried quickly. "Do you want to do something for me?"

"What?"

"Don't ask what! Will you do something for me, blindfold? Will you promise to do what I ask?"

And he answered, "Yes, Miss Yvonne. I'd be glad."

"Then have our horses saddled early in the morning, at dawn, yours and mine. Will you? And we'll go for a ride, you and I."

"But —" he began.

"You've promised! And you may get drunk, Hal, and you may shoot a man, but you won't break your word!" She turned abruptly and left him, going across the corral. Then she stopped and came back. "I don't ask you to promise this," she said, smiling at him a little, and trying to keep him from seeing the look which she could not keep out of her eyes when they rested upon his haggard face. "I'm just going to ask a favour for you to grant or not. Please don't drink any more to-day."

When she was gone he stood swaying a little, gazing after her.

"He's a man, if he is a preacher," he muttered, as he fumbled for his tobacco. "An' she's a pardner, if she is a lady! An' I wish the whisky wasn't all gone — jes' so's I could do what she asks without havin' to do it."

CHAPTER
SEVENTEEN

The Gates to Paradise

When the day was breaking tremulously across the mountain-tops, and the sky was all soft blue and tender green, and the little breeze was just springing up and frolicking with the first wisp of smoke from the range-house chimney, they rode out of the corrals. It was already autumn, one of those clear, crisp, crystalline days that are like the first days of spring, with a lure and a call and an urge to the drop of gipsy blood that is in all of us. One of those days when the trail winding underfoot promises vague, wonderful things of the land just beyond the next hilltop, when it is a joy to move on, no matter where, when the heart within you sings, and it is a gay, glad, golden thing just to be young.

Yvonne rode a little ahead of him upon Starlight, the white-stockinged colt he had broken for her. He could see the curve of her cheek with a warm flush upon it like the flush of the coming day. He was glad that she had ridden ahead of him, glad that she had not spoken beyond saying a bright, "Good-morning," when he had first lifted his hat to her, and a smiling, "Thank you," when he had taken her foot in his hand to help her into the saddle. For the shame of yesterday had been a small thing compared to the shame of this morning. Had he not given her his word, had he not known that she knew that what he said he would do he would do, he would not have met her this morning. It was not that he regretted the folly of the day before, not even with the dizzy ache in his temples reminding him of his folly. But he regretted deeply that he had forgotten her, that he had hurt her with the sight of him, that he had not gone away where she would not know.

He watched her as she galloped ahead and he swung along just behind her, musing. He saw the tender curve of her cheek, the soft brown tendril of hair that brushed against it, the creamy whiteness of her throat peeping out through the loose folds of her scarf. He noted the grace of her carriage and knew that she rode with confidence and fearlessness and in the way he had taught her. And he knew that he was very content just to ride behind her, to watch the rise and fall of her body to the rhythm of Starlight's pounding hoofs, and realised dimly, with no analysis of emotion, that she was the one being in the world whose company he would prefer this morning to the solitude of the hills.

Thus they rode across the sweep of the meadow, and turned into the trail which leads into the jaws of Big Pine Canyon, still with no spoken word between them, still with Yvonne's horse a length in front of him. Here suddenly she drew in her horse, stopping him as cowboys do, with a quick touch on the reins so that he slid a little in the dust of his own making, his fore feet set close together. Hal came to her side and stopped with her.

She turned to him, smiling, and he saw that her eyes were bright with the joy of the morning, that the life which was thrilling and throbbing everywhere about them was racing riotously through her. As she wreathed her gauntleted fingers in Starlight's golden mane and leaned back in the saddle, drinking deep with swelling breast of the wine of the tingling air, he wondered dully that he had been so blind to the exquisite, dainty beauty of her.

"I wonder" — and he leaned forward a little to catch her low tones — "if you mind giving over your day to me?"

He stammered over his answer, and she ran on quickly:

"For Oscar said that you could be spared to-day, and my heart is set upon a visit to the Valley of the Waterfalls. I have a little lunch" — laying her hand upon the parcel tied to the strings of her saddle. "No doubt" — lightly — "it is bold and unmaidenly. But when it is the fate of one to be a woman all her life she sometimes gets tired of being properly maidenly! Do you mind?"

Now at last he had to answer, and he spoke hastily, looking at her and away from her in one swift glance.

"I'd be happy, Miss Yvonne." He meant to go on, to tell her how much her friendship meant to him after all that he was, all that she knew of him. But he couldn't find the words, so said simply, "I'd be happy."

She thanked him as simply, and again they rode on, side by side now when the widening trail allowed, silent again. Gradually the fresh morning grew warmer about them, the shadows thinned in the canyon, the colours paled in the sky, the sun found out the still tops of the taller pines, and crowned them with light. As the sunlight crept down through the branches and ran down the straight, tapering trunks, they turned from the canyon, crossed the spine of Big Pine Ridge, and dropped down into a little valley.

Here already the sun had run before them, so that the myriad tiny webs that the little brush spiders had left to trail from each bush looked like thin-drawn threads of silver. About them the deep, serene stillness of the night still clung to the mountain-slopes, broken only by the quick, liquid call of startled quail, or the scampering feet of the little blue brush rabbits, that went bobbing across the dry leaves lying in the trail. And the wordless silence between them that had been before a little strained now was a natural, sense-soothing thing, a part of the stillness of the solitudes.

Their horses dropped down to a gentle canter, slowed to a walk. They stopped a little, by common accord, to watch a deer pass through a cleared space in the chaparral upon the mountain-side. When they rode on again they had slipped into easy, companionly conversation. There were so many things about them calling for a word or two, or for a swift pointing finger. The swinging oriole's nest, so wonderful a house where it rocked in the dying breeze high above them, the noisy woodpeckers with their discordant *ickety-ickety-ickety* and incessant carpenter work, the sudden splash of sunlight across a cliff that a moment ago had been black with shadow, the slinking gaunt body of a coyote, the thicket yonder that was scarlet with the new berries of the wild holly, the eagle clinging with crooked claws to the dead limb of a lightning-blighted pine and dropping clumsily into flight as they came nearer — all of these old, frequently seen sights were as full of interest now as they always are.

So slowly did they ride now, so often pause or turn aside to follow an unexplored, inviting trail, that it was after ten o'clock when they came to the Valley of the Waterfalls. Side by side they went through the narrow pass which led along the frothing creek under the thick branches of the great pines, and side by side they drew rein upon the valley's rim.

"Of all spots in the world, this is the most wonderful," cried Yvonne happily. "I think that if I had my cabin there, built of great logs, with wide doors and a big rock fireplace — there upon the knoll where the five oaks are — with little shelves for dishes, and big shelves for books — I could find the contentment which all of us dream about and so few of us find. It makes me wonder — does it you? — what cities are for?"

"It's gover'ment land, miss," he told her, smiling under her bright enthusiasm. "It's anybody's as wants it — and the logs and rocks are all handy!"

The valley was no bigger than her secluded, favourite corner of Central Park. On all sides rose the cliffs steeply, bare and rugged and back here, all covered with trailing vines there. Behind the oak-crested knoll where Yvonne's fancy saw the Cabin of Content, the cliffs towered so tall and straight that it seemed that they must lean forward at the top. 'Way up there it had been nature's mood to set two monster cedar trees, the only two big cedars to be seen from here, their longer, lower branches brushing each other in the breeze which never died upon the heights.

Between the rugged boles sped the valley creek, leaping far out, churned into white froth and flying spray, to fall upon a ledge of rocks fifty feet below, to go mad there with the delirium of its joyous leap, to gather itself in fury and foam to leap outward and downward again, a white veil now against the smooth black of the rocks, to race on, lost for a little in the pool of its own carving, to flash and sparkle in the sun, and then with a thunderous noise of its victory to fling itself far out and to the floor of the valley, hissing and boiling and bubbling along its pebbly bed as it shot by the knoll and sought its way into the outside world.

He staked out the horses and slowly went up the knoll where Yvonne had gone already. There he found her seated with her back to the biggest of the tree trunks, her hands clasped about her knees, her hat flung to the grass beside her. He dropped down at her side and made his cigarette. The whole valley was murmurous with the echoing fall of the water. The air was sweet with the down-dropping perfumes of the growing green things upon the cliffs above and the fresh smell of the new grass about them. As always here so far, so very far from the world, there was in the very majesty of the oaks and of the weather-beaten cliffs a sense of deep, ineffable peace.

Yesterday, last night, he had been drunk. A few short hours ago his soul had been seething with rebellion, bitter and reckless. He frowned and lay back, staring up at the clear blue of the sky, forgetful for the moment that Yvonne sat near him with wide, musing eyes, feeling only the lack of something within him. His thoughts touched upon Sibyl, and she was like some vague, unreal being already in another world. His thoughts touched her and ran on, and he hardly knew that she had entered them. He remembered how Charley had looked as he slipped from his chair to lie huddled upon the floor. Last night he had laughed. Now his frown deepened a little as he wondered why he had laughed. He remembered Big John Brent, the glass of whisky he had brought from the range-house, the strange gentleness of his voice, of his hand. John Brent was a man; he was big inside as he was outside. He remembered how Yvonne had come to him, the look that had been whipped into her eyes, the other look which drove that one out. He did not turn to her, but lay still, staring into the sky.

A moment he saw the scenes of yesterday as though they stood out, painted upon a canvas before him. Then, gradually, they blurred and drew back into the distance, until at last they were shut out by the sheer walls of the valley. His eyes came down from the sky and followed a long broken seam in the cliffs. It was so still in the valley, with only the murmur of the water making a crooning lullaby. There were two worlds: the

208

world outside, where there was the jumble and confusion of sordid motives ranging from cattle-stealing and murder to petty vanity and selfishness; the world here, that was so small when you looked at it, shut in by steep walls of rock, so big when you shut your eyes and let the eternal, still voice talk to your soul. Out there a man must fight to find his happiness, fight to hold it. Here peace sang to him with the murmur of the water, crept into his being with the smells of the green, growing things. Yvonne was right. If one only had a cabin here!

His tired brain and body yielded to the stillness with the lullaby of the water running through it, and he slipped into still another world, the world of sleep. Yvonne saw, and in her eyes was a half smile, like the smile of a young mother watching over her baby. And behind the smile was the look of a young mother who is waiting for the coming of the day and praying God to save her baby to her. For we are all children, and she was a true woman, and Hal was a child in a fever.

He slept only a moment and started up, his eyes startled. Then, as they found her out where she had not moved, he laughed softly, running his hand across his brow.

"I musta been asleep," he apologised. "I — I thought that you were gone!"

"I haven't stirred a step. And we are not going until we have had lunch —"

"I don't mean that," he explained. "I was dreamin', guess. I thought you'd gone away, back to the East."

"We'll be going before long," she told him, watching the frolic of the stream. "Father will be coming out soon — I don't know what has delayed him so long — and then we'll all be going."

He sought for his tobacco and papers, his eyes going whither hers had gone and seeing as little as hers saw. Yes, they'd all be going soon. He hadn't thought of that. Sibyl and Mrs. Estabrook would go. That made little difference. Fern Winston would stay probably, if Oscar stayed, and there would be a wedding upon the Bear Track. That too made little difference. But Yvonne was going . . .

And only now did he see the light that had been throwing its soft radiance over him so long, only now, it seemed to him, did he see anything clearly. Not one day had he spent with Sibyl; his spare hours had all been with Yvonne. He had ridden with her, he had talked with her about herself and about himself, he had gone to her to be taught, she had come to him to learn how to saddle her own horse, how to ride. With Yvonne had been the brightest days of his life, the happiest. They had laughed together, they had come to understand each other, there had grown to be a strong bond of sympathy between them. When the way had been hard and he had faltered he had always thought of what his "teacher" would say to her "pupil," what she would think of him, and he had gone on. He had taken her as a matter of course, and one does not see the glory in the matter-of-course things about him. The best in him had grown with her, the worst in him had been slowly dying. And he had not seen!

Now ... Soon there would be no more days with her. There would be no more bending together over the same book, no more gay rides together across the fields, no more climbing to the cliffs to look out over the level lands, to hearken to the sermon to the soul and taste of the medicine to the body. There would be no more thinking at night of being with her in the morning. There would be only the old places they had visited together, the old spots where they had stood, and they would be empty, empty.

The summer had been a long, bright day, and only now at the dusk of that day was it given him to see what had brought the brightness into it. She had been a friend — but he had had friends before, and knew that no one of them had ever entered into his life as she had done. He had been blind and a fool, and a new bitterness surged up within him.

"I'm sorry," he said lamely, and he did not look at her. "It's goin' to be — all diff'rent when you go."

"Don't let's talk about it," she said quickly. "I don't know that I want to go. It's been so wonderful out here. And now" — brightly, getting to her feet and going for her little parcel of lunch — "we're going to have our lunch. Oh, I know it's not noon yet, but we were up early, and neither of us had much breakfast, I'll venture. If you'll make the fire for coffee, I'll set the table!"

He went about the building of the fire in a heavy silence. It was so natural to do this, they had done it together so many times before, and now there was coming the end of it. But if Yvonne's thoughts ran with his she at least gave no sign of it as she went singing over her work.

Now that she was not looking at him he watched her, watched her every movement, saw how her will and faith and common sense had done what the doctor could not do, and had made her ankle strong again so that her little limp was gone, saw how there was a sweet grace in everything she did, how the warm colour in her cheeks, the tender curve of her throat, the deep, misty grey of her eyes, were wonderful things. And most of all he saw that here was a woman whom a man need not clothe with any other glory than her own to love. A real woman, a true woman, something to slip deeper into a man's heart than any idol his fancy had ever built for him.

The coffee had boiled and he had set it aside, when he heard her voice calling gaily to him that dinner was served. He drove a smile into his eyes as he got up from his knees and joined her under her oak, carrying the coffee with him. They sat down with the napkin spread on the grass between them ... Oh, how many, many times had they feasted thus together, as gay over it as two children, and how many, many days would come and go, bringing with them only the memory of the days like this! For a little he dropped his eyes as he felt the smile dying out of them. He saw the cold meat and sandwiches and olives, the tin cups for the coffee ... and then suddenly the blood rushed hotly into his face and ran out again, leaving it very white.

"Miss Yvonne!" he cried huskily. "I — I don't want it. And — O God, I'm ashamed!"

212

"Don't misunderstand," she said gently. "I know how it is. Father used to drink sometimes — too much. I know how he felt the next day. You need it. Please drink it, drink it" — with a brave little smile that cost her all his had cost him — "to me!"

So many things surged up in him then that he could make no answer. And then, when she said again, "Drink it. It is medicine. And — I want you to," he stood up and lifted the little glass so that the sunlight danced in it, and looking at her steadily, his face still white, he said.

"Your health, Miss Yvonne — and God bless you!"

And he drank, not slowly as was Hal's way, but taking it swiftly. The little glass he slipped into his pocket.

"Thank you," she said simply. "And now, what will you have first, chicken or ham?"

She strove to make their little meal as merry as the others had been. But already the shadow of to-morrow lay heavy across to-day, and Hal could not hold the smile in his eyes. Often silence fell over them, not the happy silence such as had crept out upon them so many times before, but the heavy silence which hangs thick and oppressive like much crêpe. When they had finished and Yvonne had leaned back against her oak, the brightness had ebbed out of her face, and the eyes which she turned upon him were frankly grave and troubled.

"I am afraid that my feast has been a failure," she said, a bit sadly. "I am sorry, for I think that this is the last time that we shall come to the Valley of the

Waterfalls. But — do you mind" — very gently — "if I speak to you very, very plainly? Like one friend to another?"

He shook the head that had lowered over his cigarette-making and made no other answer.

"I know what it is to have days when everything goes to pieces," she went on. "I can lecture you a little, can't I? A teacher should scold her pupil now and then, shouldn't she? And I have never scolded you yet! I can talk plainly perhaps because I am going away pretty soon, and it is very likely that we are never going to see each other again. But I am not going to forget. And, oh, if you only knew how glad it would make me just to remember you as you have been since I came to the Bear Track, to know that you were going ahead and being a man, that you were doing your best, that you were letting the real man in you come to the top! And, Hal, do you know that if you give up now, if you slip back into the old ways, it would make me very unhappy? One friend should not make another unhappy, should he?"

She paused a little, and he knew how hard it was for her to go on. But he did not look up at her, did not speak.

"When you drink — like that — you are killing the best that is in you. Don't you know it? It is a horrible thing, an ugly thing, and you are too good for it. I don't want you to promise me that you will never drink again, but — won't you promise me, can't you promise me, that you will never — go down again like you did yesterday?"

214

"If I promised anything," he demanded suddenly, half fiercely, "would you believe it? After —"

"After anything" — simply. "If you promised, I know that you would do what you said you would do!"

He shook his head, for the moment wondering within himself if he were even man enough to keep a promise.

"You must just go on in the way you have started," she was saying quietly. "You have done a great deal already; it is in you to do a great deal more. If you will let me I shall send you books when I go home, and will help you all I can."

"You are the sweetest, best lady in all the world!" he cried out suddenly, brokenly. "And I'll promise. All that's decent in me is there because of you . . . it belongs to you!"

He jerked up his head then and let his torn cigarette-paper flutter to the ground. And she saw the pain in his eyes and the sadness and the hunger.

"Listen to me." His voice was very low now and very steady. "This is the las' time we'll ride here — or anywhere — together. Me and the Colonel will move on to-morrow. So I can tell you — and you won't laugh because you'll understand." He was standing above her now, and she saw the shiver that ran over his body as he strove to keep the calmness in his words. "I'll go on and be a man anyway. I'll promise, and I'll keep my promise. And it's because — why, it's jes' because I love you!"

He broke off suddenly, and turned away, already cursing himself for a fool. She, too, was on her feet, a wide wonder in her eyes.

"But Sibyl? You —"

"Sibyl was only Sibyl — and I was blind for a spell — and you — are You!"

"Hal!"

Then he turned swiftly and saw that the startled wonder had gone out of her eyes, that another light was there. And he knew then that the gates to Paradise had swung open to him, and that he was all unworthy to enter — and he dropped to his knees before her, his face in his hands, a sob catching in his throat.

CHAPTER
EIGHTEEN

Shadows in a Man's Soul

There were two men who were often at the Bear
Track, where they found always a ready welcome, and
who were frequently gone for many days at a time.
One of them was Big John Brent, how, bestriding the
stubborn, sturdy Nicodemus, journeyed far afield to
many little mining and lumber camps to carry the
Word of the Lord. He found many men who shrugged
their shoulders and turned away from him in
contempt. But he found, too, many men, rough and
with little enough thought of God in their souls, who
knew the man in the preacher, and who gave him their
hands heartily and were glad to see him. When he
came upon an outfit that was short-handed he shed
his coat and dropped into the vacant place, doing the
work of two men, so that they forgot that he was a
preacher, and saw only that he was a man with a
great, hearty, contagious laugh and a broad sympathy
and an understanding that was greater than theirs.
When there was a man hurt by a falling timber John
Brent found him out and nursed him like a woman.
Once there was a baby born, and he drove the
bewildered men from the place and, lifting his voice a

little to his God, rolled up his sleeves and saved two lives.

The other man who came and went freely upon the Bear Track was Prince Victor, the gambler. Men said that he was harvesting a rich crop this year, that he too sought out the outlying camps, where his quick smile and generous hand made him as generally liked as was John Brent, and that in the little black satchel which hung from his saddle strings he carried new decks of cards and poker chips.

He it was who brought back word one day that young Andy Holloway, who had disappeared from the Bear Track so abruptly, had been taken with the gold fever and was prospecting in the dry hills beyond Russian Gulch. There was no change in Dufresne's manner, nothing to hint that he so much as remembered that he had driven a knife into a man's back. Nor was there a hint anywhere that he should ever be called to account for the thing which he had done.

Hal had not spoken. If he accused now he knew that the investigation his words would set afoot would not stop with the matter of Andy Holloway. Men hereabouts had a way of dealing swiftly with murderers, and Victor Dufresne's slate was none too clean already. There would come merciless inquiries, there would be stern questions set why Dufresne and Yellow Jim and Club Jordan had met in the rock-rimmed hollow at night, why Oscar Estabrook had joined them. Then, because the whole deal had been so bold and because the men who would ask questions were not fools, it would not be many days until the cattle country, from end to end of it, ran with the news of Oscar Estabrook's connivance with thieves to rob his own father. And, in Hal's way of thinking, justice would come to meet the gambler soon or late, and Andy was as dead now as he would ever be.

Hal knew, too, that five hundred steers that had been driven back into the mountains from the level lands were still browsing in the narrow valleys, that not yet had they been turned over to Willoughby of the Double Triangle. For twice, at night, when Yvonne thought that he was working in his cave, he had ridden as far as the border line, and had seen that Yellow Jim and Shifty Ward still had their camp there and that all was well. Since the night of the wild storm there had been only clear days and nights. Perhaps that was the reason that nothing had been done, or perhaps there had been a hitch somewhere that had delayed Willoughby.

Now again Dufresne was at the Bear Track, the same smiling, urbane, courteous Dufresne that he had ever been. One would have said that there was nothing of weight on his mind, no tiny fleck of shadow across his horizon. He waited upon Mrs. Estabrook as though she had been the great lady, he the gallant courtier. She compared him with John Brent, and confided in whoever would listen that the Prince came very much nearer being *her* idea of what a man of God should be than the great, lumbering, uncouth savage with the voice of a bull and the manners of a bear. He danced attendance upon Sibyl and made her delicate little speeches which, plainly pleasing her, began to make

Louis Dabner vaguely uneasy. Since the wild night upon the mountain Sibyl had had no eyes for John Brent, who, agreeing for the once with her mother, she dubbed a barbarian. A little piqued that Hal had not come back at his allegiance to her, she had at first thought to draw him by indifference, then, that failing, had resorted to methods which a few weeks ago would have sent the blood hammering in his temples. But now Hal looked her straight in the eyes, and she did not like the clear candour of his regard. So Sibyl, never content with such tame allegiance as Louis gave her, responded quickly to Dufresne's polite notice.

It seemed the gambler's one aim to be affable to every one. Although he was quick to see that Fern Winston distrusted him and that Yvonne disliked him, he never lost the opportunity to anticipate their little wants, to serve them at table, to place a chair, or find a shawl.

Hal, keeping an eye upon him whenever there was the opportunity, was long in seeing anything but the polished exterior of the man and the gently courteous manner. If there was one thing in the world which Victor Dufresne did to perfection, it was the masking of his own soul from the gaze of the curious.

But there came an evening when Hal looked through the mask and saw something standing back of it. The cowboy had come up from the bunk-house to meet Yvonne outside. She had been delayed a little by the querulous insistence of her mother. Hal, drawn back into the shadows, saw Oscar and Fern come out, saw Oscar's arm run about the girl's waist. Then, before they passed down the porch, he saw Dufresne standing at the door, looking after them. Dufresne's eyes were upon Fern, Dufresne did not know that Hal was in the shadows. And the mask was off.

Into the gambler's eyes came a look that Hal had never dreamed to see there — the look that had been in Hal's own eyes when he had known the truth and had cried out to Yvonne "I love you!" — the look that comes into any man's eyes, be he good man or bad, when his heart yearns and hungers for a woman.

"He loves her like that!" The thought startled, coming as it did with the swiftness of lightning from a serene sky. "An' she never guessed it!"

The shock of the thing lay in this: Victor Dufresne, card-cheat, man-killer, and God knows what, else, was just a man after all! And to him at last there had come a woman. To say why he had loved no other woman, to say why now he loved Fern and not Sibyl or Yvonne, were to seek to understand the great mystery of mysteries. Hard man as he was, cool-brained, selfish, unscrupulous, he had a soul, and to it a woman was speaking.

Never again was Hal to think quite the same of Dufresne; never, though the grim determination in his heart remained unchanged, was he to think of the man without a vague feeling of sympathy. For back of the yearning and hunger for the woman, there had been in the gambler's eyes a pathetic, intensely human sadness.

Then and there Hal felt that he could go down upon his knees and thank God for His goodness to him. For it had been God's sweet will to let Yvonne come to him while his life was in the shaping — before it was too late.

But, after that night, not once did Hal or another see what lay under the mask. As the days passed Dufresne was more the courtly, polished gentleman than ever. Under stress of fatigue or excitement or a great emotion other men might forget themselves; not Dufresne. He was always affable, always urbane, always in the seeming what perhaps God meant him to be, a courtly gentleman with a kindly heart. For in the little things which add to the happiness of others it was the gambler's policy to be unselfish and keenly thoughtful of them. When opportunity arose he was almost tenderly attentive to Fern Winston. But the attentions went unmarked since they were no less to the other women. And his reward was always to see in Fern's eyes distrust of him and a vague fear.

Hal, turning from Dufresne to Oscar, found here, in the nervous, anxious eyes, a barometer which he could not misread. He knew that Oscar was standing upon the brink of the last, greatest wrong-doing.

"And it ain't many days off," he told himself heavily. "How'm I goin' to stop it?"

To-night the light burned late in Oscar's room. Hal, going by to the bunk-house, stopped a little, and went on, shaking his head. For he heard Oscar's voice and Dufresne's, heard that other sound he knew so well — the rattle and click of poker chips.

"The poor fool," he muttered. "The poor fool."

To-night it had been Oscar who, when the others had gone to bed, had rapped softly at Dufresne's door, and had suggested that they play cards, just the two of them. Dufresne had looked up with as much of surprise in his eyes as he ever allowed to show there, and had demurred, saying that it was late, that he was sleepy.

"You've got to play," retorted Oscar hotly. "I want my revenge. I can win to-night, and I know it! And you've got to give me my chance."

"I'm always willing to do my part," smiled Dufresne. "Only — I beg your pardon for mentioning it — I hold a good deal of your paper already, Estabrook."

Oscar flushed at the cool meaning which lay under the polite phrasing, and jerked his hand out of his pocket, showing it full of crumpled bank-notes.

"I borrowed it from my mother," he said harshly. "And if you're not afraid I'll give it back to her in the morning and will relieve you of some of my paper."

"Again I ask your pardon," laughed Dufresne, getting to his feet and following his host into the other room. "Your luck's been bad enough, Estabrook. I honestly hope it will break a little to-night."

Oscar made no answer as he poured himself a drink from the bottle on the table. Jerking off his coat he dropped into a chair, smoothing out the bank-notes upon the table.

"There's five hundred dollars there," he said, tossing the money over to Dufresne to count. "It's on the table and it's table stakes to-night."

Dufresne glanced at the bills and pushed them back across the table without seeming to have counted them.

"Five hundred dollars," he mused softly, "is a good deal of money for a lady to be carrying about with her."

"My father," retorted Estabrook, "is not stingy — with any one except me." He drew chips and cards from the table drawer. "Straight jack-pots, sweetened five dollars every time. Cut!"

"You are out for blood," smiled Dufresne. "Well, it's late, and that's a man's way to get to the end of it."

He cut and Oscar won the deal. They played in silence for the most part, Oscar feverishly anxious over every card which he picked up as they fell before him, one by one, Dufresne winning and losing and eternally smiling or yawning a little sleepily. He clicked his chips carelessly, and stared about the room, his eyes resting more often upon the photograph of the merry-eyed girl upon the dresser than upon the eager-faced young fellow across the table from him. There was a vague hint of admiration in his look when it went to the picture, and a vaguer hint of contempt in it when it came back to Estabrook.

Once, when Oscar had lost heavily, he got up and went to the other table where the bottle was and drank. Dufresne, carelessly raking in the pile of chips, did not turn, but said gently:

"You've got the making of a great poker player in you, Estabrook. Some day you'll learn that a man mustn't touch that stuff while he is playing. It's just as well" — shuffling with swift, delicate fingers — "not to touch it at all. My deal, isn't it? Yes, you lost that on your own deal." It was just as well to impress it upon him, for presently he was going to lose again — on Dufresne's deal. He yawned again, and again his eyes

224

went to the picture on the dresser. "Next time you've got to give yourself a better hand."

Oscar made no reply as he came back to his chair and picked up his cards as they fell before him. As he looked at them he smiled quickly, and covered the smile with pursed lips. Dufresne's eyes dropped swiftly. That time Oscar won, and the next time. Dufresne glanced at the little clock across the room and noted that it was already after eleven o'clock. He was both tired from his day's ride and sleepy. After that Oscar won but little. At half-past twelve Dufresne got to his feet, slipped the roll of bills into his vest pocket, and sighed a little.

Aloud he said, laying his hand gently upon Estabrook's arm, "You have run into the toughest vein of hard luck I ever saw." And to himself, contemptuously, "What a man for a woman to love!"

Oscar did not move as he sat at the table, his elbow upon the scattered cards, his chin sunk in his palm, his eyes moody and restless. Dufresne stood over him, a little behind him, smiling openly, the contempt in his eyes unveiled now.

"I'm sorry, Estabrook," he said quietly, when Oscar did not look up. "You may not believe it, but I'm sorry. I'd have been glad to have lost to you for a change. But — it was all in the cards."

Oscar threw out his arm suddenly, sweeping the cards to the floor, and threw up his head. In his eyes was a look that startled even the man so used to seeing down into men's souls raw and quivering.

"Damn your sorrow!" cried the young fellow hoarsely. "You've cleaned me again and that's all you care. I — I — What are you waiting for? Haven't I said that you've cleaned me?"

"Good-night," said Dufresne, quietly from the door. When Estabrook made no answer but strode to the window to flip up the shade and stare out into the night, he opened the door, went out, and closed it quietly behind him.

For a moment Estabrook frowned moodily into the darkness. Then, as he heard the knob of his door turn again and some one come in, thinking that it was Dufresne come back, he swung about, crying out irritably:

"Well? What do you —"

He broke off suddenly, and the anger went out of his eyes, a look like a strange sort of dread springing up in them. It was Fern Winston. She came in quietly, and very gently closed the door behind her. He saw that she was in her nightdress, he could see the dainty white of her gown peeping out under the kimono she had thrown loosely about her. He saw her bare feet in her little slippers, saw the flash of her throat across which hung the black braid of her hair, the stirring of her breasts as she breathed deeply. Never had her girlish beauty looked so soft and wonderful a thing, never had she seemed so womanly.

"Fern!" he cried, quickly jerking down the window-shade. "You mustn't come here like this! At this hour —"

226

She didn't answer, nor did she look at him. Instead her eyes went slowly about the disordered room, wandering from the table with its confusion of cards and chips to the cards scattered across the floor, to the bottle and glass on the other table, to the picture on his dresser.

"Fern," he said again, his voice guardedly low and shaken a little with the same anxiety that shone in his eyes and spoke through his nervous manner, "you don't understand. It is after midnight. They would think . . . if any one knew that you were here . . ."

"It doesn't matter what people think!" She lifted her head a little and looked at him. In the depths of her eyes he saw only weariness and hopelessness, in the low voice he sensed that she was tired and heart-sick. "I don't care what people think, Oscar."

"But, Fern, dear —" He came to her, putting out his arms impulsively to take her to him. She lifted her hand; for a moment it touched his breast, gently pushing him back, and then dropped to her side.

"I'd rather you wouldn't touch me, Oscar," she said, with a tone so quiet that it was almost devoid of expression. "I want to talk with you, and I think we can talk better if you don't put your arms around me."

She paused and stood very still, looking at him steadily as though she were searching for something deep down in his soul. For a little he met her regard questioningly, then there crept a dull flush into his face and glint of defiance into his eyes . . . and then the red deepened and brightened in his cheeks and his eyes dropped before hers. Her breast rose with a deeper intake of breath, but she gave no other sign of having seen, of having been further disappointed in the man to whom she had given her love freely, to whom she so yearned to give freely of her faith.

"I don't think that I am unreasonable, Oscar," she went on gently. "I don't want to be unreasonable. We have to look at things clearly, you and I. I couldn't sleep to-night. I knew that you were playing cards. And the only thing to do was to come to you. Love does not blind a woman, Oscar. It makes her see very, very clearly. It makes her see the good, true impulses in the man she loves. And it makes her see his faults. I know that I am not perfect, Oscar, and that you are not perfect, and I don't want either of us to be perfect. But I do want you to be honest with me and with yourself . . . I want you to be a *man* . . . .You failed at home, and I thought that it was just because you were young. You have had your opportunity here and . . . are you failing again?"

"What do you mean?" he asked, with a note of challenge in his voice.

"You are gambling again, and you promised me that you were through with it. You cannot afford to gamble, and you are getting in debt, I don't know how heavily. You have troubles, and I don't know what they are. I just know that every day they bear down more and more heavily on you. You" — for the first time she faltered a little, and then went on bravely — "you forgot to kiss me last night. You are not keeping your promise to me. You are not holding to what you know is

228

right. You are doing the things which you know can end with only one ending."

When again he muttered, "What do you mean?" the challenge had given way to the alarm which her words bred within him.

"I mean that you know that if you go on as you have been doing you are going to kill our happiness. You are going to dig the grave for all our dreams. You are going to go your way and leave me to go mine."

"You don't love me!" he cried bitterly! "If you loved me you would not say those things, you would not draw back from me, you would make allowances for me!"

"Haven't I made allowances, Oscar?" She sighed a little, and all the girlishness of her was gone before her sweet, yearning womanliness. "And I do love you so deeply that nothing else in all the world matters. That is why I came to-night. Victor Dufresne is a man who stands for all those things which you should have left behind you. Yet you see more of him than you do of me. I tell you, Oscar, that it is because I love you that I see things which other people cannot see. I know that you have your glorious chance to be a man, a strong, manly man. And I know that you are letting your chance go by you, that you are not being strong, that you are being weak. I have said to myself as long as I could that it is just because you are young. You are old enough to know whether you want the sort of thing that Dufresne can offer, whether you want to go on with the other things of which I know nothing except that they are making you unable to look at me with frank, untroubled eyes . . . or whether you want me!"

"You are hard on me!" he muttered querulously. "Your *love* makes you see only my faults. You don't see that I am trying —"

"I don't want to be hard on you." Her hands were twisting the loose folds of her gown, a blur of mist was in her eyes. "And I do see the good in you, the good that I love so, so hard! But I feel all the time, I *know* that you are doing things that you could not tell me about! You are not keeping your promise to me — a promise is a sacred thing sometimes. I think that I would die, Oscar, very gladly, before I broke my word to you!"

Maybe he misread the misery in her eyes, the softening in her voice. He flung up his head and a little of his defiance came back.

"I am not perfect. No man is. I have done wrong. Every man does. You don't know how hard things have been for me. Now" — and he broke into a shivery laugh which drove a quick shudder over her — "what are you going to do? Is your *love*" — and in his recklessness it came with a hint of a sneer — "great enough for you to stand by me? Or do you want to end everything?"

She stood and looked at him, and it seemed that she did not breathe. Her hands had slipped away from the gown which they had been twisting and fell to her sides. She did not speak. She did not look at him, but at the picture on his dresser. He could not tell what she was thinking. It seemed that she was no longer thinking of anything. And almost before he knew it she had opened the door and had gone out, and it had closed swiftly behind her.

Then in an instant the gods granted him a great clarity of vision. He looked deep into his own soul, he saw far into hers.

"Fern!"

It was only a hoarse whisper that he himself did not hear. But the whisper reached through the heavy door and ran after her, and the love in her heart heard it. With no hesitation she turned and came back to him.

Now the vacillating man of him had knelt to the tender steadfastness of her. Now his arms were about her knees and his head was bent. She could feel him trembling.

"Fern! My God, Fern, how I love you! And I have been a coward and a fool. I have done wrong, Fern . . . Oh, you can't guess all that I have done . . . and to make it right I have done wrong again! I think if you went away from me, Fern . . . you would be happier. You are so good . . . the man you loved should be a good man . . . and I have been wrong all the time . . . I am not fit to look at you . . . and . . . Oh, my God, my God, how I love you!"

She did not speak. Bending a little over him, her hand went out slowly until it rested upon his head, her fingers wandering gently through his hair.

"If you only knew, Fern," he went on brokenly, his arms tightening about her with his flux of emotion until they hurt her, "you would never want to see me again. If it were just that I had broken my promise to you — just that I had gambled my money and my father's

231

money — you might forgive me. But that's not the worst of it! I have tried, Fern, tried so hard. And I have wanted to be worthy of you. And I have gone on slipping down and down until . . . oh, you would hate me!"

"Oscar," she said then, her words dropping down to him with a sweetness which hurt him, "what you have done doesn't matter. If you have done wrong I am sorry, so sorry for you, dear, but it doesn't matter now. I don't care what you have done, Oscar, what the world would say of it if the world knew. Yesterday is dead, dear. It is to-morrow that counts. Do you love me enough to make a new start now? Do you want me enough to stop now in the way you are going? Are you strong enough to do it? It doesn't matter what the consequences are. If you can begin *now* to be honest with yourself and with me, to be straight and to begin an absolutely new life with an absolutely clean slate . . . if you can do that, Oscar, that is all that matters. But, dear, there must be no more . . . mistakes."

When he did not answer she loosened his hands from about her knees and drew him up so that he stood close to her. Still she held his hands, and, as he lifted his head slowly, she looked deep into his eyes.

"Do you love me enough, do you want me enough to break the old life short off? If there are consequences to suffer we will suffer them together. And we won't care, for we will have the world before us, and our life ahead of us, and our dreams won't be dead. I won't find fault, Oscar. We will just take things together. And we will forget. For I know you have tried."

232

"Fern —"

Her heart heard the thing he was going to say. And the love which does not blind a woman, but which makes her see so clearly the thing which is hidden to other eyes, saw the thing that was breaking through the shadows in the man's soul.

She laid her finger across his lips, and drew his arms about her, her lips moving a little to the unspoken words which gushed up from her heart. She was thanking God for to-night that He had called and that she had heard, and she was praying God for to-morrow.

CHAPTER
NINETEEN

What Hal Found in the Ravine

Victor Dufresne in reality had been both very tired and very sleepy. Because, upon going back to his room, he had thrown himself down upon his bed and had dropped asleep without putting out his light, the course of events upon the Bear Track was thrown sharply into a new groove.

Hal had gone his way toward the bunk-house, and had stopped suddenly in the shadow of the big oak between the two buildings. That Estabrook and the gambler were together might mean simply that they were going to give the evening to poker. It might mean more. Some night both of them, or at least Dufresne, would ride back into the mountains to join Yellow Jim Gates and Shifty Ward to give the signal for rushing the five hundred steers across the border. The cowboy knew that Club Jordan had not come into the bunk-house to-night, and little things aroused his suspicions.

So he sat down in the shadows and watched and waited. An hour, two hours — he did not know the time — dragged by, and he too grew sleepy. But still he sat, leaning back against the bole of the tree, waiting.

He saw Oscar flip up the window-shade and stand staring out into the darkness. Dufresne must have gone back to his own room. In a little he would put out his lamp and go to bed. But still Hal waited to be certain.

He saw that Oscar had wheeled about, he guessed that some one had come into the room, he saw the shade jerked down. Had Dufresne rejoined him? Hal could not tell. He only knew, or thought that he knew, that the gambler had not gone to bed, for he could see the yellow light of his lamp at the edge of the window-curtain. Naturally, his suspicions led him into an error, and he supposed that it was Dufresne with Estabrook. Supposing that, it was again natural that his suspicions should be sharpened at the hasty way in which Oscar drew down his window-shade. And he was stubborn in his resolution not to move until after the lights were out in both rooms.

After what seemed to him a very long time the light in Oscar's room was extinguished. Still he waited, for he could not know that Dufresne was already asleep. His eyes rested now always upon the gambler's window.

He heard a little sound that at first he could not make out. Then he knew that it was the noise of a window being raised very slowly, very cautiously. There were six windows along this side of the house. He could not tell which one of them it was. It was not a window in Dufresne's room — the light there told him that. But everywhere else along the wall of the building the shadows lay thick and black.

He heard the window-catch, heard the rattle of the window-hook swinging free. And in a moment, his eyes straining into the darkness, he made out a form under Ocsar's window. Some one had got out there, and was moving swiftly along toward the far corner of the house. In another moment the moving form had turned the corner and was lost to him.

"Headed toward the mountains!"

Hal got quickly to his feet, ran through a little patch of starlight, and, turning into the shadow lying close to the house, walking now, swiftly but noiselessly, followed where the other had gone. He thought of his horse, but there was no time to drop back. He would follow the other a little, until he knew if it were Dufresne or Oscar and until he saw if the man took to horse and rode into the canyon. He was confident that he would find the man to be Dufresne, confident that he would go straight to a horse already saddled and waiting somewhere for him, and head on straight into the mountains.

Cautiously he came to the corner of the house about which the hurrying figure had gone. Here he paused a moment, his eyes running eagerly here and there among the dense shadows of the oaks, his ears alert for the sound of hastening footsteps. And yonder, already just beyond the edge of the grove of oaks, walking swiftly toward the broken ground where the foothills ran down into the level land, he saw the man he had followed. And now, although the night was too dark for him to see anything clearly, he recognised something in the man's carriage and knew that it was not Victor Dufresne but Oscar Estabrook.

236

For a second the cowboy hesitated, balanced upon the ball of his foot, in uncertainty whether to go on or to swing about and go back to the bunk-house. He had little enough desire to spy upon young Estabrook. But he made up his mind swiftly, and although he liked it little enough, he moved on, following noiselessly.

"They've roped the poor devil in and are playin' him for the fall guy," was the thought which decided Hal. "If he don't get jerked up somehow, he's goin' straight to hell in a hand-basket. And it looks like it was my job to get the deadwood on him and scare him into bein' good."

Oscar did not turn. It was very late, and there was no reason for him to suspect any one other than himself of being about. Now he was in the open beyond the grove, still moving swiftly toward the canyon. And now he had passed down into a little hollow, had gone on and out upon the farther slope, and had dropped down beyond a knoll, leaving the trail.

When the cowboy came upon him he was a half-mile from the range-house, upon his hands and knees in a rock-strewn ravine. It was dark here, but not so dark that Hal could not see what he was doing. The cowboy stopped twenty paces away and watched, puzzled to see Estabrook working with clawing fingers about the base of a flat rock which might have weighed seventy-five or a hundred pounds. He was cleaning the loose soil and grass from about the bottom of it so that he might get his hands under it.

Very slowly now, making no sound as he moved, Hal came closer, step by step, until he was not ten feet away, where he crouched down among the scattered boulders. He could hear Estabrook's quick breathing, could hear him mutter a little as the rock he had chosen refused to come away, could see him straighten up when at last he had turned it over.

Oscar stood for a little looking about him, listening. Then, stooping again, he took something from his coat pocket, make a little hole with his hands where the rock had been, scooping out the soft dirt, and dropped into it the thing he had taken from his pocket.

"Money!" was Hal's quick thought. "Dufresne's got scared at something and has passed over, for him to keep, the money they've taken in on crooked cattle work!"

The thing, whatever it was, would soon be hidden. Estabrook had already laid his hands again on the flat rock, and was tilting it upon edge to send it toppling back to cover the hole he had made. Hal saw his opportunity and took it. He rose from among the shadows, and as he came forward said abruptly, but none the less quietly:

"I want to talk to you a minute, Estabrook."

Oscar had straightened up and jerked back at the first word as though a man had struck him. The little cry whipped from his lips was one of startled terror. Hal came on, and stopped when only the freshly moved stone lay between them.

"I been dyin' for a smoke for two hours," he said lightly, as his hand went to the pocket of his unbuttoned vest. "We can smoke now. I guess there won't be anybody around?"

238

"You damned spying sneak!" cried Estabrook hoarsely, both rage and fear in his voice now.

"I know it. And I don't like my job none to speak on. But it don't do much good to cuss about it, Estabrook."

He made his cigarette and lighted it before he spoke further, seeking for the beginning, while Oscar stood waiting for him to go on, eyeing him anxiously. "Now, I'm goin' to lay my cards on the table, every one of 'em, and face up, Estabrook. I guess it's the bes' way. And I'm doin' it because I don't believe you're so much a bad man as a fool! That's plain enough for a start, ain't it?"

"Do you know whom you're talking to?" fumed Estabrook.

"Yes," coolly. "To my boss who can fire me as soon as he gets good and ready. But I'm goin' to talk jes' the same . . . and he ain't goin' to fire me. You've been trottin' with men as it ain't good and ain't wise to call pardners. Which means the Prince and Club Jordan. And you've got in bad somewhere, and got in deep — damn' deep. You're goin' to break with them jaspers short off! It's kinda late now to do it, but I guess it ain't too late —"

"When you go to telling me what I'm to do —"

"Which I'm doin' right now," sternly. "You jes' listen. I don't know as it's up to you to say anything this trip. I ain't goin' even to ask you any questions. Things has happened so I know purty near all I want to know."

"What do you mean?" The little spurt of anger was gone; there was only the growing fear left. "What do you know?"

"That's jes' what I'm goin' to tell you. I know firs'," blurting it out suddenly, dropping his voice a little, "all about that stick-up party at Swayne's Road-house!"

"My God!" cried Oscar. "You —"

"Your tryin' to talk like a ignorant cowpunch didn't fool me any more'n the rag you tied about your face did! I knowed your walk and I knowed your voice. I was kinda sorry after I'd stepped in, 'cause I guessed it was jes' a fool joke you was playin' on your Eastern frien's, that you was jes' figgerin' on givin' 'em a little Wild West stuff to make things sorta romantic for 'em. It was only some time later," dryly, "that I doped it up diff'rent. You needed the money so bad you was goin' to take it wherever you could get it."

"You're crazy. I don't know what you are talking about."

"That's all right. *I* know and I'm doin' the talkin'. In the beginning it wasn't none of my business and I was goin' to keep my mouth shut. But that ain't all. I said I was goin' to show you my hand, and I'm goin' to do it. On top of that come this here crooked cattle work —"

The little hope which shot up in Oscar's heart that the cowboy knew of nothing save of the affair at Swayne's Road-house was gone and forgotten. The stifled cry that broke from him now was like that of some wounded animal in a steel trap.

"I got wise to that too. And it's a miracle and a big run of luck for you that every man in two hundred miles don't know about it. It's fool business, and such things can't be pulled off without makin' a smell somewhere. So you won't make no mistakes, I'm goin'

240

to tell you what I know. The Prince and Club Jordan is runnin' the deal, with you lookin' on and the Prince doin' most of the head work. Yellow Jim and Shifty Ward is in on it, and some of the other boys I don't know about. Andy Holloway was, but Andy is — gone. You been sellin' stock to Willoughby of the Double Triangle, and the money ain't been goin' to your old man back East. Right now you're gettin' ready to crowd them five hundred steers acrost the border to Willoughby —"

Oscar's body had grown tense as the cowboy spoke, and now it was shivering in the grip of the fear upon him as he saw, yawning about him, only the blackness of the pit he had digged for himself, into which he had been so steadily descending.

"What are you going to do about it?" he cried, hoarsely.

Hal stared at him with something that was half contempt, half pity.

"He ain't no bad man," he was telling himself, feeling a queer sort of shame at looking down into this man's shrinking soul. "Jes' a poor fool."

"What am I goin' to do?" he said aloud. "That's what we're goin' to talk about. You know what I could do. I could send you to the pen for a good long time, and I reckon you know it. But what's the use? I ain't after you. I told you you got to split with them yellow dogs. I guess if you didn't want to," with deep significance, "I could come purty close to makin' you, couldn't I? Jes' holdin' over you what I know?"

"I was a fool," muttered Oscar bitterly "I knew all the time that something like this would happen. And now —" He broke off, staring at his accuser. Then running on wildly, "It was just now, not half an hour ago, that I knew what I must do, that I must break with them! And now you know everything — and it's too late!"

"The old lady as said it ain't never too late was a wise old female lady." Hal drew meditatively at his cigarette. "You see, it happens I ain't out after your scalp none. You're goin' to pull out while you can, and I'm goin' to help you."

"Help me?" wonderingly "You?"

"Yes, me. And you got to be plumb square with me from right now on. You got to stand up like a man and do your share. Sometimes one head is better'n two. This is one of them times. You're goin' to leave it up to me what to do, and you're goin' to do what I say. Can you see your way right now to come to them terms?"

"What are you going to do?" demanded Oscar quickly.

"Firs' thing, I'm goin' to head off this big steal of five hundred cattle. You'd oughta had more sense that try that on. Nex' I'm goin' to collec' the money as has already come in from sellin' cattle to Willoughby, and send it where it belongs, to the old man back East. Or else you will buy some more stock to take the place of them as is gone. That might be the bes' way, and we'd be apt to get away with it without stirrin' up a lot of talk."

242

Oscar tried to laugh a little, and his nervous attempt jarred on both of them.

"You are going to collect that money? You talk as if all you had to do was to ask for it and have it handed over to you!"

"Which comes purty near being true. The Prince has been keepin' it, ain't he? He got scared about something to-night and handed it over to you, didn't he?"

"No!" with sharp emphasis. "We were together, but we were just playing poker —"

"I was outside," cut in Hal. "I guess I know what happened. You played him, and I guess you didn't win heavy. He went to his room and you went to your window and shot up the shade and stood lookin' out and cussin' your luck. In about a minute some one come in —"

"You cur!" Oscar spat at him. "You dirty, sneaking cur!"

A sudden wrath flamed up in the cowboy's eyes. His hand fell heavily upon Estabrook's shoulder.

"I don't like them kinda words," he said sternly. "And you ain't jes' the man to use 'em to me right now! Besides, I told you once I didn't like my job. I saw what I saw, and it's a good thing for you I did. Else maybe we wouldn't have had this talk to-night."

"You seem to have seen pretty nearly everything," said Oscar hotly. "But you have no right to misunderstand, to misjudge. She came to me just to show me what I must do, to make me —"

243

"Wait a minute!" Hal snapped out the words suddenly. "I didn't say anything about a *she*. Wasn't it Dufresne who came into your room?"

"You didn't see that?"

"No, I didn't. If it wasn't Dufresne I don't want to know about it. You jerked down the shade, and I didn't see."

"Then — well, suppose that it was Dufresne?"

The first glimmer of respect for his employer that had ever burned in the cowboy's heart came into it now. For he had guessed who *she* was, he had not misjudged her, and he had seen that at least Oscar was man enough to want to shield her from the results of her imprudence.

"I thought it was the Prince. I thought that he had come back to you to give you the money to keep, and — that that was what you were hidin' out here."

"What I am doing here," blustered Oscar with a tardy attempt at independence, "is my affair. I do not deny the things you accuse me of. But that does not give you the right to dictate to me on every point upon my own personal business."

"I ain't askin' for any right, Estabrook." It was very calmly spoken, yet there was a deal more determination in his words than in Oscar's bluster. "But I know there's jes' one way to put this thing through, and it's goin' that way. I'm goin' to see what you've stuck away in that hole, and if it's the money, why, I'm goin' to take charge of it for a spell."

"If you dare lay a hand on that —"

244

"It's jes' what I'm goin' to do." Again very quietly spoken, but for all that there was a note in the low voice that made the other hesitate and drop his uplifted hand. "Don't be a plumb fool any longer. I can han'le you, and you know it."

He stooped quickly and picked up the thing that lay in the hollow at his foot. Oscar Estabrook, although he cried out angrily, still held back, hesitating.

"Money, all right," grunted Hal. "A wad big enough to choke a cow! And paper!" He looked up curiously from the thick roll of banknotes. "When did Willoughby get the Eastern habit of rag money? Well, a man as goes crooked once does some funny things. Now, we're goin' to see how much there is. And, Estabrook, you jes' remember I ain't mixin' in this dirty mess jes' for fun. Don't go makin' no mistakes."

He passed so close to Oscar as he moved a little deeper into the ravine that their sleeves brushed. And yet Oscar put out no hand to stop him. When he had reached a sheltered place among the rocks where he felt certain that no one would see him even if another than themselves were about, Hal struck a match and looked at the roll of bills.

There was a string about it, and he slipped it off. The bills were all of large denominations, and although he was little used to "rag money," he counted swiftly. His match burned down and he lighted another. That burned out and he had lighted a third. And at last he had finished counting.

He whistled softly. He had never dreamed of holding so large a sum of money in his hands.

"Four thousand and five hundred dollars! The pickin' sure *was* good while it lasted! Now listen to me, Estabrook. This here mazuma goes in my tail pocket — in the same tail pocket I carry a damn' good gun nowadays — and it stays there until it goes to a bank. And then you and me are goin' —"

He had started back to where Oscar stood. Now he broke off sharply, and stopped dead in his tracks, a fresh suspicion upon him that brought a sharp fear with it.

"*Where did you get this money?*"

With long strides he had come on. His hand fell upon Oscar's shoulder, jerking him about as though he were a child.

"Dufresne," muttered Oscar, and Hal, bending close, could see the workings of the muscles about his mouth, the terror, even, that had leaped into his eyes. "Dufresne made me —"

"You lie! *Where is the other five hundred?*"

"What do you mean? I — I don't —"

"I mean," Hal snarled at him, shaking him in a powerful grip and hurling him backward, "that Willoughby never gave you that money. Whatever Willoughby gave you was in gold. And I mean that the man that held up the stage at Bear Creek Crossing got away with five thousand dollars . . . in bills! And that same man shot Bill Cutter down like a dog!"

CHAPTER
TWENTY

Certain Light Upon the
Bear Creek Robbery

"I didn't kill Bill Cutter!" cried Oscar wildly, the words coming almost inarticulately from his dry throat. "So help me God! I swear I didn't kill him."

Hal did not see him, hardly heard him. There, through the darkness, Yvonne's face came before him as he thought of what the disgrace would mean to her. And the sorrow within him was greater than the anger.

"You'd better tell the truth to me, Estabrook," he said wearily. "I ain't exac'ly a frien' of yours, but I been tryin' to help you out to-night. I guess I can't help you much now. But there ain't no use lyin' —"

"It's the truth, man, the truth! Can't you see I am telling you the truth?" Oscar's voice died in his throat and he dropped his face into his hands. After a moment, in which the silence was heavy about them, he lifted his head and spoke a bit more quietly. "You will believe me, you will have to believe me, I have gone from bad to worse, I have done things that are — crimes! But, my God, I haven't gone so far as — murder!"

He broke off with a shudder. Hal was not listening. He could think only of Yvonne's face — and of the

247

dead face of poor Bill Cutter. All along he had seen the difficulty of the work ahead of him. Now he felt smothered under its hopelessness. For a moment he hung upon his heel, of a mind to go back to the bunk-house and let things run on as they would.

"I am goin' to ask you some questions," he said at last, very coldly, indifferently. "You can do as you please, answer 'em or not. Firs': Did you hold up your own frien's at Swayne's?"

"Yes," came the answer with no hesitation, desperately.

"For fun, or meanin' business?"

"Because I had to have money!"

"Have you been in cahoots with Dufresne and Jordan to steal your old man's cattle all along?"

"Yes."

"Did Dufresne give you this money?"

"No."

"Where did you get it?"

"I got it —"

Then only did he hesitate, and again he buried his face in his hands. Hal waited in silence.

"This thing is killing me!" burst out Oscar at last, throwing his arms wide out and then letting them drop listlessly to his sides. "Will you listen to me while I tell you why I did these damned things?"

"Estabrook, I guess we're jes' wastin' time. You've lied to me already, and I ain't goin' to believe a word you say unless you can prove it. If you didn't do for Bill Cutter I don't give a damn what you've done, and I'll stick with you. But if you did, then I guess you got to

248

take your med'cine. And I wish to God you wasn't the only one that had to take it! If *you* didn't do it, who did? And where's this money come from?"

"I didn't kill him! I tell you I didn't kill him!" moaned Oscar. "Everything I did I meant to make right after a while, don't you see? I couldn't have made it right if I had killed a man, could I? I'm going to tell you the truth, and you've got to know it's the truth!"

"Talk fas'. And if you're lyin' to me you're jes' wastin' time."

"In the beginning, the very beginning" — Oscar spoke swiftly, the strange calm of desperation in his tone now — "things went wrong for me. Dad gave me some money to build a range-house here. It wasn't enough. I wanted to do the right thing, to make it a home that I could bring — my wife to in a couple of years. I meant to steady down when I came out here, and cut out gambling, and everything looked so bright I thought that we were going to be so happy here when — when we were married. That was the beginning. Dad wouldn't give me enough money, and I wanted to build the house right then — and I met Dufresne. He had plenty of money then — he had just been winning heavily and he let me have a thousand dollars. I gave him just my note. Then when the money was due to him he came out here and stayed a couple of weeks. You remember? That was a year ago. I didn't have all the money, and when he suggested that we play for it, double or nothing, I thought I saw my chance. I played him and lost. God! I was a fool!"

249

"Go ahead," grunted the cowboy. "That remark's sunk in. And you don't have to prove it."

"Two thousand dollars I owed him, and I couldn't call on Dad. Dufresne was decent about it. He took my note and let it run on, without interest. I began saving out what I could of my own money, and banking it. But after a while I saw the utter hopelessness of it. The range has paid precious little since I have had it, and what profits there have been have gone to my father. I have had only my salary. Dufresne came again, and I got reckless and played cards with, him again. And I won! If I hadn't won then maybe all the rest wouldn't have happened! It looked as though my luck were turning." Hal smiled grimly but made no interruption. "He went on to the mining camps and when he came back I played him again. And my luck had gone and I lost.

"I went on like that and I got in deeper and deeper. All I wanted to do was to get square and then quit. Then Dufresne told me that he had been losing and that he had to have money. I couldn't pay him. Just before mother and the girls came he wrote saying that he was coming out and that he had to have five hundred dollars. I was afraid that if I didn't pay him he would send word of my notes to Dad. The thing drove me almost mad . . . That's why I tried to get the money from them at Swayne's. I knew that they could spare it and not miss it, but I didn't dare borrow from them for fear that they would tell Dad and he would begin to guess that things weren't going right. And I was going to return it some day, just as soon as I could!"

"Go on," said Hal curtly.

"You know what happened. You let me go, and since you never said a word I began to be sure that you didn't have an idea who had done it. I came back to the Bear Track that night and met the folks the next day. I waited for Dufresne. And then — then he drove me to this! He told me that he had waited long enough for his money and that if I couldn't let him have at least five hundred he'd write to the old man. And — Dad told me when he sent me out here that he was giving me my last chance, and that if I fell down on it he was through with me. He meant it. My God, don't you see the position I was in?"

"I see," with no change in the cold tones. "Go on."

"What could I do? I couldn't see any way until Dufresne laughed at me for a blind man and showed me the way. And I took it! I had to take it."

"Meanin' that you begun to sell your old man's stock on the sly so he wouldn't get wind of it, and keep the money?"

Oscar stood still a little, moistening his lips.

"Yes. He explained it all to me. He told me that Willoughby of the Double Triangle would take the cattle if I undersold them a little, and would get them out of the country before anybody saw the brand and got to talking. The thing was to be done at night — the cows were to be put into cattle-cars at a siding at night and rushed to Chicago. Club Jordan was to attend to the work, and to get a couple of men to help out. I was to get the money, Dufresne was to be paid, and he and Jordan were each to get ten per cent of the money. I —

I didn't want to do it, but it was either that or have Dufresne write to my father. In the light in which I came to see the thing it wasn't a crime! Dad had told me that if I made good out here he was going to give me the range and the brand — it was as though they were already my cattle —"

"There ain't no use wastin' time excusin' yourself," said Hal shortly. "A man generally makes himse'f see things the way he wants to."

"Well, that's how I was dragged and driven into it. The whole thing would have been done and over with now if I hadn't, time and again, thought that I could win back from Dufresne what I had lost to him. That man has the luck of the devil! Every time we played, almost, he pocketed another I O U. Always I knew that the luck would have to break some time, if I could only stay with it."

"Luck!" snorted Hal. "Luck! There ain't no such thing as luck in poker, not with a man like Victor Dufresne settin' in! Go on!"

"Even to-night," ran on Oscar hurriedly, seeking to get the thing over with, "I tried to win back some of the thousands that I have lost to him. You asked where the other five hundred was! Dufresne has it!"

"Then" — quickly — "you ain't denyin' that there was five thousand in this roll?"

"No. There were five thousand dollars there. They have been in the bottom of my trunk all along. To-night — I couldn't go to sleep with this money in my room. I had to get it out, to hide it somewhere. I tell you that I had already made up my mind to be straight," he cried fiercely. "I was going to return it to the express company —"

"You ain't denyin' then that this money was took from the stage at the Bear Creek Crossin'?"

"I am not going to deny anything that is the truth from now on. I am sick of —"

"And you are the man that held up the stage?"

"Yes" — desperately.

"Then," cried Hal hotly, "there's jes' one reason why I don't drop you where you stand for a damn' coward and a murderer —"

"Stop! I tell you I did hold up the stage — I was driven to it by fresh losses to Dufresne, by new threats from him. I told you I was going to make it good as soon as I could — it was just like borrowing — I was even going to pay interest. Could I have made it up if I had killed a man? I did not kill Bill Cutter!"

"*Then who did?*"

"I don't know! I would give five years off my life to know. I haven't been able to sleep at nights since the thing happened! I have suspected everybody. I — I have suspected — you!"

"Estabrook, don't lie to me!" There was a sternness in his voice that had never been there until now. "You held up the stage, and you ain't denyin' it. How can you deny the rest?"

"You've heard how it happened. It has been talked over and over and harped on until every man, woman, and child in the whole country knows as much about it as I do. Right at the crossing I rode out in front of the stage and threw a rifle on Bill Cutter. It wasn't too dark

253

yet to see clearly. He put up his hands, and Martin, the express agent, put up his. And the one passenger put up his. I made Martin open the express-box. I knew that the money was there, and it was going to the Rock Creek mines. I made him throw it out into the road. Then I got down and got it and got back on my horse. It was all so easy that I was surprised at it. You know how at the Crossing the road winds on into the canyon? I turned and rode into the mouth of the canyon, going slowly, making the three of them keep their hands up."

"Well?" snapped Hal, when Oscar stopped suddenly, his tongue running back and forth between his parched lips.

"I knew that they couldn't see me now, I was so deep in the shadows of the canyon. But I could see them, and I called back to them for the last time to keep their hands up. Then, just across that pile of rocks from where I was, the one all topped with manzanita, I saw a spurt of flame. There was the crack of a rifle not over twenty steps from me. I heard Cutter cry out. I saw him jerk to his feet and stand a second with his arms still high above his head, and then plunge straight down under his horse's feet. I remember jerking in my horse and staring at him. Then all I know is that I was shaking with horror of the thing and fear for myself, and I was running away from it all!"

"And the man who shot him?"

"I don't think that I even thought of him then. I only wanted to get away. I only wanted to get away. I tell you. I even forgot the roll of bills I had stuffed into my

254

pocket. I knew that it was murder, and that the man who had held up the stage would be accused of it."

"Do you fool yourse'f for one minute," said Hal dryly, "thinkin' that that yarn would go down any jury's throat in the world?"

"No, I don't. My God, man, I tell you it has been driving me mad! But it's the truth, the truth, so help me!"

"How would the other man happen to be there?" — candidly cynical. "And why would he want to do for Cutter?"

"I don't know. Oh, I know it sounds like a lie. But can't you see I'm telling the truth now? And, think, man! Why should I have wanted to kill him? After I had got clean away? Don't you see I wouldn't have done that?"

There fell a long silence. When at last the cowboy broke it he spoke very slowly.

"Estabrook, I guess you know you're standin' right now so close to the end of a rope you oughta feel it 'round your neck. The sheriff ain't quit on the job, and if you know Dan Nesbit you know he ain't goin' to quit until somebody swings. I've thought things over, and I ain't goin' to take a hand in nailin' the top on your coffin. Why I ain't is jes' my business and it ain't yours. I'll see that this money gets back where it belongs, and then I'll drop the whole rotten mess. So you don't need to be scared of what I know. You look at it straight. If you're lyin', if you did kill Bill Cutter, why, you better, clear out of this neck of the woods, and clear out damn' fas', and keep goin'. That's open and shut. If you don't, they'll get you, sooner or later."

"I won't go," cried Estabrook hysterically. "I didn't kill him. And I promised — just to-night — that I'd be square from now on, and that I'd take my medicine. I promised — Fern! And I'm not going to break my word to her again, I don't care what happens!"

"I ain't finished," went on Hal coolly. "If you're tellin' the truth, and you can make me believe that story of yours about the other jasper, why, I'll stick to you until the snow's ten foot deep in hell! You're a fool to stick around if you're lyin'. Now, it's up to you."

"I'm going to stay," said Oscar doggedly. "I didn't kill him."

"Then," brusquely, with a quick tightening of the lips, "me and you has got some work to do! We're goin' to find who did kill him. And we're goin' to head off the rest of this cattle-rus'lin'. You're goin' to walk straight with me, and you're goin' to open wide up everything as is in you. And you're goin' to start in right now. When do them jaspers plan to pull off the stealin' of them five hundred steers?"

"That's what brought Dufresne back. It's to happen to-morrow night."

"Then you and me had better be gettin' some sleep." Hal strode by him, headed toward the bunk-house. "I'm thinkin' to-morrow is goin' to be a real busy day!"

256

CHAPTER
TWENTY-ONE

What the Mountains Have Hidden
They May Disclose

That night Hal slept little, Oscar Estabrook not at all. Yet neither of them knew when Victor Dufresne slipped quietly from the house and hurried down to the stable for his horse.

In the dim half-light before the dawn Hal opened the front door of the range-house, and going quickly to Oscar's room, rapped gently. As Oscar opened his door and the cowboy stepped inside, a glance at the young fellow's haggard eyes and at the smooth coverlet of the bed told him that all night Estabrook had walked restlessly up and down, or sat staring into the utter blackness his own hand had gathered about him.

Hal stood facing him steadily, his hat pushed well back from his eyes, his thumbs hooked in his belt.

"Estabrook," he said in slow, matter-of-fact tones, "I've framed you up all the time for a fool rather than a bad man. I told you that. So it ain't hard to believe what you told me about the hold-up at the Crossin'. Now, what I want to know is, have you any idea who the other man in the canyon was?"

"I've suspected every one — Club Jordan and Yellow Jim and Shifty Ward and — you! For none of you four men were at the bunk-house that night, and I don't know where you were."

"You haven't any reasons to pick out any one in particular?"

"No."

"That's one question, and your answerin' don't help much. Now, for another. You said las' night you knowed that the stage would be carryin' a lot of money to Rock Creek mine. How'd you know it?"

"Dufresne happened to drop it. He was just back from the mines and had learned it there somehow. He had been playing cards with Nelson, the superintendent, and won all Nelson had. The superintendent told him that in a few days there would be money in camp, and that he would play him again."

"So the Prince knowed it, huh?" Hal paused thoughtfully. Then, "Who else heard about it?"

"Jordan. We were together, the three of us, when Dufresne mentioned it."

"I wish only one of 'em had been in on it. It would make it easier for us. Well, we'll trail that down after a while. Firs' thing is to put a stop to the deal with Willoughby to-night. Let's wake the Prince up and have a heart-to-heart talk with him."

As he turned his back to go out, he loosened his belt a little, and saw that the revolver which he had thrust into the waistband of his overalls was free. Then, with Oscar at his heels, he went to Dufresne's room.

It had been a warm night, and they saw almost before they crossed the threshold that what sleep the gambler had taken had been with his clothes on. The imprint of his body was there upon the bedspread, a dent in the pillow.

"Where's he gone to?" Hal demanded sharply.

"I don't know. He was to join Yellow Jim and Ward to-day, and to see that Willoughby had everything in readiness. I did not expect him to go so early."

"Did he get a tip somehow of what was doin'? Has he cleaned out?"

Oscar shook his head, staring vacantly from the disordered bed to the other's keen eyes.

"I don't see how he could. He was asleep when I came in. I could hear him snoring when I stood by my open window."

"His snores might have been real and might have been fake," grunted Hal.

They had closed the door so that their low tones might not reach any ears other than their own. The cowboy was looking swiftly about the room for some sign to tell him if Dufresne's going had been in the way of a flight, or if he had suspected nothing and expected to return.

"It's the wrong time of year to waste time guessin' riddles," he muttered. "There ain't no way to tell — unless," — and with the sudden thought he wheeled about upon Estabrook — "unless you happen to know where he keeps the money you fellers has already took in from Willoughby?"

"Yes, I do know," answered Oscar bitterly. "I think he enjoys letting me know where it is all the time. He knows how much I need money, and he knows that I wouldn't dare touch it without his consent. For a word from him —"

"Would put a beautiful crimp in your game!" interrupted Hal sharply. "Does his hidin'-place happen to be anywhere near here?"

For answer Oscar went across the room to the old-fashioned bureau. He dragged it away from its place in the corner of the wall, stooped, and threw back the corner of the carpet, and jerked up a loose board from the floor. There, lying in a careless heap, were three buckskin bags, each half filled.

"He's coming back then." Hal knelt, slipped his arm down into the opening, and drew the bags out. "See if it's all here."

He went to the bed and, untying the strings at the mouths of the bags, poured the contents out upon a pillow. There was handful after handful of minted gold, all in twenty-dollar or ten-dollar pieces.

"He's sure figgerin' on comin' back. And he let you know where he kep' it all the time? And you needin' money like that?" There was something like admiration in his eyes as they turned thoughtfully toward the mountains into which he knew that Dufresne had ridden. "That man's sure got an awful cold nerve. He musta had you buffaloed to a freeze-out!"

He gathered up the gold again, putting it all into one bag. Then he stood frowning at it as he weighed it in his hand.

"It looks like it was all there?"

Oscar nodded.

"All right. You're goin' to take care of it to-day. I'll hold on to the rag money, but I can't tote this around with me. You put it in a good place and just roost on top of it until I come back. I guess," — very sternly, as he surrendered the bag into Estabrook's hands — "you won't make any kind of mistake with it. It's your one las' bet to square yourse'f."

"And you?"

"I'm goin' to do a little ridin', seein' as the Prince beat us to it. And you're goin' to write me a coupla nice little letters."

They went back to Estabrook's room, and as Hal dictated Oscar wrote, asking no questions, thankful that at last he had some one to lean on, some one who would assume the responsibility and strive to straighten out his muddled affairs.

"I want a order firs' to turn them steers back onto the flats, and to call the deal off with Willoughby. It might come in handy. Write it this way:

"Mr. Dufresne and Mr. Jordan,
    "DEAR SIRS, — I've changed my mind. Tell Willoughby I'm not sellin' any more cows to him. Drive the five hundred steers back to the flats."

"Got it? Now sign it."

Oscar signed the order and handed it to Hal.

"Dufresne has an order too," he said listlessly. "He said that it would be as well to have it if anything

261

unexpected came up. It's an order to him to sell what cattle he thinks advisable."

"The bets as that man misses ain't worth takin'," was the cowboy's grunted comment. "Well, we'll try it on, anyway. Date this one, date it for to-day. It'll be later than his'n, anyway. Now for the other order. Make it to Club Jordan, and tell him in it that he's fired, and that I'm foreman until fu'ther notice. In case he bucks at the firs' order I can slip this one on him. We're apt to have a little trouble, Estabrook, and it ain't goin' to hurt none to have every trick we can pick up from now on, so if we get mixed up with the law things'll look right."

Again Oscar wrote, dated, and signed. Hal, blotting and folding the two pieces of paper carefully, thrust them into his vest pocket.

"Now I'm goin', and there's goin' to be things happenin', and all you got to do is keep a damn' stiff upper lip and your eyes open. The sheriff has been stickin' around the Crossin' the last coupla days tryin' to pick up something, and I guess he's staying nights at the old camp six miles the other side. He's goin' to be on the job to-day, but he ain't goin' to smell your trail if you jes' keep your tongue in your face. I'm goin' down and saddle up now. I want you to mosey to the bunk-house and call Dick Sperry out. Tell him to come down to the corrals, and that he's to do what I say to-day. And" — turning, with a last glance at the pillow under which Oscar had thrust the buckskin bag — "don't forget to set tight on that, and that's it your one show to break even."

They passed out into the yard together and by the bunk-house met John Brent, who, rising early as was his custom, had just been to throw down some hay to Nicodemus. He called a breezy good morning to them, and as they went on stood with his legs wide apart, his great hands on his hips, drinking deep of the freshness of the morning and watching the glorious colours brightening across the path of the new day.

Hal had brought out the Colonel, saddled and watered, and was buckling on his spurs when Dick Sperry came into the corral.

"What's up?" asked Sperry, eyeing his fellow-worker curiously. "Estabrook's jes' come down an' shook me out an' tol' me I was to take orders off'n you to-day. He looks all shot to pieces, like a man with the devil astraddle his wish-bone!"

Hal swung up into the saddle, holding the Colonel back with a strong hand.

"Feed yourse'f real fas', Dick," he said shortly. "Then you climb on a hoss and hit the trail for the old camp the other side the Crossing. Mos' likely you'll find Dan Nesbit there. If he ain't there, why you jes' keep on' till you find him. Tell him I'm ridin' straight to the little pass where the old north trail runs across into the Double Triangle. I'm goin' by the Death Trap way. You tell him to foller me as fas' as he knows how, and I'll show him a man he can put his rope around."

Dick's quick questions were lost as the Colonel was given his head and shot away across the corral, through the open gate, and out across the meadow. He stared a moment after the horse and rider, and then, with much

263

grave speculation in his eyes, turned back to the bunk-house and the beginning of the new day's work allotted him.

Gradually Hal soothed the Colonel and brought him down to the swinging stride which did not wear him out and yet which ate up the miles as fast as an impatient man could wish. For there was a long ride ahead and rough trails, and the end of the day might call upon horse and man alike for a reserve of strength. It was early, Dufresne could not have much the start of him, and they would wait until night to conclude the deal with Willoughby.

He would go, not the shortest way, but the way of the better trails. That led by the Death Trap, fifteen miles away, and then on across the spine of the mountains another twenty miles to the pass where Willoughby was to meet them. He knew that there was no other horse upon the range with the speed and the endurance and the fine spirit of the Colonel, that the heavier bulk of Dufresne would make itself felt upon the cow-pony he rode. He hoped to come to the Double Triangle upon the heels of the gambler, if not before him.

"Five hundred big steers," he muttered. "Fat as butter, every one of 'em, and worth money in Chicago. Even if they're goin' to Willoughby dirt cheap they're worth ten thousand dollars! And Estabrook thinks that the Prince and Jordan would fork it all over to him, jes' keepin' out their commissions! When they've got him where he couldn't squeal if they cut his throat! That boy oughtn't never to have come so far from home."

The splendour of the breaking day had surged up across the eastern sky as he was leaving the corrals. The sun was up when he came to the cliffs at the base of Death Trap mine. Here he took the shorter trail, the one he and Yvonne had taken that day when he had first brought her here. His eyes softened as he remembered. He drew rein abruptly and swung down from the saddle.

"There's no use takin' extra chances," he told himself. "And this is as good a place to leave it as any."

For the thought had come to him that if anything happened to him at the hands of the men he was rushing onward to meet, it would be as well if he did not have the roll of bills upon him. He went straight to the wreck of a cabin and, sitting down upon the old bunk, took out the scrap of paper and stub of pencil which he always carried nowadays, and wrote a brief note. There was little time for careful composition, so he wrote hurriedly:

"The money as was took from the stage in the Bear Creek Crossin' hold-up is hid back of the cabin under some rocks."

Then he drew off his boot, thrust the paper into the toe, and pulled the boot on again.

"If anything happens to me," he thought grimly, "they'll find that before the funeral. Now we'll cache the long green and hit the trail again."

He knew that just behind the cabin there was a washout where the downpour of the other night had swept away the loose soil and deadwood that had sifted down from the mountain above. His thought was to scoop out a little hollow just as he had seen Oscar doing, to put the bank-notes in it, and cover them with a few stones, scattered in seeming carelessness.

He glanced about him quickly, making certain that there was no one to see. Then he went swiftly behind the cabin, into the wash-out, and dropped to his knees. He saw where the bank had crumbled away, and where the rushing, rocky avalanche had swept it across the little tableland, hurling it toward the cliffs below. Here, where he knelt, not ten feet behind the cabin, there had evidently been a narrow belt of loose soil, for the cloud-burst had carried it away so that it looked now almost as though a neat house-keeper had been over it with her broom. The cut was six or eight feet wide and a couple of feet deep.

He sought about until he found a little hollow that the water had scooped out, and set to work to clean it out and make it a little deeper. Into the hole he had made he dropped the roll of bank-notes, covering them swiftly with the loose dirt he had removed to make their hiding-place. Then, in order to make the place take on again the look that nature had given it, to remove the traces that he had made, he scattered over it the loose pebbles lying about him. Upon these he began to pile the few rocks which were to mark the place so that he could find it readily again, or so that, if anything happened to him, the person into whose hands his note came would have little difficulty in finding the spot.

He had piled three or four rocks together, seeking to make of them a sign that would not attract a man's notice unless he were looking for it. Turning to go, he saw that the storm had made other little heaps of stone here and there, and that his was in no way differentiated from its fellows. At his feet, half embedded in the ground, was a flat stone which he stooped to get, thinking to lay it upon the top of the others. It did not come away easily in his hands, and he struck it with his boot-heel to dislodge it. He saw that he had shaken it, stooped again to lift it — and suddenly went down on his knees beside it, his heart thumping wildly.

Where his boot had struck a bit of ragged edge had broken off, crumbling like dry clay. And in the light of the sun just peeping over the ridge above, the broken surface gleamed into his eyes with a soft, dull yellow glow! Bold! Pure, yellow, soft crumbling gold!

He sought with pounding temples for the particle that had been broken off, and found it lying among the strewn pebbles. He rubbed it against his overalls, wiping it clean of the dirt that had gathered upon it. It was as large as the end of his thumb, it was heavy in the palm of his hand, its broken edge shone in the sunlight with the same dull yellow glow. With fingers which he could not make altogether steady he drew out his knife, opening the little blade, and scratched at the surfaces dulled by weather and accumulated soil. And he knew then that the thing he had discovered because of the careless stroke of a boot-heel was the biggest nugget he had ever seen.

Already he had forgotten the four thousand five hundred dollars he had hidden. Little feverish spots were burning through the tan of his cheeks, his eyes sparkled with the leaping fire which the finding of gold puts into a man's blood. His hands were trembling as he strove with the rock, dragging it from its bed. He hacked at it with his knife, scraping here and there, making long scratches. The weight alone of the thing in his hands set his heart pounding with redoubled excitement. When he saw again and again the soft, pale colour, when he knew that it was all shot through with gold, his mouth was dry and the breath was catching in his throat.

He flung it down, as though it too were a thing of no moment, a sudden, greater hope clutching at his I eart. He ran here and there, up and down the wash-out, snatching up pebbles, digging with his hands or with the blade of his knife, muttering to himself. There was only one thing in his brain, just one question clamouring to be answered. And while he sought feverishly, his imagination leaping to new, wonderful heights, he was half afraid to come to the answer.

"Was this the one bit of gold the storm had brought down from the mountains, or had the landslide here uncovered the old vein of the Yellow Boy?"

In a little he was standing with his back to the cabin wall, gone suddenly weak, shaking like a man with a chill. And still he felt hot, feverishly hot, and little drops of sweat stood out on his forehead. His mind went back to the night of the storm. It had shown him the true gold of a woman's nature. It had uncovered for him the old, lost lode upon Death Trap Mountain!

He stared ahead of him, seeing nothing. A moment age he had been a cow puncher for the Bear Track, with nothing in the world but his horse and his daily wage. And now — why, now he had found the richest goldmine that had ever been worked and lost in the State — now he was a millionaire!

Still he stared, seeing nothing. Then, little by little, there came something to take form before his eyes. It was not the scarred breast of the mountain rising before him. It was a log cabin in the Valley of the Waterfalls, a cabin built of great logs, with wide doors and a big rock fireplace — with little shelves for dishes — and big shelves for books —

"And she won't know until it's all done!" he whispered. "Until the shelves is all filled and the fire's goin' in the fireplace. And then, some day —"

CHAPTER
TWENTY-TWO

The Prince Calls for a Show Down

But there was the day's work still ahead of him, a grim, merciless thing that rose up to cast its shadow over the glitter of gold and the softer, warmer glow of a woman's love. Hal slipped the nugget he had broken from the rock into his pocket, thought swiftly of the likelihood of another man coming here before he could come back and stake cut his claim, and then hurried down the trail to the Colonel. He realised that he had lost time already, and that he must hasten if he came to the herd of steers before Dufresne.

Again, now with a thousand thoughts riding at his elbow, he gave his horse his head and made what speed he might along the rocky trail. He had frowning impatience for the steep ups and downs of the way, eager impatience for the short, level stretches where his way ran through the little valleys. And as he went he wondered if Sperry had found the sheriff, and if they were even now thundering along behind him.

It was not yet noon when he came to the crest of the hills looking down upon Live Oak Valley. Here he knew the steers he sought had been grazing, here where it had been possible for a very few men to keep them from breaking away and scattering through the canyons. He had ridden slowly as he came up the steepening trail, he drew rein when he could catch his first glimpse of the rolling floor of the valley below him. His eyes were very grave as they swept from end to end of the hollow shut in by the mountains and saw nowhere a single steer.

"They haven't waited for night!" was his quick, startled thought. "They've pushed 'em on to the Double Triangle! Well," and he shook out his reins and shot down into the valley, "if Willoughby's got 'em on the run already he's goin' to bring 'em back! And Dufresne's goin' to cough up all he's swallered!"

It was but three miles farther to the boundary line running between the Bear Track and the Double Triangle, and from here on a man might let his horse run and not miss the broad trail the big band of cattle had left behind. He swept on through the valley, left it behind him, and at last, leaving the trail a little, came to the top of another rise from which he could look down upon the pass where the old north trail crossed into Willoughby's territory. Now he saw that if he were to save Oscar Estabrook from this last great criminal blunder he had come not a moment too soon.

The pass was an old water-worn gully, fifty yards across, where with steep clay banks it debouched into the Double Triangle, the hills rising close upon each side. Yonder, where the banks came closest together, they had built a high fence of freshly-cut timbers, leaving in the middle a gap through which a single steer might pass at the time, or two, when they pressed their big bodies close together and crowded each other for room. Beyond the gap, on Willoughby's range, there was a slight rise, a flat-topped knoll, upon which sat two men on horseback. From where he looked at them Hal was quick to recognise the big, burly frame of Willoughby upon a sorrel mare, and he caught the glint of the sun upon a diamond in the other man's tie.

Down in the gulley, on the Bear Track side of the line, were four men — Club Jordan, Yellow Jim Gates, Shifty Ward, and a man they called Dandy Miller, a man whom Club Jordan had hired with the other two. They rode upon the outskirts of the herd that was pressing into the gulch, their swishing ropes and short cries urging the cattle towards the gap. Already a score of the frightened brutes had found the opening in the high fence and were running out toward the east, across the Double Triangle. It was easy to see that Willoughby and Dufresne, sitting side by side, were counting them as they ran.

"Here's hopin'," grunted Hal, "that I get a show to work my new mine! Go to it, Colonel."

The Colonel asked nothing better than to go to it. He carried his master down the short slope as though they had been out upon the level lands, in his fine nostrils the odour rising from the hot bodies of many cattle, eager as a range horse always is to be among them, working his will and his master's upon them. The six men down below him had ears only for the bawling cattle, eyes only for the plunging bodies and tossing horns, and knew nothing of the coming of Hal until he was down among the hindermost steers. Then he shot into the herd, shouting at them, urging them to right and left, making his path through them. Club Jordan saw him first, and was yelling curses at him, calling to his men to head off the steers that were breaking back from his onrush and making for the canyon behind or the wooded slopes.

"Yell, Jordan, yell!" he muttered in his throat. "You've given jes' about the las' orders you'll cut loose on this range!"

He rode on, the Colonel carrying him with what speed he could through the jam of cattle, ploughing through them here where they fell back to each side with lowered, threatening horns, swinging there to right or left where he saw an opening, scattering them until the four men behind him grew hot with their own curses and their horses' sides dripped with sweat. In the thick of them Hal felt his legs being crushed into the Colonel's panting sides. Where the gulley was narrowest, just before he came to the fence, it seemed as if he could never fight his way on through the tight-packed bodies. But at last he was through, the Colonel stood in the gap with his four feet braced and his ears laid back, and only sixty or eighty steers had gone through.

Club Jordan was yelling things that Hal could not make out, the words reaching him in a blur of sound through the din in the gulch about him. But he guessed their import as with the tail of his eye he saw the frantic breaks for the open upon the rear of the herd, and he smiled grimly, deeply pleased at the anger which he knew to be burning in the foreman's heart. He sat still, allowing no steer to pass him, watching the man who was the brain of the thing — and the nerve!

Dufresne, unlike Jordan, had not spoken, and his habitual smile had not left his lips. He was riding forward, a little before Willoughby, and as he rode drew slowly at a freshly lighted cigar. Yes, the smile was still on his lips. But now he was near enough for a man to look into his eyes — and they were not smiling.

"So you've mixed into the game at last, have you?" There was only a quiet, polite interest in his voice. He flicked a bit of cigar ash from his vest with the little finger upon which his biggest diamond shone.

"Yes," just as quietly, just as expressionlessly, with eyes as unsmiling and watchful as the other's. "I've sure mixed in."

"I've half-way expected it." Dufresne sighed, and broke off to draw again at his cigar. "I told Jordan to get rid of you. Jordan's a fool and always will be a fool."

Willoughby had come up to them and sat heavily in his saddle, silent, his big face flushed a little, his eyes going from man to man. As for a second Hal glanced away from Dufresne he saw that there was a buckskin bag tied at Willoughby's saddle-horn.

"The days are getting short," Dufresne went on. "We have a good deal to do before sundown. Spread your cards out, Hal, so that we can look at your hand."

"Your little game's up, Dufresne," returned Hal, turning just a little in the saddle, his eyes never leaving Dufresne's now, the memory upon him of the ending of things for young Andy Holloway. "I guess you know when you're beat, and ain't goin' to try to make things worse'n you've made 'em already. Them steers is goin' back to the Bear Track."

"Your long suit is surprising people, Hal," laughed Dufresne. "Why are they going back?"

"Because the deal with Willoughby is off, and the Bear Track ain't sellin' no more cattle at a sacrifice."

"At a sacrifice?" Dufresne lifted the black lines of his brows. "Willoughby is paying all they are worth to him at this time of year, with winter coming on. And it's a fair price. We don't have to waste time talking, Willoughby," he said, turning a little to the Double Triangle man. "But you can spare a few minutes, can't you?" Willoughby nodded heavily, but did not speak, the eyes under his shaggy brows still going back and forth between the two men, waiting the outcome. "You would seem to give the impression" — once more to Hal — "that there was something irregular in this sale?"

"I didn't say so," with no rising of his steady voice. "I jes' said the deal was off."

"You've got in wrong somewhere, Hal." Dufresne was very pleasant about it — if one had looked at his lips he would have seen that the smile there had broadened good-humouredly, but the cowboy saw only his eyes, and saw that there was no change in them. "And you are putting Jordan and the boys out there to a lot of trouble. Now, look here. Do you happen to know that these cattle belong to old Pompey Estabrook?"

"I seen the brand as I come through 'em," carelessly.

"And do you happen to know that Pompey Estabrook has made his son his representative here, authorising him to make what sales, forced or otherwise, that he thinks advisable?"

"Yes."

"All right. You see, Willoughby, we are getting along like little ducks learning to swim! Do you happen to know also that Oscar Estabrook has empowered me to make this sale, to deliver the cattle to Willoughby, and to collect for them?"

"Yes."

"Then, what's the matter? Where do *you* get any authority to tell us to stop? Why shouldn't Willoughby buy if he is ready to pay and Estabrook is ready to sell?"

"Estabrook ain't ready to sell," retorted Hal bluntly.

"But I talked with him last night —"

"And he's changed his mind this mornin'. The deal ain't made until the money's paid over. And the money ain't paid yet. Estabrook wants it called off."

Dufresne sat silent for a little, his eyes roving out over the herd that was taxing the resources and patience of four men to keep in the gully, then coming back to the cigar smoke floating aloft, pale in the sunlight. Only then did they come to rest upon Hal's.

"If Estabrook wanted the deal called off why didn't he tell me? If he just changed his mind this morning why didn't he come out to tell me about it?"

"He had something else to do. So I come in his place."

"Do you realise," with a certain curious inflection in his voice and a quick, sharp glance at Willoughby, "that it is a trifle strange for Estabrook to have entrusted you with an errand of this kind? You two

276

have never had much to do with each other. A man who didn't know you very well, Hal, might think that you were lying!"

"Then it's good you know me real well, Dufresne."

"But just the same, I have my orders from Estabrook. The sale is going on. Are you going to move out of the gap so the cattle can get through? Or — you'll notice that there are six of us, and the boys back there are getting tired of fooling — do you want us to make you get out?"

"When I get out I'm goin' back behind a herd of five hundred steers," returned Hal, his eyes narrowing as he spoke. "Willoughby, you've heard what I said. Are you still countin' on tryin' to buy them cattle?"

"I been listenin'," rumbled Willoughby's deep voice. "I've talked with Estabrook an' I've heard him say for Dufresne to go ahead an' sell me the stock. I ain't out for no fireworks, but I'm ready to pay good money for them cattle jes' as soon as they're runnin' on Double Triangle dirt."

"Dufresne," went on Hal, his thumb hooked in the belt of his overalls, "I ain't lookin' for trouble neither. But I'm standin' pat this time. I thought maybe you might reckon as I hadn't understood Estabrook right, so I fetched this along." With the fingers of his left hand he drew a bit of paper from his vest pocket, and held it out so that the gambler could see it. "No, I'm keepin' it in my hands. It might come in handy if there's any of this mess leakin' into court. It's wrote big so I guess you can make it out."

Dufresne pushed his horse a little nearer and, leaning from his saddle, read the brief order at a glance. Having read it, he sat back and shrugged his shoulders.

"Very pretty, Hal. You've drawn nicely to your hand, haven't you? Only that isn't worth anything. You might as well roll it around some tobacco and smoke it." He took from his coat pocket a thick wallet, opened it, and drew out a neatly folded piece of paper. "Here's an order, signed by Oscar Estabrook, authorising me to sell what cattle I thought wise to sell to any purchaser and at any price! I think" — the smile in his eyes now as well as upon his lips — "that we can go ahead?"

Hal smiled back at him.

"It jes' happens, Prince, that my card tops yours. This here is dated this mornin'!"

"So?" No shade of annoyance crossed Dufresne's smiling face. He took from his vest pocket a fountain pen, removed the cap, shook out a drop of ink, laid the paper upon his wallet, and wrote in a date in a small, girlish, neat hand. "When I made this out" — between puffs of his cigar — "I left the date out. Now" — and he waved it slowly back and forth to dry the ink — "my hand tops yours. It's dated — this afternoon!"

Hal, without turning in his saddle, without moving his eyes from Dufresne's, held out Estabrook's order so that Willoughby could see it.

"It's an order, Willoughby," he said quietly, "sayin' that them steers ain't for sale. Estabrook wrote it this mornin'. If you go on with this deal it'll jes' be buyin' stolen cattle. Do you figger as you want to do that?"

Willoughby lifted his heavy shoulders and answered equally without hesitation and without haste:

"I'd be glad to have them steers at my price. I seen your order an' I seen Dufresne's. I don't know nothin' about it. If the cattle is delivered on my land, an' delivered damn quick, I'm ready to pay for 'em."

"They'll be delivered as quick as you can count them on the run," said Dufresne crisply. "Now, Hal, we've used up all the time we can spare, being polite to each other. There's a bunch of money in this thing for Wiloughby, and there's something in it for Jordan and his men out there — and for me. You've shot your wad and it hasn't done any damage. Have you got brains enough to pull out now while the trail's open?"

"I've give you jes' one barrel," laughed the cowboy lightly, although with full realisation of the danger of the thing he was going to say. "Here's the other: Dan Nesbit's headed this way on a dead run. He's lookin' for somebody and he's got blood in his eye. He's after the man as held up the stage at the Crossin', and *he's after the man as did for Andy Holloway!*"

"Holloway?" Dufresne frowned as though he did not understand, and there was no quiver of an eyelid, no tremor of his lips to show that he did understand. "What's the matter with him?"

"Nothin' — only he's dead," answered Hal quietly. "He's been dead some time and he didn't die natural. Some one of a bunch of cattle-thieves mos' likely did for him. If you fellers want to make things look worse for you than they are already, runnin' off stock when Estabrook says to bring 'em back, go to it." He gathered up his reins quickly, and threw the Colonel about on his haunches and back upon Bear Track soil. "The gap's open!"

Even then as he went back through the jam of cattle he did not let his eyes wander from Dufresne. Not until he had ridden a hundred yards and had come to where Club Jordan was waiting for him with red rage in his eyes.

"What in hell do you mean by this?" Jordan yelled at him.

"I'm jes' bein' a peaceable errand-boy," laughed Hal into the wrath-distorted features. "Estabrook sent me out with word to call this deal off."

"Hey, Jim," shouted Jordan, wheeling his horse to cut off the retreat of two red-bodied, long-horned steers running side by side. "Drive them cows on into the cut! Get a move on. Ward, bring them brutes in on the run."

Hal jerked his own horse in close to Jordan's side.

"Better listen to me a minute, Jordan," he called to him. "There's a sheriff headed this way real fas' —"

"Sheriff?" snapped Jordan. "What's a sheriff got to do with it?"

"He's after the man as killed young Andy Holloway one night up on the cliffs," retorted Hal sharply. "Know anything about it?"

He saw Jordan's eyes widen suddenly and then narrow until they were mere slits. He saw surprise and a something like the stirring of a quick uneasiness. Jordan, jerking in his sweating horse, let half-a-dozen steers break back by him.

280

"What do you mean?" he demanded, his tone one of bluster but at the same time with a hint of anxiety in it.

"I mean that there's been a lot of crooked business on the Bear Track lately. There's been crooked cattle work, but you've got a chance to squirm out'n that, seein' as you took orders from Estabrook all the time. There's the hold-up at the Crossin' as was did by somebody on the range. There's the killin' of Bill Cutter, with his hands up! There's the slippin' a knife into Andy Holloway — *when he was stoopin' over to grab his money!*"

He stopped a second and saw that a sick pallor had crept into Jordan's bronzed face.

"You know when Dan Nesbit gets as hot on the trail as he is now there's mighty apt to be hell poppin'. Here's an order from Estabrook to turn them steers back. If you go on with 'em you're stealin' 'em with a sheriff as means business campin' under your nose. A sheriff," with deep significance, "as counts on cleanin' out this neck of the woods while he's here. If you didn't do none of them things I mentioned some one of your gang did. If you go on stickin' with 'em, if you put this cattle deal through with Willoughby, you're makin' things look purty bad for yourse'f. And the law's got jes' about as quick a way handlin' a man as puts in with a murderer as it has handlin' the murderer himse'f."

Jordan sat for a moment, staring into Hal's eyes. As he stared he bit his lips and thought — thought fast.

"Let's see that order," he snapped.

Hal held it out to him as he had shown it to Dufresne and Willoughby, slipping it back into his

281

pocket when Jordan's frowning eyes had finished with it.

"Remember," he said quietly, "we're all goin' to have a chance to talk with Nesbit before sundown. Ain't you figgerin' you got enough on your ches' to explain already without goin' ahead with this thing?"

Jordan's face had gone merely stern. The little wave of surprise and anxiety had left his eyes, his jaw had squared, his expression was guarded and told nothing. Hal, eyeing him keenly, could form no idea of what the man was going to do as for a little he sat, head down, frowning at the ground. Then, suddenly, the big foreman lifted his head.

"Hey, there, Jim!" he shouted. "Shifty! You, Miller! Turn them cattle back! Estabrook has sent word to call the deal off. Bring them other steers back off'n the Triangle. Put every damn' head of 'em on the run-back to the Bear Track flats!"

And driving his spurs into his horse's flanks he shot through the scattering herd to where Dufresne and Willoughby were waiting.

CHAPTER
TWENTY-THREE

A Wager With the Sheriff

Already had these other men seen that something had gone wrong. They knew Jordan well enough to obey his snapping command. As each steer ran by them, plunging back through the cut to their old stamping grounds on the home range, Yellow Jim and Shifty Ward and Dandy Miller saw the money running out of their pockets, and there was lust of murder in the black faces they turned upon the man who had come at the eleventh hour to block the final move. But they did not hesitate, for they knew that the money was running faster out of their foreman's pockets than out of their own, and that there must be a strong reason for the order he had shot at them.

They drew together in the gully, letting the running cattle seek their own devices, and spoke in short, angry tones which came in a confused rumble to where Hal sat making his cigarette and watching them from under the lowered brim of his hat. Then, riding three abreast, they raced on through the cut and toward the gap in the fence where Club Jordan had already jerked in his horse beside Dufresne and Willoughby.

Jordan had cried out something to Dufresne, and the two men drew a little aside, leaving Willoughby to stare at them with curious, watchful eyes. Hal thought that he could guess what it was Jordan was saying. When the other men came up, and the foreman called sharply to Yellow Jim to come on, and for the other two to hold back a minute, it was still clear that they were speaking of Andy Holloway, speculating swiftly as to what Hal knew, how he knew, and if others knew what he did?

"I thought it would stop 'em," mused Hal, as he saw that no man of them moved to head off the cattle that were already scattering widely along the Bear Track foot-hills. "And don't think I played it wrong. Dufresne thinks as somebody stumbled on the place they buried Andy, and that I was bluffin' a good deal. And he ain't goin' to show his hand by tryin' to sneak out'n the country. And he ain't goin' to leave without goin' back to the Bear Track and tryin' for the money he lef' there. And before he travels very far I'm goin' to introduce Dan Nesbit to him."

So he made his cigarette and smoked it and watched them. He saw Dufresne shrug his shoulders, wave his half-burned cigar carelessly, and ride back to join Willoughby. He saw Ward and Miller come up with Jordan, the four falling into earnest talk. Then when Willoughby turned back along the Double Triangle trail, and Dufresne rode with him a little, talking swiftly while Willoughby did little beyond listen, Jordan and Miller swung back into the gully and gathered up the steers. Ward and Yellow Jim gallopped after the strays

284

upon the Double Triangle, setting them all on the trot back toward the home pastures.

Hal saw that Dufresne and Willoughby had stopped together upon a little knoll, that Dufresne was still talking, Willoughby listening, and then he touched the Colonel with the spur and rode around the flank of the running herd, saying nothing to the men pushing them on, but hastening to pass them and to hurry back over the home trail.

"They ain't pleasant jaspers to ride with anyway," he grinned, a keen enjoyment upon him as he glimpsed Club Jordan's scowling face. "And it's up to me to get back to the range-house before the Prince does. There's jes' the chance," and he shrugged his shoulders at it, "that he's scared out'n goin' back and is goin' to try to beat it. And I don't care if he does! Dan Nesbit'll go after him like a hound-dog after a cotton-tail, and I'd jes' as lief there wasn't a sheriff stickin' around till I get another chance to talk to Jordan and Ward and Gates. When I can show Dan Nesbit who done for Bill Cutter it ain't goin' to be hard to tease him away from lookin' for the man as got away with the money. Especial when the five thousand's forked over."

So he swung into the trail, let the Colonel out into the pace that swallowed the miles, and looked ahead eagerly at each rise for the coming of the sheriff.

Mile after mile slipped away behind him, and when again and again he lifted himself in the stirrups, his eyes running ahead along the winding trail until a sharp turn hid its further twistings, he began to wonder if Dick Sperry had loitered on his errand, or if Nesbit had moved on somewhere else, and had left the country. The afternoon wore on; be came at last to the cliffs standing below the cabin and Death Trap mine, and still no one came to meet him.

At the cliffs he stopped and scrambled up, hastening to the rear of the cabin for the bank-notes he had left there. He found them readily, stuffed them into his pocket, gazed a moment with brightening eyes over the wash-out that spelled riches — and a log-cabin! — and hurried back to the cliffs. From there, looking down into the level lands, he saw three men on horse back riding toward the Bear Track range-house, recognised even from that distance the white-stockinged mare Sperry so often rode, and guessed one of the other men to be Nesbit. He went back to the Colonel, mounted, and raced down the slope to join them.

He came at a hammering gallop to the mouth of the canyon where the trail runs out of the mountains and down to the level lands. Nesbit and Sperry and the other man had just passed — but they *had* passed! They were not turning aside into the trail which led to the Double Triangle, they were not following him as he had directed them to do. Even while he wondered he called out to them, and they stopped, swinging about in their saddles.

"Did you tell Nesbit?" he demanded sharply of Sperry, with a glance at the third man — a little man with a sharp nose, and much bushy hair, and very bright eyes, whom he knew to be Cop Kelley, one of Nesbit's deputies.

286

"It took me all day to find him," returned Sperry. "An' then I tol' him what you said."

Nesbit, a very big man already passed middle age, grave-eyed, stern-featured, extended a large hand, and said quietly:

"Hello, Hal. Yes, Dick told me."

"But you were ridin' by. Why didn't you cut across toward the Triangle, like I said?"

"I was countin'," smiled Nesbit, "on ridin' on to the Bear Track first."

Hal looked at him curiously. It was not Dan Nesbit's way to turn aside when there was in front of him a man the law wanted. He could not understand.

"Dick told you I could put you wise to a man you wanted? What's the matter you didn't take my tip? Did you figger I didn't know what I was talkin' about?"

"No" — slowly. "Not just that, Hal. I figgered that if you knew there might be others as knew, and I'd better hurry up and get my hands on the man I'm after before he got wise and drifted. That's all, Hal."

"But you know — already?"

"Yes. I know."

Hal felt his heart stop, and go on, tripping irregularly. Nesbit knew something, Nesbit was riding straight to the Bear Track, where he was going to arrest a man — and there was nobody there but Oscar Estabrook!

"Maybe we're shootin' at diff'rent marks," he said, trying to speak lightly. "Do you mind sayin' who you're after?"

"Not a bit, pardner. Seein' as I'm goin' straight for him now, and nobody's goin' to get a show to break away and go on ahead and put him wise! I'm after the man as held up the stage down to the Crossin'."

"And you know who he is?"

"Sure enough to take him in," laughed the sheriff. "Goin' our way? Let's be ridin'."

Hal drew in the Colonel beside him, and the four men rode on toward the range-house. For a little there was silence, broken only by the thud of the galloping hoofs on the soft soil.

"Mos' of the boys is back yonder in the mountains," offered the cowboy after a moment.

"The one I want ain't," said Nesbit shortly.

And then Hal blurted out:

"You said you didn't mind tellin' who he was. I'd like to know."

"It's Estabrook," announced Nesbit, watching the other to see the surprise which should appear in his eyes. But there was nothing there but a brooding interest.

"A man makes a mistake sometimes," Hal replied slowly. "What makes you so sure?"

"A good many things, first and last, Hal. I've found out he's got so deep in a hole he can't see daylight up above him. And he's got himself in the claws of a man called Dufresne. You oughta know him," with a twinkle driving the gravity out of the grave eyes. "And Estabrook was missin' the night the thing was pulled off. Then Martin, the express agent, is willin' to swear it was a man just about Estabrook's build. Them things made me suspicious. And I've picked up some more. Anyway, Estabrook's got a lot of mighty tall explainin' to do, and he's goin' to do it to a judge."

Hal lifted his eyes to the clutter of range-buildings drawing nearer and nearer. Nesbit would arrest Estabrook, the boy would be frightened out of his wits, he would become entangled in his own flimsy defences, he would finally confess that he had held up the stage. Then he would be accused of the murder of Bill Cutter, and he would deny, and the story he would tell would sound to the sheriff, as it had to him, like a lie, a poor lie at that.

If he had had only a little more time, just a few days! If he could only have pointed out to the sheriff the man who had fired that cowardly shot from the canyon, if he could have had the five thousand dollars returned to the express company, then might the lesser crime have been forgotten in the larger, then might he have found a way to have saved Oscar Estabrook from the penitentiary — to have saved Yvonne from a great sorrow, and the smear of a great disgrace! But now —

His eyes suddenly brightened, he opened his lips to speak — and then he closed them, saying nothing. He must think it over. He must be sure.

They galloped on, dropped into a little hollow, rode out upon the crest of a gentle rise. The range-house looked very near.

"Look here, Dan," he said casually. "Like I said jes' now, a man makes mistakes sometimes. I'm bettin' you you got the wrong man."

"What are you bettin', Hal?" grinned the sheriff. "A sack of cigarette tobacco against a sack of pipe?"

"I'm bettin'," returned Hal soberly, "jes' four thousand five hundred dollars! Can you cover it?"

Nesbit laughed.

"You're talkin' like a man as has just found a goldmine!" he chuckled, and wondered at Hal's start.

"Maybe I have," Hal laughed back at him. "Anyway, look at that!"

As he spoke he whipped something from his pocket and held it out to the sheriff. And Nesbit, as he saw what it was, jerked his horse down to a dead stop, his eyes boring into the cowboy's.

"Where did you get that?" he snapped.

"Count it." He surrendered it into Nesbit's hands, reining the Colonel close up to him. "See if it, ain't just four thousand five hundred."

Nesbit counted swiftly, and again demanded sharply:

"Where did you get it?"

"I told Dick to tell you I'd show you a man you could take in with you," smiled Hal, allowing no tremor of the misgivings within him to show in face or voice. "I reckon it looks like what turned up missin' after the hold-up at the Crossin', don't it? And I'm about the same build as Estabrook, ain't I?"

Dick Sperry with bulging eyes, Cop Kelly with eyes which were low-lidded and very, very bright, had jerked in their horses alongside. Nesbit, staring incredulously at Hal, muttered dully:

"You mean — you was the hold-up man?"

And Hal, returning his stare, answered steadily:

290

"It looks like it, don't it? And I guess we don't have to go on to the Bear Track now, huh?" He laughed into Nesbit's puzzled face, and ended, "It's quite some time since I was entertained in Queen City — in their little old ten-foot jail!"

But they did not turn back. And as they rode into the corrals below the bunk-house Hal cried out aloud, a sudden new fear in his heart, and, forgetful of the sheriff, drove his spurs into his horse's flanks and rushed on to the range-house.

For in the dust of the corral lay a saddle-horse, dead! It was the horse that Dufresne had ridden to-day — and Dufresne had killed it in getting back to the house.

CHAPTER
TWENTY-FOUR

Estabrook Takes His One
Desperate Chance

What Victor Dufresne had seen ahead of him had not shown in his eyes. He had glanced carelessly toward the herd that was being forced back to the Bear Track, and there had come no change in his voice as he went on talking earnestly but calmly to Willoughby. He had seen Hal ride around the running steers, climb the hill, and drop out of sight upon the farther side. Then if his eyes showed anything, Willoughby did not see it. For the gambler had shot his spurs home with no word of his going, had jerked his horse into the south trail, and had headed straight back toward the Bear Track range-house. And that he might save what few precious moments he could, he had killed his horse getting back to the home corrals.

As the animal had, for the last time, gone to its knees with wide-staring eyes which told of a bursting heart, he had slipped quickly from the saddle. With no glance behind him he walked swiftly to the bunk-house. Charley, the cook, was getting his fire laid.

"Charley," he said sharply. "Come here."

Since the most independent man upon the range is the cook, since Charley was busy with his own work, and since, further, he did not like the gambler, he stared insolently a moment, and then jerked his bony shoulders up in a shrug.

"Heap busy," he retorted. "No gottee time."

Dufresne came swiftly across the bunk-house floor, and stood so close to the Chinaman that their bodies touched, looking steadily down into the little slant eyes.

"You take time," he said sternly. "My horse is out in the corral, dead! You get the saddle off him, and put it on the big roan in the stable. I'm going up to the house and I'll be right back. You have that horse saddled by the time I get back or I'll kill you! Sabe?"

Now at last there was something in the gambler's eyes that any man might read, and the same something was in the voice he had even lowered a little. Charley's yellow face went suddenly white, there was a quick patter of flopping sandals upon the rough floor, and with his queue escaping from the coil about his head and flying behind him, Charley fled upon his errand.

Dufresne stepped to the kitchen table, picked up two thick slices of coarse bread, slipped between them a piece of the cold steak Charley was going to make into a stew, found time to snatch up a scrap of paper to wrap about the great sandwich, and, stuffing it into his pocket as he went, turned to the range-house.

He saw Mrs. Estabrook and her two daughters lounging in hammock and easy-chairs out under one of the oaks to the east of the house, lifted his hat to them, and went on, walking swiftly. Upon the steps he came upon Fern Winston, reading. Again he lifted his hat, this time stopping a moment. As he stood over her, upon the steps, his eyes ran for a little out over her head, and he saw four men riding towards the house, out on the level lands.

"Miss Winston," he said gently, the look of frank admiration in his eyes that was always there when he looked at her, or at her picture upon Oscar's dresser, "Mrs. Estabrook and the girls are out there under their oak. They called to me to ask you to come out."

Fern got to her feet quickly, and ran down the steps, as frank in her eagerness as she always was to escape from his company. Dufresne, glancing again at the four men who, it seemed, had stopped a little, estimated quickly that they could not reach the corrals for half an hour yet, and went on into the house.

He hurried to his room, went in, and closed the door softly. There was no sign that the old-fashioned bureau in the corner had been moved. He laid his hands upon it, swung it about, jerked back the corner of the carpet, and, dropping to his knees, lifted the loose board. For a second he did not move, frowning down into the empty space disclosed to him.

"If Hal's got it," he muttered, "I'm playing a losing game. But if young Estabrook has it —"

Speculation took time; speculation was useless at a moment like this. And Dufresne had no time to waste. He got to his feet quickly, went down the hall and to Estabrook's door. He did not knock — that also took time. The door was unlocked. He threw it open, entered, and shut it behind him.

294

Oscar Estabrook was sitting before his table, upon which he had put Fern Winston's picture. He looked up quickly as Dufresne came in, and started to his feet. Their eyes met, and for once Estabrook's were as steady as the other's and did not drop before him. There was in the young fellow's look something that had never been there before, that Dufresne was quick to see, that told simply and with a force which mere words could not have expressed that at last Oscar Estabrook had become a man.

"It's Fern's work!" was Dufresne's first thought, even as his eyes left Estabrook's to sweep the room for the hiding-place of the thing he sought. "There's a woman for you!"

Estabrook had not moved again; there came no change into his eyes as they rested steady and stern upon Dufresne.

"I'm glad you've come, Dufresne," he said quietly. "I wanted to talk with you."

"I haven't come to talk and I haven't time to talk," said the gambler sharply. "You know what I've come for."

"I've come to see things differently," went on Oscar earnestly. "I've been a fool, worse than a fool, long enough. And we've both come to an end of this crooked business."

"I tell you I haven't time to talk!" snapped Dufresne. "Where's that money? And don't lie to me!"

"I'm not lying to anybody. I'm sick and tired of lying!"

295

"Then where is it? Quick, man! Can't you see I'm not here to fool with you?"

"It's here, in this room. And *I* am taking care of it now."

Yes, here was a different man to the Oscar Estabrook Dufresne had so long driven at his will. Dufresne's manner changed swiftly, his voice was suddenly soft as he said:

"And what you owe me — on the notes I hold —"

"I am going to pay, in full!" He turned to his bed, and jerked away the pillow, taking up one of the two buckskin bags there, the one that was the less bulky. "Here it is. You can count it, and you can have it when you give me back my notes."

Dufresne took it, but, making no move to count it, he dropped it into his coat pocket. As he took it he moved a step nearer, closer to Oscar and what lay under the pillow that Estabrook had thrown back to its place.

"Estabrook," he said sternly, "I tell you I mean business to-day. I want the rest of it, all of it. And I'm going to have it!"

Estabrook stood without stirring, the little pallor creeping into his cheeks, the sudden brightening of his eyes, and the quick clenching of the hands at his sides showing that he had heard, that he had understood.

"You are not going to have it, Dufresne," he said as calmly as he could.

But Dufresne had seen his answer coming and did not wait for it. He sprang forward without warning, his clenched fist driving with all his weight behind it into Oscar's face, sending him reeling backward so that he

296

fell across the bed. As Oscar fell Dufresne's eyes left him, Dufresne's hands tossed away the pillow and found the heavy bag under it. Still clutching it in his hand he turned and ran to the door, jerking it open.

But Estabrook was again upon his feet and had flung himself forward. Before the door had closed his arms tightened about Dufresne's body. The heavier man jerked back, striking again, and Oscar's arms slipped until they were about Dufresne's knees. But there they held, tightening.

"Let me go!" snarled Dufresne. "Let me go, I tell you!"

Oscar made no answer. He put his head back, looking up into Dufresne's face. His lips were cut, the blood from them smeared across his cheek. There was no fear in his eyes, no doubting or hesitation, but a sort of fierce determination that was not a part of the man of yesterday.

"Let me go, you fool!" cried Dufresne again. "I don't want to kill you!"

"Not with that money," panted Oscar doggedly. He sought to draw himself up, to shift his arms about Dufresne's body.

There came a quick step upon the walk leading to the front door, and then some one, a woman, was running up the steps. The gambler had shifted the bag of gold to his left hand. His right hand had gone to his hip pocket, and Oscar knew what the gesture meant, knew and realised before he saw the revolver in Dufresne's white fingers.

"Let go!" It was merely a whisper now, as Dufresne jerked back and could not break the clutch of the arms about his knees. "Do you want to make me kill you?"

"It's my money," panted Oscar. "My money. You don't dare shoot. It's mur —"

He didn't finish. The gambler heard the front door bang back against the wall as it was jerked open, heard a woman cry out, heard even the rustling of her skirts. He struck at the man clinging to him with the barrel of the revolver, and as he struck Oscar jerked his head to one side and the thing fell heavily upon his shoulder. He did not let go, he did not believe that Dufresne would shoot, he knew only that there in that buckskin bag was "his one chance to square himself." And he clung to Dufresne's legs, seeking to trip him, trying to draw himself up —

Then Dufresne fired, fired and heard Oscar cry out as the bullet stabbed into his body, heard the scream from the woman whose form he could see already darkening the hallway. And yet the arms about him did not relax, but rather tightened spasmodically, threatening to throw him to the floor. He fired again, the muzzle close to Oscar's throat — and then he was free, with a limp form huddling at his feet, and was running to the door, carrying with him a blurred impression of a man with a white face and wild eyes and a woman moaning over him.

As he ran down the steps he saw four men out in the level land riding swiftly toward the house. He saw Mrs. Estabrook with her face in her hands, heard her shrill shrieks, saw Sibyl with staring, terror-stricken eyes, saw

Yvonne running toward him. And in the corral he saw Charley throwing a saddle upon a big roan horse.

He shot by Yvonne, his eyes no longer for anything but what lay ahead. Charley was fastening the latigo as he came to him. He jerked the thing out of the Chinaman's hands.

"Give it to me," he commanded sharply. "Go into the stable and turn every horse loose. Quick. Run them out of the corrals."

Again Charley understood, and with the fear of death upon him, obeyed. Dufresne tightened the cinch with a jerk, swung into the saddle, and turned his horse's head toward the canyon back of the house, through the grove of oaks. As he went, bending low in the saddle, his spurs already red and dripping, he saw that the corral gate was open and that half a dozen horses were running out across the fields with Charley shouting at them and waving his arms.

CHAPTER
TWENTY-FIVE

And at Last is a Man

Big John Brent and Louis Dabner had been loitering upon the slope of the knoll upon the farther side of the house, and at the sound of shots came running. John Brent, plunging on ahead, came upon Mrs. Estabrook and Sybil in the yard, saw Mrs. Estabrook wringing her hands, and ran by her, leaping up the steps. In the hallway, as he came in at the door, there was the smell of powder. He stopped short, his face going black with wrath, his big hands clenching at his sides, when he saw.

Fern had reached Oscar first. She was down on the floor at his side, his head upon her lap, her hand red and hot with the blood from the great hole in his throat. His face was very white, his eyes had closed, and if he were not dead, then death was very, very near him. Yvonne was standing near Fern, her face as white as Fern's and as Oscar's, looking with mute misery into her brother's face.

They lifted his limp body, John Brent and Dabner, carrying him gently to his room. And when they had laid him upon his bed John Brent drove them back while he cut away the shirt and did what a man might do to bandage the hole in his chest and at the base of his throat, and to stop the flow of blood. Then he stood back, and his lips moved a little, though he said nothing for them to hear.

Dabner stole out and went to Sibyl and Oscar's mother. Fern had dropped down upon her knees at the bedside, her hand going so naturally to smooth back the hair from the forehead, stooping closer now and then to lay her cheek against his. Yvonne drew back a little, and laid her hand upon John Brent's arm. He saw the question in her eyes as she lifted her face to him, and she saw the answer in his and dropped her face into her hands.

"God is with us," he whispered, his great hand upon her shoulder. "He knows best. And He is merciful."

Oscar had opened his eyes, his hand had slipped into Fern's.

"Fern," he whispered. He tried to lift his head and a spasm of pain ran across his face and contracted his brows. He lay still again, and again his eyes had closed. And then, painfully, each word coming with an obvious effort and huskily so that it did not carry across the room, "Is . . . he . . . gone?"

"Yes, Oscar," her poor tortured lips whispered back. "But it doesn't matter. Nothing matters, dear, except for you to lie very still and save your strength."

He didn't answer. So long was he still that the fear in Fern's heart had begun to force out the last, yearning hope. But at last he opened his eyes, and they rested upon hers with a pain in them and a longing that forced a little sob from her dry throat. From her he looked to

John Brent and Yvonne. They saw and understood, and went silently out of the room, closing the door gently behind them.

"I want to tell you . . . everything, Fern."

She leaned over him and kissed him upon the lips, and sank back upon her knees beside him, his hand pressed close to her breast.

"Don't tell me anything, dear." She strove so hard to keep the anguish out of her voice. "Just that you love me, Oscar. And I know you do. That is all that matters."

"No. Let me tell you. I think . . . I haven't . . . long."

Then she saw that it would make him rest easier, and she drew closer to him, and listened.

"I was going to be . . . square! And now . . . it's too late. For I can't . . . get well . . . can I, Fern?"

"Don't, Oscar," she said gently. "You are badly hurt, but I am going to take care of you and . . ."

His hand pressed hers a little, and he tried to smile.

"Poor Fern! I've just . . . brought you . . . unhappiness all along. And now . . . I was just beginning to be honest with myself, and . . . I am going to be honest with you, Fern. Maybe, when you know . . . you won't be so sad."

Each laboured word drove a fresh pain into her heart. But again she saw that this man could not rest in silence under the weight of the thing upon his soul, and she pressed his hand closer to her breast and waited.

"I meant all the time," he went on, stopping between the words to gather and hold the strength that was flowing out of him, "to return all that I was taking. I gambled more heavily than you knew, Fern. I broke my

302

promise to you over and over. Dufresne wanted his money, threatened to write to Father. That is why I tried to rob my own friends at Swayne's that night."

He paused, figthing for breath, his eyes anxiously upon hers, looking for the start of swift horror and shrinking there which must follow his words. And all that he saw was a deeper tenderness, a misty, yearning pity for him.

"That isn't all." His eyes left hers and went slowly to the square of light where the window was. "I thought I saw the way to get money, and I have been selling father's cattle . . . without his knowing it. I have been . . . stealing them. And," his voice so faint now that she had to bend closer to hear, "I held up the stage at the Crossing!"

"Oscar!" Her lips were as white as his own; one would have said that she too were losing her life's blood. "You didn't —"

"No. I should have let them shoot me before I would have killed a man. I don't know who —"

"My poor Oscar." She put her arm about his shoulders and again kissed him upon the lips. "Didn't I tell you that it didn't matter what you had done? I knew you had made mistakes. But you were willing to take the consequences of the things you had done, and I was so glad to take them with you. And you are square *now*, and good and true and a man! And you love me, and I love you, and that's all that matters, dear."

Now he brought his eyes back to Fern's eyes, and his tears gathered suddenly as he saw what kind of woman this was and what it would be to die and so leave her.

303

"Love does not blind — it just makes us see clearly, Oscar. And I see in you to-day the man I have always wanted!"

She felt his fingers stir in hers as she tried to press the hand that she had not drawn back from. His eyes closed again, wearily, and his breathing came more gently in a little sigh which spoke of a thing that was almost happiness.

In the hallway John Brent had driven back Mrs. Estabrook with her hysterical moaning and sobbing, and now opened the door and came in quietly, bringing with him the little satchel containing the few simple medicines that always went where he and Nicodemus journeyed upon their errands of mercy. Stooping, he laid his hand upon Fern's bowed head.

"I have sent a man to Queen City for a doctor," he whispered. "Until he comes we are going to do what we can."

When she lifted her eyes to him and he saw in them the same question that had shone in Yvonne's, he answered her gently:

"I don't know. But there is always hope. God knows what is best, but maybe He will help us now." As she got to her feet and made room for him, he even smiled softly as he whispered, "You are a wonderful brave girl! And you going to help me do our best for him."

Then it was that Hal had come to the house and had had his question answered before it was asked by Yvonne's grief-stricken eyes. He had gathered her tenderly into his arms, holding her tight, his lips upon

304

her hair, the anger in his eyes suddenly softening as he felt her fighting not to let herself go. When at last she raised her head, he asked softly:

"Is he hurt bad?"

She nodded, pressing tight together the lips which she did not dare to trust with spoken words. And she wondered when he asked again, swiftly:

"Has he — said anything?"

"He was talking with Fern," she answered steadily. "She and John Brent are with him now."

He glanced over his shoulder and saw Nesbit and the others in the yard.

"Tell her," he said quickly, "I want to see her. I got to see her right now! It's about — Estabrook."

Yvonne looked at him curiously, but turned and went to where Fern was helping the preacher minister as best she knew how with the wounded man. She took the bandage from Fern's fingers, and Fern, with a lingering look at the white face upon the blood-covered pillow, went swiftly to where Hal was waiting for her.

"Has he said anything to you?" he demanded quickly.

"What do you mean?"

"About — did he — confess anything?"

"Yes," very simply. "He has told me everything."

"Has he told anyone else?"

"No."

"Then don't let him! And don't you say anything. The sheriff is outside now, and — There's no use now, don't you see?"

Nesbit's big form was already filling the doorway. Hal turned towards him quickly, and Fern went back to Oscar's side.

"Come here, Dan," he said, drawing the sheriff aside and back upon the porch. "You can't forget about the man as stuck up the stage. You've got back mos' of the money, and the man as took it ain't the same man as killed Bill Cutter, anyhow."

"What do you know about this business, Hal?" snapped Nesbit suspiciously. "And how's it happen you know so much?"

"What I know you can pump out'n me after a while. I ain't goin' to run away. But there's a man runnin' away now, and he's goin' like hell. He's jes' put two holes into young Estabrook, close up. And you want him anyway. He murdered Andy Holloway one night back in the hills!"

Nesbit, a man used to surprises, stared at him with frowning eyes. But because he was a man of action, because he saw that at least there was no chance of Estabrook getting away from him, he asked no questions.

"Dufresne ain't got much head start of us," he muttered. "But he's got a fresh horse. And he's made the Chink turn the others out."

"Dick's bringin' 'em up," returned Hal shortly. "Put your saddle on the big bay with the white star. I'm goin' on now. The Colonel's as good as a fresh horse right now." He ran down the steps and threw himself into the saddle. "He's gone back through the trees and into the canyon. Headed mos' likely for the Triangle. Sperry'll show you the way."

Already he had turned the Colonel's head the way Dufresne had gone when he heard Yvonne calling to him, and he drew his horse close into the porch where she was. If she should ask him not to go . . . But:

"God go with you, dear," was all that she said.

And she leaned out toward him and lifted her lips up to him.

CHAPTER
TWENTY-SIX

The Blue Sky for a Limit

Hal knew that upon his own shoulders rested the weight of the thing that had happened. He had told Dufresne that it was known that Andy Holloway had been murdered. He told Jordan that the man who had killed Holloway had done it with a knife, when the young fellow was stooping over to pick up his money. Jordan had told Dufresne. And the gambler, knowing that within a few hours he would be sought by a sheriff who never gave up the trail so long as the man he wanted was at liberty, knew that without money he would have little chance of escaping. It was his business to take risks, and he did not hesitate to return to the range-house. And he had shot Oscar Estabrook . . . and it was because of the things that Hal had said.

This day the Colonel had already carried his rider seventy miles. But his muscles were hard and his spirit was the spirit of a thoroughbred . . . and it would soon be night in the canyons. A man must not loiter, no, not even for a fresh horse now.

Dufresne had ridden straight back into the canyon, and for a couple of miles there was no place where he could turn aside. For there lay much rough country on either side of the main trail here with much thick chaparral which a man must ride around, losing time. And seconds now to the fleeing man would be like bright gold pieces to a miser. So the cowboy looked only ahead and followed the main trail with unslacking speed. But as the miles fled behind him and he pushed deeper and deeper into the mountains, he stopped now and then to lean out from his saddle, his frowning eyes keen for a sign that the gambler had turned aside into one of the many trails leading to north and south.

He saw no sign until he had ridden some six miles and had come to a little creek sprawling across the trail. And there he saw what he looked for, the imprint of the hoof of a shod horse, so fresh that the water was still trickling into it, breaking down the little rim of earth it had pushed up about it in the wet, sandy soil. Dufresne had not turned aside, and Hal felt that he was not going to turn aside until he had put many miles between him and the Bear Track.

"We won't get him to-night," muttered Hal as he jerked the Colonel's head up from the water and swept on. "And he's got an awful good chance of gettin' clean out'n the country. He's got the nerve, and he's got the money."

Whether or not there is such a thing as luck does not matter. Victor Dufresne was, above all things, a gambler. And every gambler is as thoroughly convinced that he is going to win upon his "lucky days" and lose upon his "unlucky days" as he is that half of the cards in his deck are red, half black. His "streak of luck" had been long and he had played it heavily. And he had known that, soon or late, it would break, that his losing days would follow as naturally and as inevitably as the winter was following the summer.

To-day, when at the very end of his game there had come the interruption in the deal with Willoughby, he had sensed that the luck had broken. Then, on top of that, had come mention of Andy Holloway. He had seen that his one hope now lay in getting back to the Bear Track and getting the gold there. And he had done it only after shooting Estabrook, and with the sheriff at his heels.

And now, half a dozen miles ahead of his foremost pursuer, a small thing happened that was a big thing, because he was a gambler and a gambler has his superstitions that are uncannily more than superstitions. The thin arc of the new moon had floated up above the mountain along whose base he rode. It was pale, glowing wan and dim through a little mist. And he saw it over the wrong shoulder.

Whether or not there is such a thing as luck does not matter. But the thing which happened to him before his eyes had left the pallid new moon, all unexpected as it was, did not surprise him. His big roan was carrying him easily, swiftly, across the grass-matted floor of a little valley. There, in the soft dirt, a squirrel had dug a hole. The horse's foot slipped into it, the animal stumbled, fighting for its balance. But it could not check the headlong speed, could not jerk its foot out again. It went down, floundering, with a broken leg. And for a little

Dufresne, who had been thrown over its head, lay still. Then, when he got slowly to his feet, he went on on foot, and limping a little.

They came upon him in the thick darkness just after midnight. Hal had come first upon the crippled roan. He had swung down from the saddle, and after lighting many matches had found the prints of Dufresne's boot-heels. He had seen that the gambler, even now, was making no attempt to leave the main trail. He was headed for the Double Triangle, and was going the shortest way now.

Half a mile farther the cowboy swung down from the saddle again. There was another crossing here, and with lighted matches he once more sought the tracks of the man who had gone on before him. When he found them their story was plain. Dufresne was still walking toward the Double Triangle. He was walking slowly now, and the imprint of the boot upon his left foot was deep and clearly defined, while there was a long scratch in the sand where the right foot had been dragged over it.

After that Hal lighted no more matches. He rode slowly, peering into the shadows about him, listening for the snapping of a twig or the clatter of a stone sent rolling down some rocky bank.

The night was clear and the stars made here and there spaces of dim light. Hal was riding through one of these open spaces when a sudden thought that was like a premonition came to him. If he were in Dufresne's boots, knowing that he was followed and that the word of his flight would run out to-morrow across the whole country, he would waste no time in getting away. If he were hurt, as the gambler surely was, so that he limped and must walk slowly, he would get a horse, no matter what risk he would run. And since there would be no horses to be had except those his pursuers rode, he would tempt his fate one last time and chance everything in trying to get one of these horses! He would lie in the shadows somewhere close to the trail, close enough for him to shoot the first man who came by and seize his horse's reins.

The swift thought upon him, Hal swung his horse out of the starlit open and into the darkness that clung close about the tree trunks upon the farther side of the trail. Then he knew that the thought had not come a second too soon. For he saw the darkness not twenty feet from him cut in two by the red spurt of fire from a revolver, heard the sharp, angry report, and felt the sting of lead like a hot iron laid against his side. He gave the Colonel the spurs and shot deeper into the thickest of the darkness, turning in the saddle and firing as he rode. Again he saw the red spurt of flame, and again, and the third time he heard the whiz of flying lead. But he knew that at the right moment he had turned from the clearing into the dense darkness under the trees, and that now the gambler's firing was but guesswork.

And again Victor Dufresne, a true gambler that he was, saw that his luck had left him, that he had missed when he should have shot unerringly, that he had played his last card and lost.

Hal threw himself from his horse, dropped the Colonel's reins over his head to the ground, and came forward a little, walking slowly, watchful, listening. He felt a warm trickle down his side but paid scant attention to it, knowing that his wound was scarcely more than a scratch. Dufresne had not fired after the third time, and the cowboy could not make out his form. The gambler had chosen the place of ambush well. Before him was the open space through which Hal had ridden a little way. Behind him was a rocky ridge of the mountain, strewn with great boulders, one of them hanging out over him where he crouched in its shadow. He had chosen his place well for his purpose. And his purpose was not retreat.

Hal still drew nearer, his gun in the hand hanging at his side. He saw nothing but the unbroken blackness of the overhanging rocks, and above the sharp crags against the skyline. He had fired several times at the spit of Dufresne's revolver, and began to wonder if one of his shots had found its mark. It was so silent there, with no sign of a moving, living thing. But he knew Dufresne, and he stopped, his brows drawn into a heavy scowl as he tried to make his straining eyes see through the thick veil of the night.

"Dufresne!" he called sharply.

"Well?" It was Dufresne's voice, what Dufresne's voice had always been, calm, unmoved, with no trace of emotion in it. "It's Hal, isn't it?"

"Yes. You haven't got a chance in the world, Dufresne. You'd better finish the game out in the courts."

He moved a little bit, stepping quickly, to the left, expecting his voice to draw the gambler's fire. But there came no fourth shot.

"I think you are right, Hal. I've about played to the "end of my string. But the courts?" He laughed softly. "They're a cold deck, Hal." And then, a little change in the quiet voice, "Where are the rest? Where's Nesbit?"

"They'll be here in a minute now. You never were a fool, Dufresne. And you know you haven't a chance."

"No," thoughtfully, "I never was a fool, or anyway, I have thought so." He grew silent, and Hal, trying to locate him, began to think that he had slipped behind one of the big rocks lying at the foot of the abrupt slope, and was crouching behind it. "Hal," he went on, after a little, "how did you find Estabrook. Is he dead?"

"No. But he is another man whose chances are mighty small."

"I didn't want to shoot the fool. He made me do it. I hope he pulls through."

"You needn't try to smooth things over with me," cried Hal sharply.

"I'm not trying to. I wouldn't care . . . *for him*. It's for *her* sake . . . I wonder why a woman like her loves a shrimp like him?"

From the meditative, gentle tone one would have said that if in these mountains there were two men with revolvers in their hands, watching for each other, it must be a long way from here. Before either had spoken again there came to them through the stillness of the night the pound of galloping hoofs. Hal, waiting until he knew from the sounds that the sheriff and the men

314

with him were in earshot, called out to them loudly, still watchful for any move on Dufresne's part.

Five minutes later Nesbit, Dick Sperry, and Cop Kelley had joined him, and the four men moved out in a widening arc so that they could come in on three sides of the man in hiding. But although they had called out again and again no answer came to them.

So they waited for the light of the coming day, knowing that he could not get away from them across the broken slope behind him, listening for a rolling stone, watchful for a moving figure against the sky or among the thinning shadows. Then came the first glint of day, and they saw him. And they knew that he too was ready and waiting.

He had made his way back a little from the trail, a little higher on the slope, and had taken his place upon a level space shut in on three sides by great boulders. They saw him get to his feet, look at the flush lying close to the horizon, and stretch himself like a man awaking from sound sleep. He was fumbling with something in his pocket, and they could not guess what he was doing. Then they saw him strike a match and light his cigar — the last cigar which he had saved all night until now.

He lighted it carefully, turning it round and round to get it burning evenly, as careful about it as he always was, as though there were no other thing in all the world this morning that so called for his undivided attention. They saw the glow of the burning cigar-end, saw the little puff of smoke held all but motionless by the still air. Then they saw him turn and look out at them, and they fancied that he was smiling.

"I've had my sleep, boys," he called to them. "And I've dreamed all my best dreams over again. Now, if you're ready —"

"Dufresne," cried Nesbit sharply, standing with his rifle across the hollow of his arm, "I call on you in the name of the law to surrender. You haven't a chance in God's world to get away."

"I don't know that I want to get away," laughed the gambler insolently. "I'm tired and . . . I'm ready, if you are. And if you'll come one at a time you'll last longer!"

Nesbit made no answer. He turned and walked away from him, calling to the others to come to him. When they came to his side he said shortly:

"He's goin' to fight to the finish. And he's a dead shot. Cop, you move out that way, and there's no sense in getting too close to him. You and me both have got rifles and we can make him see sense, maybe. Hal, you and Sperry move out to the sides, and see he don't make a break for it."

He watched them take the places he had assigned to them, strode to the spot he had chosen for himself, from which Dufresne would not be sheltered by the boulders among which he stood, and jerked his rifle to his shoulder.

"So that's it!" It was Dufresne's voice again, taunting, filled with contempt. "You're not coming any closer than you have to, eh, Nesbit? Well, I don't blame you."

316

His hand hung idly at his side and they could see that he held his revolver in it, ready.

"Steady, boys," cried Nesbit sternly. And to Dufresne "I'm calling on you for the last time! Will you drop your gun and put up your hands?"

Dufresne didn't answer. He stepped quickly to one side, so as to be hidden for a little from Cop Kelley, and as he moved he jerked his arm up quickly and fired. The bullet sped close enough to Nesbit to draw his curse after it, and to send his rifle to his shoulder. The sheriff's first bullet flattened upon the rock two feet to the left of where the gambler stood, his second cut into the dirt at his feet, his third, hissing through the smoke of the two others, had passed through the loose cloth of Dufresne's coat.

Meantime the gambler had not ceased firing. The light was uncertain, the distance was rather too great for accurate revolver shooting, and yet he had not emptied his cylinder when Nesbit's curse was a half-choked cry, and the sheriff's left arm dropped to his side.

For a moment there was silence, unbroken. Dufresne had thrown himself to the ground, out of sight, and was slipping fresh cartridges into the emptied cylinder. Then he stood up again, and even moved a step nearer, in plain sight of them all. As he moved they could see the glowing fire of his cigar, and again they fancied that he was smiling.

Nesbit, with his left arm useless, had dropped down behind a rock, resting his rifle upon it. Kelley, moving a little so that he could see the gambler, had lifted his rifle. It was brighter now. They could not miss . . .

Hal suddenly jammed his revolver back into his hip pocket and turned away, growing a little sick. The man didn't have a chance. It was like shooting down an unarmed man. He deserved it, yes. But it was like murder. Dufresne was standing there, not trying to keep his body under cover, smoking his last cigar, a laugh in his voice as he called to them:

"My last game, gentlemen . . . the blue sky for a limit! Bad light, Nesbit, or I wouldn't have missed your heart a foot that way. So, Kelley, you're in it now? Hal doesn't like the rat killing! Take that, Nesbit. Miss again? Next time . . . Ah!"

Together Nesbit's rifle and Kelley's had spat their hissing lead at him, and he was down. Down upon his knees, swaying until he steadied himself with his hand against the rock at his side. Down, but still shooting. And as he fired he still called out to them, and although there were little pauses between his words, they came with the old quiet coolness:

"Once more, boys . . . and we can . . . all go . . . home!"

"All nerve," came in a mutter from between Nesbit's set teeth. There was only admiration in the sheriff's tone. And there was only respect and regret in his eyes as he steadied his rifle upon his rock.

Close together again came his shot and Kelley's. Victor Dufresne's hand dropped to his side, his smoking revolver clattered down among the stones about him, and he settled a little, swayed, settled lower,

318

and then went down on his side, his wide eyes upon the last star fading at the horizon.

They came to him and stood about him, the four men looking down at him where he lay. There was blood on his hands and face, blood soaking through his shirt, blood gushing down into his shoe. And yet, as he stared up at them, he tried to smile.

"It was all in the cards, boys." His voice was a faint, wavering whisper, at last no longer the thing he could make obey his will. "But the cards — were stacked."

"You made us do it, Victor," muttered Nesbit. "Damn it, I'm sorry."

"I'm glad." It was very simply said, and yet already the lips were growing white, and he had to fight hard for each word. Then, looking up into Hal's darkening eyes, his whisper so faint that they all bent lower over him, and Hal dropped down upon his knees to catch the faltering words, "In my pocket. I wrote it last night. A note to . . . Miss Winston. You boys read it first. Tell her I'm sorry . . . about Oscar . . . I hope he . . . gets well."

Then his eyes went back to the last star at the horizon. He did not speak again. Gradually the day brightened over the mountains. The star paled . . . and was gone. And Victor Dufresne's life had gone out with it.

The note he had written in the darkness of his last night was very short.

"DEAR MISS WINSTON, — Had there been a woman like you in my life things might have been different. I am sorry I shot the man you love. If he gets well . . . well, I am sending you my wedding present anyway. —

Faithfully yours,   VICTOR DUFRESNE."

And upon a separate piece of paper he had written and signed a full confession to the murder of Bill Cutter, and to the holding up of the stage at Bear Creek Crossing.

CHAPTER
TWENTY-SEVEN

The Valley of the Waterfalls

"So he held up the stage!" There was a world of surprise in the sheriff's voice. "I'd have swore it was young Estabrook."

Hal turned away, and in silence went back to where the Colonel was tied. All the hardness had long ago gone out of his eyes. He knew that he would never again be able to think of the gambler as he knew he should think of him. That he would always remember Victor Dufresne as he had seen him one night, looking with yearning eyes at the girl whose lover his fate had driven him to shoot.

Dufresne's confession, written with difficulty in the darkness, was brief, but it was amply full. He even gave his reasons for the murder of Bill Cutter. He said that they had had trouble before, that Cutter knew of a "crooked deal that he had put over in Rawhide," and had threatened lately to expose him. He gave the names of two men in Queen City who had heard Cutter threaten him.

Hal came back to the Bear Track, riding alone, not waiting for the others. Under the oaks he found Yvonne and Fern, their arms about each other, their faces white

321

and drawn from the vigil of last night. As he swung down from the saddle Yvonne came to meet him, her two hands held out, her question in her eyes.

"It's all over," he told her simply. "And he died like a gentleman."

"You" — she hesitated, her eyes asking that other question that her lips faltered to put into words — "you didn't —"

"No. He fought to the finish, but Nesbit and Kelley had their rifles —"

He drew her close to him as he felt the little shudder run through her body. And he saw through the pain in her eyes a misty gladness that at least he did not come back to her with this man's blood upon his hands.

In answer to his question she told him that John Brent was a God-blessed man, that his prayers had been short and his hours over Oscar's bed had been long, and this morning he had laughed his old boyish laugh again, and had put his hand upon Fern's head and had told her that God had seen fit to save her lover to her.

Then they went to where Fern was waiting for them, and Hal gave her the things that Dufresne had written. For a little she looked at him with puzzled eyes when she had read. Then suddenly he saw that she had understood, that the gambler who had come so near to robbing her of all that was in life for her had made reparation, that he had been thoughtful of her during the last hours in which he saved his last cigar, that he had given Oscar his chance. And she dropped her face

322

in her hands and turned away from them, going swiftly back to where her lover lay.

John Brent, when he heard of the passing of Victor Dufresne, professional gambler, stood with clenched hands, the muscles of his face twitching. Slowly two great tears formed in his eyes. Unchecked and unhidden they rolled down his sunburnt cheeks.

"God dealt you a hard hand to play in this life," he whispered, as though Dufresne were there listening. "Somewhere He will give you another chance. For you were a man, Brother Victor! And He plays square!"

The last thing to say — to be sure it is all unnecessary, but the story of the "Outlaw" ends there and another story begins — is that one day Hal rode away into Queen City to take out the necessary papers for the new mine. It had been the Yellow Boy and the Death Trap. Now it was the Heart of Gold. When he came back he brought with him many men and tools. But he did not put them to work upon the mine at first.

Spring came. Upon a morning that was eloquent with bursting seeds and opening flowers of the birth of the merry season, he saddled the Colonel and Starlight, and called softly under Yvonne's window. Riding side by side they came into the Valley of the Waterfalls. And in the mouth of the pass which led into this home of down-dropping odours from the green things along the cliffs and of the murmur of leaping water, they drew rein together.

She did not speak, but the soft light that shone out suddenly through the tender grey of her eyes told him

323

that she had seen, and that her words were lost in the rush of a gladness that was very close to tears.

The smoke from the wide-throated chimney drifted out to meet them. The doors were wide and they were open, calling to them to enter, to come home. Within there would be little shelves with their dishes, and big shelves with their books —

A big man, as shaggy as a shepherd dog from a bed in the thicket, ungainly, ill-dressed, his great form all but filling the doorway, was shouting to them. And at the import of his words the red ran into Yvonne's cheeks, and for the first time she dropped her eyes before her lover's.

Here the old, old miracle was wrought again. For a little there were three in the Valley of the Waterfalls. Then Big John Brent climbed awkwardly into his saddle and rode away upon Nicodemus. And when he had gone the two were one, together.